HELL OR HIGH WATER

Hailey Edwards

COPYRIGHT INFORMATION

Edited by Sasha Knight

Cover by Damonza

Interior format by The Killion Group

CHAPTER ONE

The golden wolf loping at my side licked her chops, her focus narrowing on our prey with laser precision, and surged ahead of me. Fur as blond as the wheat shafts pelting my forearms, she blended into the field, impossible to track except by the rustling stalks.

This was not going to end well. For our witness.

"Stop." Through my teeth, I sucked in humid air tinged with bird dander. "I need to...ask you...a few questions."

Trilling hoots erupted from two rows over. "Didn't see a thing. Not a thing. Not one. *Bye.*"

Thighs screaming from exertion, I plowed through a wall of rigid stalks that bent under my weight. "I'm an agent...with the Earthen Conclave."

One on forced leave, but he didn't have to know that.

Panicked squawks rang out, and I cursed under my breath. *Dell.* Odds were high that the feather duster was the last person to see Isaac at the gas station about an hour ago. No one had seen or heard from him since. No one had seen or heard from Aunt Dot period. The grainy labyrinth could have been a lava flow dotted with molten rocks, and I would have followed him barefoot.

He would tell me what he knew or I would toss him to the literal wolves.

This hunt would go so much faster if I shifted, but embracing my inner she-wolf meant my prey drive would skyrocket. One glimpse of my half-wolf aspect in hot pursuit, and my eyewitness would combust in a torrent of kaleidoscopic feathers.

"Just a few…" I gasped as a stitch arrowed through my side, "…questions."

"I had my eyes shut. I was napping. Didn't see a thing. Not a thing. Not even that pink-haired molly with the wide eyes who reminded me of my second cousin's daughter's boyfriend's uncle's kid."

All out of steam, I plodded to a stop, eyes darting in search of my wolfy backup. "A pink-haired girl was there?"

The shafts quit thrashing, and a series of chirrups told me he had paused to think. "Aye. Sure. Pretty thing. Smelled human, but not. That man-thing didn't mind. He hopped out of his truck when Pinky crooked her finger. Got a funny look in his eye, he did, when she patted his cheek. Walked off, followed her away, and left his vroom-vroom with a rumble in its belly at the store."

He meant the truck. Harlow had lured Isaac away from the gas station. Trapping the groan bordering on a growl in my throat, I shoved my she-wolf down again before she split my skin. Isaac must have recognized Harlow by her description. He knew about the pink hair, and how many pink-haired girls roamed a city of this size?

Bracing my palms on my upper thighs, I bent over and worked at regulating my breathing. I really ought to start jogging again. "What happened next?"

"Cheeky." A zinging trill erupted. "I didn't watch. With the eyes and the looking. I'm not that kind of bird."

He wasn't a bird at all. He was fae, a cercibis, who resembled a great horned owl with tie-dyed feathers and a distended belly that made his gut taut as a drum. His sticklike legs belonged on a flamingo and bowed, ready to snap under his weight. His eyesight, though, was that of a raptor, and his hearing matched his owlish facade. He was the next best thing to a surveillance video, if he would only cooperate.

A snort stung my nose at his flimsy lie. Cercibis loved to watch. Anything. Everything. And they had near photographic memories. "What did you hear?"

Round eyes, inky black with yellow rims, peered out at me. "Pinky didn't spout a word. Didn't have to, did she? Not with them long lashes batting."

Chills raised the fine hairs down my arms. "Do you remember anything else about her?"

"No. Not really. Yes. Well, maybe." He blinked, first one eye and then the other. "Pinky struck me as rather..." he kept winking until I got dizzy, "...*nice.*"

"Nice," I repeated.

"Nice is an obvious trap," he shrilled. "Females eat weak males. How has the man-thing survived to adulthood without knowing this?"

"Human females don't eat their males," I murmured distractedly, tracking a faint rustling on my left.

Most humans had all the magic of a freeze-dried rainbow inside them. As the mundane half of a changeling pair, Harlow wasn't strictly human, but she wasn't fae either. Doubting he would appreciate the distinction, I held my tongue.

"My own mother swallowed two of my little brothers," the cercibis reflected with a sad *hoo-hoot.* "Her talon polish chipped after she got home from the salon, and she always was an emotional eater..."

Yanked from my thoughts by a flicker of blond fur, I offered my condolences. "I'm sorry to hear about your brothers."

"It's all right." A whistling sniffle. "It was a few centuries ago. You move on, you know?"

"I— Yes. You do." I caught Dell's eye and shook my head. "I have a gift for you to show my gratitude."

"Oh?" He bounced on his twiggy legs, exposing the bright red and orange swirl of his face. "Don't be a tease. Where is it? Where?"

"Wait here. I have to get it from my..." *mate* sounded too permanent a fixture in the life of a transient fae, but that's what he was, even if the scope of that one single word terrified me, "...Graeson."

The springing action petered out to nothing. "Oh. I can wait. I guess. I'm not fond of waiting, it's quite dull, actually, but for a gift..."

The susurration of wheat tassels behind me broke sweat down my spine. Wading in after the cercibis with Dell as backup might not have been the smartest decision I'd ever made. Isaac's disappearance had given her usually playful warg teeth. Pulling recalled magic through my veins to heighten my sense of smell, I found a fresh reason to panic.

"Oh crap." I turned my back on the fae and flung my arms wide. "Graeson, no. We talked about this."

A rangy wolf with sterling fur emerged with a large sack of birdseed slung across his back. He glided forward and nudged my leg with his shoulder in greeting. I hadn't expected him back so soon. A shudder moved through him as he shook off his cargo. It hit the dry soil with a dull thump and toppled onto its side.

"Is that it?" the cercibis warbled from behind me. "Is that my gift? Smells furry. Is it a coat? A bit out of season, isn't it?"

Not waiting for my reply, he rushed forward and bumped the back of my knees. Prancing around me, wings aflutter, he shook his vivid red tail feathers in a cha-cha swish.

Fixated on the back and forth of those curling tendrils, I experienced a moment of disconnection where my brain flipped the card from *temporary ally* to *future meal*. I had only been around predators since evolving a half-wolf aspect with a mind of its own. Right now her instincts were pushing fur beneath my skin in an attempt to shift without my permission. A battle warred within me, the agent versus the wolf, and the wolf was winning.

The cercibis got its slender ankles tangled on themselves, and it stumbled forward, face-planting a foot from the tip of Graeson's wet nose.

"Oh—oh—*oh*. That is not a coat." He pushed up, beak clicking, and hopped to his feet. Flapping his stubby wings to achieve liftoff, he wailed. "This is the thanks I get. It's Mother all over again. I helped you, and you murdered me. Run," he cried to empty air. "It's a massacre."

Between his bloated stomach and the spindly legs that didn't tuck like they should, his struggle barely hoisted him up to my shoulder-height. "You're not dead." *Yet.* "He's not going to kill you." *Probably.*

On cue, Dell eased forward, lips peeled over her teeth and drool stringing from her jaw.

A tall crest of crimson feathers rose in a mohawk down his scalp, and the whites of his eyes shone.

"Lies," he squawked in my face. "You're a liar."

"You're stirring us up by flapping your wings." I almost had my arms around him. "Can you just hold still a minute?"

"Us?" Puffing up twice his size, he slapped me hard across the face. The fine hook tipping his wing slashed open my cheek, the move dipping his bulk to hip level. He had to pump his way back up to finishing hissing at me. "You're one of them? Ye gods."

A bass growl rattled my back teeth. Mine? I glanced down and swore. "No. Dell. Stop." I flung my arms around her neck, tackled her to the ground, and held on tight. "You want to find Isaac, don't you?"

The soft whine tensing her throat gutted me, and the urge to answer burned my own.

A new threat perked my ears, and I twisted back toward the cercibis, my gut pitching into my feet. "Bad wolf," I warned Graeson. "Bad."

Too late. His hackles rose at the sight of my bloodied cheek, and his eyes flashed molten gold. Fixating on the cercibis, he bunched his muscles and leapt. He snapped his jaws shut on its frilly tail feathers and yanked out a fistful of the wispy tendrils. The poor thing spun in a dramatic mini death spiral before thunking to the earth on his back, knobby legs sticking straight up in the air.

Gasping and wheezing while clutching his chest, he poked his serpentine tongue out one side of his beak.

"Are you happy now?" I pointed at the twitching fae. "He was helping us."

Spitting out a mouthful of fluorescent feathers, Graeson sneezed himself backward a step. His ear-splitting bark at Dell rang with triumph, and she yipped, encouraging his bad behavior.

Yes, my wolf was quite pleased with himself.

"Sorry about that." I nudged the cercibis with my toe to be sure the yap-fest hadn't given him a coronary. "We're leaving now."

One bony foot twitched, and he rasped, "The seed?"

"I'll leave it right here." I scooped up a feather damp with drool and tucked it in my pocket. Fisting each wolf's ruff, I dragged the pair of them with me. "Bon appétit."

The trek back to civilization required twenty minutes, not that the wolves minded. Emerging from the neat rows of tidy plantings, I breathed a sigh of relief when my boots thumped onto pavement.

Asphalt spread the next block over, carpeting a four-pump gas station slowly being devoured by rust. A shiny crew cab truck blocked one of the pumps, and it rocked as someone shifted their weight on the front bench. A dark head popped out the door, and my lungs froze with hope so powerful I couldn't breathe until I saw the man's face.

Not Isaac.

Just another human cop, this one with a sleek camera hung on a thick strap around his neck. As much as it burned me to press my nose against the glass of their investigation, I had no badge and no jurisdiction. Pursuing the cercibis had yielded positive results and burned off our restless energy, but I was eager for a conclave rep to arrive.

I had put in a call to Marshal Comeaux before leaving Chandler pack land and had yet to hear back. Until he arrived, I was stuck on the outside looking in while well-meaning humans trampled the scene.

A throttled groan announced Graeson's shift back onto two legs, and I flinched against the gruesome *pop pop pop* of bones as they snapped into a new alignment. Drawn forth by his change, Dell's metamorphosis followed a beat later.

Unable to listen to their suffering, I drifted toward a corroded milk crate I'd noticed earlier. Scuffed black boots sat in front of it, and a neat stack of men's clothing cushioned the top. Graeson's change had been controlled. Dell's... Not so much. Her clothes were scattered in the field, her shift a product of hurt and the desperation to *do* something other than waiting around for Comeaux and any answers he might bring with him.

Tempted as I was to sit while I waited them out, I caught the flash of a man's arm—banded in cypress ink—as it darted out from between the dried stalks, snagged the clothes and vanished with them.

Sometimes I forgot how fast he could change when given proper incentive. I wasn't the only one nervous about the cavalry arriving.

Rolling my boot over loose rocks, I forced out the tingle of magic warming my blood so I could be as level-headed as possible when Comeaux arrived. Wolf blood, I discovered, ran hot when emotions ran high.

A few minutes later Graeson joined me on the blacktop, and we leaned against the splintering fence while Dell's curses peppered the air behind us. The fly on his jeans hung open, and I was looking before it registered what I was seeing. Cheeks flaming, I backpedaled too fast, and my leg shot out in front of me. I windmilled my arms to regain my balance but managed to stay on both feet.

Hand on his zipper, Graeson made a production of raising it click by noisy click. "Did something spook you?"

"I thought I saw a snake in the grass." This time I dipped my gaze on purpose, the better to hide my flaming cheeks. "Then again, it was pretty scrawny. Maybe not a snake, an earthworm?"

Husky chuckles roughened his voice. "Maybe you should take another look to be sure."

Raising my chin high, I decided that deflection was better than embarrassment. "Do you know how rare cercibis are?"

"No." He tugged his shirt over his head, abs flexing with the movement. "But I've got a feeling you're about to tell me."

"Half their population was relocated to Earth in the hopes they would breed here." Faerie did that a lot, transplanted bizarre and annoying but generally harmless fae to this realm to get them out from underfoot. "There are laws against hunting them. Being earthborn won't save you from punishment."

Padding over to me, he wrapped a wide palm around the base of my neck. Heat poured down my nape and loosened taut muscles. "I yanked on his feathers." An unapologetic twitch of his lips tempted mine to respond in kind. "I think he'll survive." His thumb stroked over my pulse. "Besides, if I hadn't distracted Dell, she would have eaten him."

There was that. A fine gold band ringed her irises today and had since Graeson told her Isaac was missing.

The urge to rest my cheek against his chest left me fidgety. Wargs exalted in the physical, and the longer I spent around them, the more I craved skin on skin too. "Why did you shift in the first place?"

"You ran after prey." An undercurrent of excitement whispered through him. "You're pack. It triggered a hunting reflex."

Pointed reminders kept trickling into our conversations. Loaded words like pack, alpha, female, *mate*. The gentle caress of his hands as he claimed more territory on my body had grown so familiar I got the sense *he* was the one gentling *me*, each touch a claiming that promised more when I was ready.

He caught me staring at his mouth, and the metallic flecks in his eyes glinted before he released me and blasted out a pained breath. "You're killing me here, Ellis."

A shy grin curved my lips, and I almost regretted the worm comment. Almost.

"They're here. Finally." Relief washed through Dell's tone as she jumped the topmost rail and landed in a crouch beside me. "Let's go talk to them."

Sure enough, a black SUV crunched its tires as it turned in to the gas station with its lights strobing lazily. The white logo printed on its side wavered under its glamour, but I had no trouble identifying the Southeastern Conclave's seal.

The rush of flirtation chilled on my skin, and guilt that I had forgotten—even for a second—why we were here prickled over me seconds later.

Beside me, Graeson stomped a boot onto his foot then braced on the crate to tie his laces. "Dell, you're not getting anywhere near those humans."

A throttled snarl twitched her lips. "I didn't come all this way just to be sidelined."

"Your eyes are gold." Straightening, he hooked his hands on his hips. "Humans, if you recall, don't know about fae, and they sure as hell don't know about us. I get you're worried for Isaac. We all are. But until you get your wolf under control, you're a threat and not a help to us."

"I'll wear sunglasses," she gritted between teeth she ought to know better than to flash at her alpha.

The air crackled with building magic as Graeson accepted her challenge. "I said no."

A single gut-wrenching pop was my only warning before Dell stumbled backward and exploded into her wolf. "Oh *crap*."

Graeson tackled her, driving her to the dirt. Hand wrapped around her throat, he glanced up at me, eyes blazing. "I have to handle this." He jerked his chin toward the waiting fae. "I'll join you when I'm able."

Flashbacks of Graeson punishing his six left me nauseated with fear he might hurt Dell that way.

"Trust me," he said, eyes softening. "I won't hurt her more than it takes, but her wolf has to be reminded she can't challenge her alpha unless she thinks she can win."

Packing away the writhing in my stomach, I gave him a nod of support then strode toward the SUV, game face on.

CHAPTER TWO

A wiry man dressed to the nines and crumpled by humidity eased from behind the wheel of the dusty SUV. He raked a hand through his hair, trying and failing to tame a cowlick, while scanning the area. His hawkish gaze landed on me, and a genuine smile broke over his face.

"Agent Ellis." He moseyed my way. "I heard you closed the Charybdis file. Congratulations." Shoving his hands into his pockets to avoid shaking mine, he gestured toward the scene with his chin. "I didn't expect to see you back out this way again so soon." His tone implied *or ever.* "What's your connection?"

"That truck belongs to my cousin, Isaac Cahill." That got his attention. "He and my aunt were in town fueling up and buying supplies. He was filling gas cans when he vanished." I linked my hands at my navel to make Comeaux more comfortable. "The clerk found the vehicle abandoned, used Isaac's phone to call a number frequented in his caller ID and ended up dialing me. We talked, and here I am. I called you the second I hung up with him."

"No sign of your aunt or her vehicle?"

The words were too hard to force out, so I shook my head.

"Is there any reason to believe this might be tied to your work?" The marshal scratched the day-old stubble covering his cheek. "What we do doesn't endear us to our kin, if you catch my drift."

"My work is my life." Unable to resist, I flicked a glance back at the truck as though expecting the scene to have changed. Two of its four doors stood open, and glove box detritus littered the front passenger seat. "Or it used to be."

Yesterday I would have said I wasn't alone anymore. Today...I felt more alone than ever.

"I don't see any gas cans. Were there any present when you arrived?" Ambling away from me, he walked a slow circle around the vehicle. "How long have you been waiting?"

"Fifty minutes."

"My apologies." Smiling, he lifted a hand in response to a cop's familiar wave. "Our office is in the next county over. It takes a while to make the drive here, but the tradeoff is fewer skirmishes between the fae marshals and the Chandler wargs."

"It's no problem." The long wait had been torture, but I'd worked at my fair share of rural outposts, and sometimes the drive to cover your territory was a bear when problems arose that required immediate conclave intervention. A phone call would have been nice, though. "I expected there might be a delay."

The sandy-haired officer strolled over with a handshake and a backslap for Comeaux. "Stepping on my toes again so soon?"

"I'm a dancing man, Donaldson." Comeaux shuffled his gleaming dress shoes on the pavement. "What can I say?"

The younger man groaned. "That you won't do that again?"

Pleasantries normally didn't ruffle me, but my lip was in danger of curling as the two dragged out their manful greeting ritual. Interdepartmental relationships were critical in order for the fae to suppress what humans knew about us, but this time I was cast in the role of relative of the victim, and that act held less and less water as I waited for their attention to refocus.

Catching my eye, Comeaux returned his hands to his pockets and sobered. "What do you have so far?"

"Not much." The cop's attention wandered to me. "Nothing that warrants the FBI getting involved."

Taking the misconception in stride, Comeaux leaned in close and lowered his voice. "The suspect is on our watch list."

"How do you want to play this?" Donaldson's mood went somber. "Say the word, and the force, such as we are, is yours to command. We can line up local news coverage to get the word out if you'd like to borrow extra eyes from the community."

"The situation is...delicate. We believe he might have taken a hostage when he stole this truck." Comeaux fixed a serious expression in place. "For now, we'd like to fly this incident under the radar."

"Understood, sir." Donaldson eyeballed me again. "I don't mean to be rude by staring, ma'am. I noticed you were here when we arrived. Are you with the FBI as well?"

A cool lie prepped itself for launch, but Comeaux intercepted.

"Agent Ellis has a personal connection to this case. Her cousin is the alleged hostage." He let Donaldson absorb that. "To keep things aboveboard, she was issued strict orders not to engage with the local law enforcement until my arrival."

I extended my hand. "It's nice to meet you, Officer Donaldson."

His grip was firm, dry and utterly mundane. He was one hundred percent human. But I felt better after checking to be sure.

"Shit fire and save the matches," Comeaux muttered under his breath. "Just what I don't need."

Eyes in the back of my head weren't necessary to see what—no, *who*—had set him off.

"That guy? He going to be a problem?" Donaldson hooked a thumb through his gun belt, too near his weapon for my comfort. "I can detain him until we finish if you want."

A tendril of comforting warmth tickled my nape, a heated rush of awareness that Graeson's eyes were on me.

"That won't be necessary." Even I heard the edge in my voice. "He's with me."

"Why don't you go touch base with the techs?" Comeaux checked his phone, expression slipping before he forced a smile for Donaldson. "Wrap this up in the next hour, and we can grab a burger at Havarti's and gripe about the Mets."

"Deal." Donaldson peered over my shoulder, sizing up Graeson with seasoned focus that missed nothing. "Holler if you need assistance."

"Will do." Comeaux crossed his arms over his middle, scratched his elbow and pegged me with a wary glare. "He's with you? In what capacity?"

Evading his questions, I angled my hips toward the weathered split-rail fence across the road and savored Graeson's approach. Even at a distance, the newly minted alpha stood taller than most. Slabs of muscle packed his frame. His expression read as a man who had zero fucks left to give this town. Mind set on the future, he was done with this place that reeked of the past. Heavy bands of ink circled his wrists, and lush cypress trees erupted up his forearms. His rolling gait was that of a predator, and Comeaux tensed in anticipation of the trouble that plagued warg-on-fae interactions.

Humans loitered on the fringes of the parking lot, dipping their hands into chip bags or slurping on frosty drinks as they indulged in a little harmless voyeurism. One look at his harsh expression, and they scattered as leaves before a tornado.

"Mr. Graeson." Comeaux greeted him with all the enthusiasm of a flu diagnosis. "What brings you to town?"

Grin stretching his cheeks, the imposing warg slung his arm around my waist and tucked me against him, savoring Comeaux's apparent bewilderment. "Ellis."

Shrinking under Comeaux's scrutiny, I resisted the urge to stomp Graeson's instep for all but peeing on my leg to mark his territory. It took physical effort not to shrug him off and duck from his embrace to regain control of the situation. "He means that literally." I went for casual, despite the warg sweater I was wearing, and pointed at the gleaming truck parked on the curb. "We rode together."

"I see." Comeaux struck a casual pose that failed to hide his interest on every level. "You never said what brought you back to our neck of the woods, Agent Ellis."

"I'm following up on a case." Not an exact lie. "Is that a problem?"

"Not at all." His Southern accent thickened. "Do you often bring your family along?"

"This would be a first." His barb struck me between the ribs and stuck there. "Seeing how it turned out, it's safe to say it's also the last time I involve them in my work."

A chime rang out, and Comeaux held up a finger while he located his cell. He swiped his thumb across the screen, read the message, and his expression darkened. "Your name was flagged on my incident report, so I had my partner dig deeper. It says here you're on leave." His gaze bounced between us, judgment heavy in his eyes. "So I'm afraid I'll have to ask you again. What business do you have in Villanow?"

Any answer I gave him put me on the official record. The truth might land me in prison. A lie, well, that could end my career.

"Tell him." Graeson's fingers bit into my side, the pressure meant to convey a message that stumped me. "It'll be okay."

I wet my lips, wishing I'd had the forethought to prick his finger before making a beeline for Comeaux. A mental bond would come in handy right about now, because I had no idea what he was playing at by encouraging me to spill my guts in front of the marshal. Still uncertain, I embraced the lesser of two career-dooming evils.

"I came to visit my..." I sucked in a sharp breath then whooshed it out, "...mate."

"I wanted to meet the in-laws." Graeson rewarded me for claiming him by dropping a kiss on top of my head before adding, "That's why her family joined us here."

"I see," Comeaux said again, and it was clear he did. Both the warg's possessive hand resting on my hip and the way I had fought my instincts and lost. As though my brain were chanting *act professional* while my body made *pfft* noises and did what felt right. Leaning into him for support kept me stable. As long as I had Graeson at my side, I could survive this. "I don't expect Bessemer was thrilled with this turn of events." His smile wasn't unkind. "Wargs mating with fae is taboo in this part of the state, in most of the country if I'm blunt."

"No," Graeson answered in a clipped tone. "He wasn't."

"Graeson has severed ties with the Chandler pack and will be establishing his own." Confiding that information felt like extending a peace offering. It also made our situation so much more *real*. Tacking on, "We can't share any details beyond that," sounded better than admitting we hadn't thought that far ahead.

"Let me know when you get settled." He clapped Graeson on the back with sincerity. "A pro-fae alpha is something our office can get behind. The magistrates will be thrilled to endorse your pack. We could all use insight from a man in your position to help smooth future interactions with the warg community."

"I won't make any promises." Graeson inclined his head toward me. "I'll have to discuss it with Ellis...and our pack."

The urge to squirm returned when Comeaux's jaw fell open as Graeson's full meaning registered.

A fae alpha. Stranger things had happened.

Right?

"Sir." A tidy man wearing a crisp navy polo paused at Comeaux's shoulder. "We've finished processing the truck."

Shuffling to one side, Comeaux opened up our circle and gave the man room to join us. "What can you tell us?"

"Not much," he admitted. "An erasure spell was cast sometime in the last forty-five minutes. Our technicians made attempts to recover evidence, but the scene has been sterilized."

Report given, he turned on his heel and returned to the rest of his polo-clad crew.

"Forty-five minutes," I echoed. "That's not possible. I've been here for over an hour. I would have..."

"The cercibis," Graeson reminded me.

"I'm sorry?" Comeaux anchored his hands at his hips. "You said cercibis? Do you mean Bert?"

"I didn't ask for his name." Bert. Yeah, he looked like a Bert. "He was flighty, and I didn't want to spook him."

"Flighty," Graeson murmured.

Great. Now Dell had him poking fun at me too.

Comeaux glanced between us and chuckled. "Locals are convinced there's a chupacabra on the loose."

"He revealed himself to humans?" I had spotted him loitering on the edge of the field and assumed I'd gotten lucky. Maybe not. "That was a bold move for such a nervous guy."

"Well, it's like this. He got the name Bert in part because he resembles a reject from Jim Henson's Creature Shop and in part because he was half of a pair. See, there used to be an Ernie. It turned out she was an Earnestine. She startled some hunters last deer season, and they shot her. We couldn't prosecute, because the humans had no idea what she was to be aware she was endangered. Bert lost his mind after that. He started people-watching, getting bolder about where he goes and who he reveals himself to. A few of us are concerned he's stalking the humans responsible for his mate's death, but he can't stay cohesive for long enough to present a true threat. At least not yet." The marshal's tone sharpened. "How is he mixed up in this?"

"The cops arrived within minutes of us, so we parked on the curb to wait for you." Without a badge to grease the wheels, I didn't have much choice. The local boys wouldn't take my word that I was a law enforcement officer without proof, and admitting the truck belonged to my missing cousin would have gotten me barred from the scene before I contaminated it. "I noticed the cercibis's crest twitching in the wheat field and went to question him."

Comeaux flicked Graeson a questioning glance. "Alone?"

"No," he answered, managing to sound insulted. "A pack mate provided backup while I went across the street to the feed store."

Tactful as any seasoned alpha, he avoided mentioning that in Dell's heightened emotional state, she had exploded into her wolf form the second the cercibis's scent hit her nose and bulleted in pursuit of him, leaving Graeson no choice but to let me calm her while he purchased the necessary bribe.

"I read a paper on cercibis in the academy, which is why I knew Bert would make an ace witness if I could get him to cooperate," I explained to Comeaux. "Offer one a gift and, if they accept it, they're obliged to answer any one question truthfully in the future."

"Huh." Comeaux turned contemplative. "I'll have to remember that."

"One more thing to keep in mind," I advised him. "Get as much information as you can before you give up the seed. Cercibis are worthless after you reward them."

"Good to know." He traded his phone for a thin spiral notebook and pencil, scratching a few notes before glancing up at me. "How much information did the seed buy you?"

"Enough. He told me a pink-haired girl was on the scene." I didn't name names, but I didn't have to.

"Not Harlow." His hand froze poised over his notes. "How did she get mixed up in all this?"

"She was abducted from the last crime scene I worked before going on leave." Hating to do it, I slid a half-truth past him. "I've been trying to find her ever since."

It wasn't a total lie. I had spent weeks searching for her before finding and losing her again.

"I didn't know." He scratched the pencil thoughtfully against his cheek. "I sure hate to hear that."

That he cared made me like him that much more. Most of her coworkers had been fine with writing her off as a loss, a life for a life. Harlow was a good kid who had made a terrible mistake that got a man killed. Did that mean she ought to be punished? Maybe. Did that mean she deserved what she got? No. I couldn't believe that. Damn it, she was worth saving.

"Right now I'm not sure what it means that Harlow is tangled up in Isaac's disappearance, but I'll get to the bottom of it." Besides the fact she was acting as the latest avatar for Charybdis, and that he saw my family as a means of settling some imagined score, I had pitiful few clues to go on. Telling Comeaux might endanger my family. Factor in Vause's disappearance, and any whiff of suspicion might bring the conclave down on all our heads. So I kept that knowledge to myself. "Hopefully, when I locate him, I'll find her too."

"You're doing all this off the grid?" He whistled. "You've got balls, Ellis. I knew I liked you for a reason."

The absent caress of Graeson's fingers over my hip spoke of his approval in Comeaux's tastes.

"Agent Ellis." Polo returned with a clipboard in hand. "Give us another ten to finish processing the scene, and we'll release the vehicle into your custody as you're the next of kin."

Next of kin. The chilling phrase sent a shiver zinging through me that Graeson rubbed away.

"We'll process what evidence our techs collected and start proceedings to acquire what the cops found." He caught the tech's eye. "The local PD was first on scene. The erasure spell was cast prior to our arrival, but their samples might not be tainted."

Erasure spell or not, they wouldn't find much. Of that I was certain. Charybdis had eluded us this long for a reason.

Thank the gods the quirky cercibis had been staking out the gas pumps when he had, or we'd have nothing to go on.

"I should go help wrap up the paperwork." Comeaux speared Graeson with a cajoling smile. "Keep my offer in mind. You could do a lot of good for your people—and ours."

The tight grin pinned on Graeson's lips didn't reach his eyes. "I'll be in touch."

To offer a polite decline, I was guessing.

Left alone to count down the promised ten minutes, Graeson hauled me into his arms and massaged my shoulders. The urge to resist his comforting embrace flickered and died as his warmth seeped into my bones. I wasn't great at this, at allowing myself to indulge after a lifetime of deprivation, of feeling unworthy for being the sister who lived, and we both knew it. He spared me the embarrassment of admitting as much. Instead he taught me with selfless patience to accept what he gave in the hopes one day I might take what I needed from him instead. He asked for nothing from me, content to nibble on my affection in tiny bites as I offered them.

Considering he was the one with a wild spirit, I got the feeling I was the one being tamed.

Fifteen minutes later, the cops left the parking lot. Five minutes later, the marshals did too. Comeaux was last, his dusty black SUV idling at the curb as his ride waited for him. The rumpled marshal did the honors, dropping Isaac's keys into my palm.

"Can I ask you for a favor?" I folded my hand over the cluttered ring as though protecting them might extend to Isaac too.

"Depends on what you want," he said frankly. "I like you, but I like steady paychecks more."

Didn't we all? "I could use some help locating my parents."

He shoved his hands into his pockets, glanced at the SUV, and I sensed him wriggling off the hook.

"I'll give you the favor Bert owes me." I wouldn't be back here to collect anyway. "An informant like that might come in handy."

"All right." A slow grin took his face. "I'll take that offer. I have your number in my phone. I'll call when I find something."

Passing over one of the feathers Graeson had spat out on the ground, I handed it to Comeaux. "Cercibis remember every feather they've ever lost. Give this to him, and tell him I sent you."

Comeaux didn't remark on its dampness. "I'll do that." He tipped his head. "Safe travels."

The moment we were alone, I cut my gaze to Graeson. "I'll meet you at home."

"Ellis," he growled.

"I'm okay." I hooked a smile on my lips. "It's just that I haven't talked to Theo in…a long time." Isaac's twin brother was not my favorite person, but he was all the family I could locate. "I'd like to break the news to him alone."

More than that, I required focus for this next part. Theo's reaction, both to my call and Isaac's disappearance, would be all the proof I got that he was untainted by Charybdis.

Unhappy but understanding, Graeson stole a brief kiss that startled me with its suddenness.

One day I would be prepared for his affection. One day I would rise up on my toes, link my arms around his neck and put my gratitude into the reverent press of my mouth on his. But not today. Not while my bleeding heart weighted my heels flat on the ground.

"I'll see you at home." He made it sound like a dare. As if I'd run from him. I was in too deep now. "Call if you need me."

With the pack bond severed, he was carrying a cheap prepaid phone for a change. Dell too, but she kept losing hers. Speaking of my shadow... "Take Dell with you."

His jaw worked over an instant denial. "Charybdis is hunting you, hunting your family. I respect your right to privacy, but respect my right to keep you safe." For the first time since I'd left the two wargs to settle their differences, Graeson acknowledged Dell with a jerk of his chin that brought her loping toward us. "She'll wait here, in plain sight. Drive as far as you can and still see her, and she won't overhear you." Muscle ticked in his cheek. "Is that fair?"

"Okay," I agreed, because it was a good compromise. He was trying, and I didn't want to be alone despite what I'd told him. "This won't take long." A flicker of a smile warmed me. "I would promise to check in once we're headed your way, but I'm sure Dell will let you know without me having to ask."

Graeson's silence stood as agreement, not the least bit chagrined that I was right. She was my friend, but orders given by someone more dominant stuck. Though that same willingness to bodyguard me and then report back to him must be one of her most endearing qualities as far as he was concerned.

Following Graeson's instructions, I drove as far as I could while keeping Dell visible in my rearview mirror, then pulled off to the side of the road where I dissolved into tears I wasn't strong enough to share with anyone—not even Graeson—yet.

Old habits die hard it seems.

Tears wet on my cheeks, I forced my hands to stop shaking long enough for me to palm Isaac's cell. The techs had left it on the seat spotted with fingerprint dust, and it stained my hands as I checked his call history and retrieved Theo's number. His name popped up three times more often than mine or Aunt Dot's. I hadn't realized he and Isaac spoke so often. Or at all really, Isaac being so averse to speaking on phones, in texts or not.

One more deep breath, then I dialed and punched send. I fingered the pearl bracelet Harlow had given me out of habit.

"What's up, bro?" a breathless voice yelled over throbbing dance music.

"Theo, it's Camille."

"Cammie?" The noise muted, filtered through the palm he must have slapped over the receiver. "Give me a sec." Slowly the pulsating bass waned. "Want to tell me what the hell you're doing with Izzy's phone?"

Throat tight, I wet my lips and broke the news. "He's missing. He vanished from a gas station a few hours ago." I flattened a palm hard against my chest like it might stop my heart from escaping through the cracks in my ribs. "No one has heard from Aunt Dot either, and her truck is missing. I think she was taken too."

"Where are you?" Icebergs ran warmer than his voice now, the chill of his words reassuring me he was himself. "Never mind. I've triangulated your signal. Keep the phone on. I'll find you."

I lowered the phone to my lap and smudged my thumb across the screen.

Never had I been happy to hear that Theo was due for a visit.

I guess there really was a first time for everything.

CHAPTER THREE

Dell and I returned home to find organized chaos. Our borrowed corner of the pack lands bustled with activity. The Chandler wargs kept to their homes while our tightknit band of exiles scurried to pack their belongings and meet their former alpha's deadline to vacate the premises.

"Like ants on a mound," Dell observed.

"And Bessemer's the kid holding the magnifying glass into a sunbeam."

An almost smile graced her lips, but she smelled like fur and regret to my heightened senses.

"We're going to get him back," I promised her, as much for her sake as my own. "Aunt Dot too."

"Yes, we will." An exhale pursed her lips. "I'm sorry. I don't mean to take away from your pain, when this is your burden. Not mine." She knuckled her chest. "My wolf is riled, that's all. Too much change too fast probably."

"You're entitled to your feelings." Dell and Isaac had been blasting mixed signals at one another since the day they met. "I'm glad you got to know Isaac well enough to worry for him. He doesn't make it easy."

The hurt wafting off her made me wonder how deep their antagonistic friendship extended.

Angling Isaac's truck into the wide clearing where four gleaming silver Airstream trailers formed a wide circle came second nature to me. Eyes on my mirrors, I shifted into reverse, lined up the hitch with ease after a lifetime of practice, then threw the gearshift in park.

The door swung open before I killed the ignition, and the surly-faced alpha of an as-yet-unnamed pack reached in and hauled me into his arms so fast my feet didn't have time to touch the ground. While my heels drummed the running board in a weak attempt to wriggle free, Dell made her escape and jogged toward the others to lend a hand.

"You smell like tears," he murmured against my neck. "Is everything all right?"

Laughter muffled against his shoulder as I turned my face into his cheek. "You mean other than my aunt and favorite cousin being kidnapped by a serial killer's changeling puppet while the cousin who's hated me since we were kids is coming to ream me out about it?"

Scruffy as he was, his smile tickled against my skin. "Yes. Other than that."

"Then yes, everything is fine." I squirmed until my boots hit dirt. "How much longer do we have?"

"Six hours." He released me with obvious reluctance, and I was reminded yet again how tactile wargs were compared to Gemini or fae in general. "Everyone is packed and ready."

"Waiting on me," I said, because it was true.

A frown cut his mouth. "No one sees it that way."

No one could have foreseen these events, except perhaps the Garzas if I'd only known to ask them, and no one would blame me for holding up our mass exodus considering we had no destination in mind, but squatting on Bessemer's land was dangerous for us all. It was past time we left.

"I have a favor to ask Dell." I fisted Isaac's keys. "I'll need help moving the trailers now that..."

My throat worked over a knot. Using all those years of practice in blocking out memories of Lori, I erected a mental barrier of questionable integrity and prayed it held until we made it out of Villanow. I had to be strong and focus on getting Aunt Dot and Isaac back safe. Grief would only slow me down.

Pushing off Graeson's warm chest, away from his comforting embrace, I headed for the milling group of nervous-smelling wargs who now belonged to Graeson.

"Alpha." Dell set the tone, her cheerful facade back in place, and the others murmured hesitant greetings. "What do you need?" She crossed to me, wiped tears I hadn't felt slide down my cheeks, and crushed me against her chest. "Other than a hug, 'cause you had to know that was incoming."

"I need you to drive Isaac's truck and trailer for me." Tongue thick, I managed to add, "I'll need help with Theo's too."

Releasing me, she turned thoughtful. "Is Graeson handling Aunt Dot's?"

"Yes—" I started.

"No." He clamped a hand on my shoulder. "You're in no shape to drive, and we have a lot to discuss."

Things like how, as leaders, we had to actually lead our people to their new home, wherever that was.

One of the men I recognized from Abbeville, Haden, smirked at the reprimand.

A pulse of recalled magic danced up my arm, and scythelike claws sprang from my fingertips. My scent changed, and the musky spice of my dominant she-wolf saturated my skin. His nostrils flared, and the nasty grin fell off his face. Unable to hold my gaze, he ducked his head, chin flush with his chest.

Graeson didn't speak a word, didn't have to, but I caught his smug grin out of the corner of my eye.

Championing me in front of the others would damage my reputation, not bolster it. I didn't need a knight in shining armor. More likely I had to get my own metaphorical sword bloody to prove the point I had earned my mate, my title.

Right now emotions ran high. These wargs were about to leave the home they had known their whole lives in search of something new, something better. It was a terrifying prospect, and I respected that. But their instincts had them itching to dominate me except when I smelled more warg than fae and, like with the selection, I would have to back up my claim with teeth and claws when necessary.

Graeson would let me fight my own battles. As foul as my mood was, I looked forward to it.

"I'll ask around and see who's comfortable driving a truck and trailer." Dell punched my shoulder. "With all these good ol' country boys at our disposal, it shouldn't be hard to find volunteers hoping to score bonus points with the new alpha."

"I'll take one off your hands."

At first I wasn't sure where the offer had originated, but Haden sneaked a peek up at me. I shared a questioning glance with Dell, who nodded approval, but I wasn't convinced. "These trailers are our homes. They're precious to us, and I need to know you'll care for them the way you would your own property. Your attitude toward me since we met hasn't exactly inspired faith."

"You're fae, and I don't much trust them." His chin lifted, his jaw working around a grievance he struggled to phrase politely. "I chose to leave my pack, my home, to follow Cord, and he believes in you." Lower, almost below my hearing, he grumbled, "My wolf does too."

Ribbons of warmth sifted through me along with the first glimmer of hope that our fledgling pack might have a bright future.

"This is a big adjustment for all of us," I allowed, Dell leaning against me, happy as a clam. "I'm still learning what it means to be part of a pack, and I'm bound to make mistakes along the way, but I am trying. That's all I ask of any of you. Try with me. It's the only way this will work."

Several heads bobbed, and low voices murmured in agreement. As a show of good faith, I retrieved the keys to all the trailers and trucks. I dropped Isaac's keys onto

Dell's palm, and she closed her fist over them with an unreadable expression. Deciding to extend a smidgen of trust, I gave Haden a set of keys too. Theo's. Just in case. Meaning he got to drive Cord's truck. That left Graeson and me hauling two trailers pulled by mine, a normal sight for our caravan, unless we scrounged up another volunteer.

"We'll take responsibility for the last one. Our pickup's over there." A man with eyes the color of sun-kissed skies stepped forward. "I'm Jensen." He gestured toward one of the three women in our group. "That's my mate, Bianca."

The fine-boned woman glided forward, hand resting on her protruding stomach, a curtain of straight brown hair concealing her features. "Alpha."

"Oh. Wow." I clenched the keys in my fist so hard they bit into my palm. "You're pregnant."

Smooth, Cam. Smooth as a baby's behind.

The burly man squared off with me. "Is that a problem?"

"No. I'm just surprised. A baby." A child Graeson and I, as alphas, would be responsible for protecting. This couple had that kind of faith in him. Abandoning the familiar, they chose to embrace a new and uncertain life. As a gesture of peace, I turned to Bianca. "Would you mind shaking hands with me?"

Submissive to the core, she extended her arm almost before I got the words out. Jensen loomed over us, gaze fixed with rapt attention on my hand while he wore an expression that spoke of familiarity with my talents.

"I won't hurt her," I promised. "She won't feel a thing."

His reluctant nod dredged a smile out of me. My fingers touched Bianca's, and the pulse of wildness that identified her as a warg blazed through that contact. Hers was a softer magic, not as potent as the other female wargs I'd touched. Dominance could be a factor, but I'd read people for a long time and had an idea of what it meant.

"You're a half-blood," I surmised, and a flush stole over her cheeks.

"Y-yes." Her palm went damp. "I am."

The trick I was about to perform only worked on a person with magical integrity of a certain level, with a pregnancy past a certain stage. Babies weren't my thing, but I'd engaged in enough watercooler chat with expectant coworkers to know a baby bump popped out around six months, for most humanoid species, meaning Bianca fell right inside that narrow window.

From what Graeson had told me, pureblood pups were rare, and wargs bred with humans easier than other wargs. A half-blood child had a fifty-fifty shot at being able to shift at puberty. Otherwise it would live out its life as little more than human, a part of the pack but held apart.

Having grown up so alone, my heart half-empty, I wouldn't wish that type of isolation on anyone, especially not a child.

"Jensen?" I held the keys out in my other hand. "Here you go."

His fingers brushed mine, and potent magic spilled up my arm. Had I never met him before and shaken his hand, I would have known a powerful wolf slumbered inside him. He was a pureblood. That gave their child better odds of being born with a wolf's spirit inside it.

Sending a featherlight pulse of tingling magic through the hand clasping Bianca's for confirmation, I gave them news that would ease their minds the last three months of her pregnancy. "Your—" I caught myself before giving away the sex of the baby, since magic is distinctly male or female, and both flavors can't coexist inside the same person naturally, "—child is wolfborn."

"How can you—?" The keys poured through his fingers, and he bent to scoop them up again. "Are you sure?"

"Magic doesn't lie." I laughed as her hand was ripped from mine when Jensen grabbed her hips, lifted her high and spun her around. "Congratulations."

"Alpha?" Cheeks flush, Bianca leaned against her mate once he set her down on pain of an evening dose of morning sickness. "You hesitated. Does that mean...? Do you know if we're having a boy or a girl?"

Jensen's head snapped toward me. "You can tell?"

An amused smile lifted one side of my mouth. "Do you want to know?"

"Hell yes" clashed with "Not now," and I stood there until the couple made their decision.

"Right now it's enough to know our little wolf truly is a little wolf." Bianca patted her mate's chest. "Can we come to you again if we change our minds?"

Their relief at getting confirmation of their child's leanings sent a pang rocketing through my chest. Predators birthing children doomed to be seen as prey amounted to a death sentence in aggressive packs. They were right to be glad. I had to stop projecting my own abandonment issues onto them. It wasn't their fault my parents had left because I was less, because I wasn't *normal*.

"Of course." A coarse hand gripped my elbow, warmth spilling up my arm, and Graeson led me away from the crowd, knowing as he always did that I needed to distance myself from the happy couple through no fault of their own. "I appreciate the rescue. I'm glad for them, but I'm not myself, and I don't want to take away from their joy."

"You were magnificent." His eyes shone golden with pride. "I had no idea." He brought my hands to his lips and kissed each finger. "Your talents never cease to amaze me."

"It's nothing. Just a trick I learned." Embarrassed, I rolled a shoulder. "It made me popular with pregnant coworkers."

"It's not a trick, it's a gift." He linked our fingers. "*You* are a gift."

Heat rose in my cheeks, and I had to look away before my vision went glassy. "You're just trying to butter me up so I'll stick around and handle my half of the pack duties."

A chuckle radiated from him, and I sneaked a glimpse at his smile.

"You're half right." He wrapped my arms around his waist, and a pleased vibration rattled his chest when I linked my fingers behind his back without prompting. "I do want to butter you up."

I leaned my cheek against his pecs and blinked at the hot prickle of tears behind my eyes. "You'll get tired of me." It was my greatest fear, letting him in, him seeing the lack in me and leaving.

"Maybe." He kissed the top of my head. "Just in case, I think we should spend the rest of our lives together to be sure."

I shut my eyes against a feeling too large to contain within my chest until I could breathe again. "Where do we go from here?"

Another press of his warm lips, this time against my temple. "You and I, or the pack?"

"The pack." Forcing myself to step out of the circle of his arms, I glanced around the clearing. "We can't stay."

"I made some calls while you were in town. I found an RV campground about an hour north, near Chattanooga. They've got room for your trailers, and they have decent security in case we end up parking there for a while. They're also the nearest location with full hookups." He tapped the end of my nose with his fingertip. "Best of all, thanks to a sewage geyser erupting from their blocked septic tank earlier in the week, the place is a ghost town. Only two slots are rented, and those just for a few days. We've leased the rest of the campground for the week, so human interactions should be minimal."

Gooseflesh rose in stinging peaks down my arms, as though someone had walked across my grave. Like death, the return trip to my honorary home state seemed inevitable.

"That sounds good." Stinky but better than the alternative, squatting in a human-filled campground with a baker's dozen wargs itching to get hairy and run under the moon. I hauled out Isaac's phone and shot Theo a quick text update with the promise of directions once I had them, though he sounded confident he could locate me on his own. "We should get moving so we can settle in before dark."

All too soon the trailers were hitched and the trucks idling. Our pack was thirteen wargs strong and required six additional vehicles, some with flatbed trailers, to get our caravan mobile. The strangest sensation swept over me, a wave of deja vu, reminding me of the summers when my extended family traveled together in a mile-long procession that drove locals crazy but made us laugh as their cars wove in and out of lanes to pass us.

The fuzzy warmth of the nostalgic moment evaporated as I tracked a blur of midnight fur rocketing through the trees. No doubt one of Bessemer's spies off to make their report. Dismissing the mild annoyance, I swept aside the fading tendrils of the family memory. Those misadventures rang hollow without someone who had been there to share them. Even if he were here, Theo would hardly be in a mood to reminisce while his mother and brother were missing.

Another layer of guilt drifted onto my shoulders, the panic I wasn't doing enough, the certainty I could try harder.

"We're going to get them back." Graeson rubbed my shoulders. "We'll make your family safe again."

His vow rang eerily similar to the one I had made Dell earlier. I hoped it being a double promise meant it was twice as likely to be kept.

"I believe you." I trusted his word. Graeson was pigheaded and stouthearted. His promises had weight. "We'll keep your people safe too."

He clicked his tongue. "*Our* people."

Pocketing the phone, I headed for my truck, thoughts divided between the family I had been born into and the one I was making.

Graeson and I cleared half the distance before an explosion rocked the ground beneath our feet and billowing clouds of blackness enveloped the sky.

CHAPTER FOUR

Ringing in my ears deafened me to what was being shouted around me. Pulling on my magic earlier meant I had summoned my wolf's sensitive ears in the bargain, and *ow*. How were Graeson and the others managing the pain?

Rugged hands cupped my cheeks, and I turned my head to find Graeson kneeling beside me. Kneeling. In the grass. I was sprawled on the ground. When had that happened?

His lips moved, and I read my name there. *"Ellis. Ellis. Ellis."* Over and over, he chanted it like a prayer.

"I'm okay." My throat vibrated, telling me I'd spoken. "I can't hear."

A nod tipped his head, and he set about massaging my scalp with a serious expression pinned in place. Sound drifted back to me in slow increments, aided by the stinging discomfort at my hairline.

"You got hit by shrapnel from the explosion." His fingers brushed my forehead. "I removed the piece of metal, and the cut isn't too deep. It's messy, though. Head wounds are bleeders."

He took my right hand, rolled his thumb over the nail concealing my spur and met my gaze.

I tried to sit up, got struck with vertigo and let him lay me back down. "Are you sure?"

He nodded and offered his palm.

Gritting my teeth against the nausea, I extended my spur, fingernail dropping to the ground, and pierced the meat of his hand. The bite of his blood hit my veins, and the vision of him—gold dust and sparkles—filled my head as a pack bond of two sprang between us.

Being alone in his headspace, cocooned by his affection, broke a flush along my skin.

"Give it a minute." His voice rang through my head. He kept a hand on my shoulder, pressing it flush with the grass. *"You've stopped bleeding, but there might be more damage we can't see."*

Aided by his donation, the world rushed back in a burst of frantic sound as the pack rallied around a column of twisting smoke beyond the trees.

"Better?" Gaze raking over me, he kept me pinned.

"I'm good." I ground my palms over my ears to scratch the healing itch of what I suspected was a set of new eardrums. "What was that?"

Clasping hands with me, he hauled me to my feet gently, so my swimming head got time to adjust to being upright. Vertical again, I spotted dozens of wolves gazing at the black column rising up to pollute the sky. Chandler wolves.

"Graeson?"

He didn't answer, and he didn't let go. He started walking toward the source of the explosion and dragged me behind him. I didn't mean to resist, but a bone-deep dread filled me the closer we got, and then my knees stopped working altogether.

My free hand flew to cover my mouth. "Oh gods, no."

A twisted metal sculpture glinted in the heart of the flames. The paint had bubbled, and the explosion had blasted out the windows, but I'd recognize the frame of Aunt Dot's vintage Ford F100 pickup anywhere.

Iron bands wrapped around my middle, yanking me to a gut-clenching halt as I ran straight for the inferno.

"You can't get any closer," Graeson yelled over the hissing and crackling. "Whoever did this used a magical accelerant. Look. Fire sprites."

Tears blurred my eyes, from the heat and the heartache, but now that he'd pointed them out, I saw them everywhere. Red, yellow and white sprites leaped and twirled through the wreckage. They wouldn't stop until the metal was molten and the spell released them back to the heart of the volcano that birthed them. The cycle would take hours to complete and leave nothing but ash.

The missing gas cans melting into plastic puddles several yards away were just overkill.

"I'll talk to Bessemer and bargain for more time." Graeson loosened his grip a fraction as he backed me away. "We'll wait it out."

"No." My voice cracked. "This kind of trouble is why he wants us gone. He's not going to cooperate and risk endangering his people. Not when he's so close to dusting us off his hands." Turning my back on the raging inferno felt like surrender, like accepting defeat, but there were more lives at stake than just those of my family. The pack was in more danger every minute we lingered, the tentative peace with Bessemer easily broken when he realized fae troubles had marked his land, his people, once again. "We should go."

The destructive spell had been cast. There was no extinguishing it without witchy intervention I couldn't afford and wouldn't ask anyone else to pay. The flame-mouthed sprites were ravenous.

"Are you sure?" A growl laced his words as he glanced around the clearing where the Chandler wargs had gathered. "Once we leave, there's no coming back."

"She wasn't in there." The steadiness of my voice surprised me. "She and Isaac are together."

Safe, I almost added, but I was afraid I had already lied to myself and didn't want to compound it.

"Come on." He tucked a strong arm around my waist and led me to my truck. "Hop up." He patted the seat, and I climbed in, let him click the strap in place over my lap and shut the door. "He needs her alive. He needs both of them alive." He circled around and slid into the driver's spot. "The girls the kelpie took were kept for a period of time before he killed them and left them out in the open for us to find. It's how Charybdis's magic works, how his mind works. This..." his fingers clenched on the wheel, "...is foreplay."

And Charybdis meant to wring every ounce of pleasure from my pain.

CHAPTER FIVE

A night breeze swirled around my ankles, kicking up the scent of fried foods and all but vibrating with the gentle hum of cicada song. The air was cooler here in Chattanooga, closer to the mountains, but I'd been jogging hard for hours. Perspiration rolled into my eyes, camouflaging wayward tears. Sweat dripped from my clothes, and my throat was drier than the Sahara, but the spiking pain in my side distracted me from the ache in my heart.

Feet made of lead, I lapped around the track circling the RV park rather than face those empty trailers and the expectant faces.

Heavy footsteps synced up with mine, and I glanced over my shoulder to find Graeson pounding the asphalt behind me, hair slicked back and droplets falling onto his damp shirt.

I might have laughed if I'd had oxygen to spare. "How long?"

Twice I had caught a whiff of almost but not quite recognizable fur, there and gone before I could identify the babysitter Graeson had sicced on me. However, his much more familiar scent had eluded me until he chose to reveal himself.

"The whole time." Winded but steady, he put on a burst of speed to even us. "You shouldn't be alone right now."

"Afraid Charybdis will jump out of a bush and grab me?" I threw back my head and let the moon beat down on my face. "There was a time when that's exactly what you wanted to happen."

A noncommittal grunt escaped him before he caught my elbow. "Enough exercise for today. Let's go. It's time."

"Time?" Legs running on autopilot, I dragged him several yards before stopping. "For what?"

"To own our titles, mate." Chest heaving, he searched my face. "We have no pack bond. Our members need that connection to keep their wolves level. It will bind us together, cement our bonds of fellowship, give them a sense of belonging to their people if not to a place. Plus, it's a more efficient means of communication." He spun me back the way we had come. "I asked them to have everything in place by the time the moon reached its apex."

Scowling up at the treacherous orb, I let him march me back to our section of the RV park. Except he kept going, past the walking trails and bathrooms, beyond the laundry hut and the main road, and into the shadowy embrace of the poplars leading into a dense forest large enough a dozen wolves might stretch their legs unnoticed by their human neighbors.

Flickering dots illuminated the ground ahead in a winding circular path, candles as bright as stars fallen to Earth. Graeson escorted me, my arm now tucked in his elbow, and stopped when we reached the dried lip of an evaporated creek bed that crumbled under my sneakers.

A sense of wonder captivated me, rooting my feet to the spot. I was about to take part in activating a pack bond, in cementing the bedrock of this group, and it was a ceremony no fae I'd ever heard of had been privy to, let alone acted as a cornerstone.

Everyone with the exception of Graeson and me had changed from their trip outfits and now wore white. The men dressed in loose-fitting linen pants with flowing tops, and the women wore fluttering dresses so sheer the tips of their breasts were visible through the fabric. Flower chains adorned their heads, and even a few of the males wore single wildflowers pinned over their hearts.

I smoothed a hand down my drenched tank and scrunched my toes up in my shoes. "I'm not dressed for this."

"That's where I come in." Dell stepped from behind me carrying a plastic sack, the kind from a grocery store, and a jug of water. Arm looping through mine, she tugged me away from Graeson. "You're with us."

"You know what that means." Jensen approached Graeson with a second bag and jug. "Step this way."

Graeson crossed to me, lifted my hand and kissed my knuckles in a dramatic farewell that made Dell snort beside me.

"Okay, girls." Dell whistled through her teeth. "Let's get our alpha ready for the ceremony."

As we peeled aside to go our own way, I saw the males rallying around Graeson and urging him in the opposite direction.

Bianca's touch whispered over my elbow, and a comforting brush of her magic followed. The last of the four females in our pack, one of the six who had accompanied Graeson to Abbeville, gripped the other. She walked so close her thigh brushed mine, and a hard lump jostled me. Glancing down through the gauzy material of her dress, I saw a bulky dagger that desperately wanted to be a sword secured in a leather holster to her upper leg.

"I'm Nathalie Wilson." She put distance between us so the handle no longer created friction. "No one's bothered to introduce us, but since I'm about to see you naked, I figured we should be on a first-name basis."

"Um, what?" I dug my heels into the decaying leaves. "Why would you see me naked?"

"The purification ceremony." Bianca squinted up at me. "Cord didn't mention it? I thought he must have since you two performed the first half together."

Casting my thoughts back over the past few hours, I struggled to pinpoint any rites I might have undergone.

"Sweating out your impurities?" Nathalie scrunched up her face. "He really didn't explain this to you?"

"Nope," Dell chimed in from up ahead. "He wanted it to be a surprise."

A groan of utter mortification escaped me. A surprise meant they had put their heads together, decided I would freak out over whatever was about to happen, and decided to ensure my cooperation via ignorance and peer pressure.

Same old Graeson.

I was so going to yank Dell's perfect hair for this later.

"Here we are." Dell arranged her supplies on the ground and tugged her dress over her head. "Get naked." She wiggled her eyebrows. "Let's get it on."

I crossed my arms over my chest, because she must be talking to someone else. Right?

Bianca carefully stepped from her gown, and Nathalie shucked hers in one smooth motion, then hung them both on a low limb to keep them wrinkle free.

I stood there in my three-quarter yoga pants, a sports bra and stained racerback tank top. Suddenly I was the overdressed one.

"Don't be such a prude." Dell linked her fingers around my wrist and hauled me into the creek bed. "Boobs are boobs are boobs."

I gripped a sapling on the way past and hung on for dear life. "Yes, but these are *my* boobs."

"We've already seen them through Cord's memory," Nathalie contributed. "His wolf saw you shower and broadcasted the images through the pack bond." She belly-laughed at my dawning horror. "It was better than pay-per-view."

I died on the spot. The elbow Dell was yanking must have belonged to my ghost, because no way had I survived the detonation of that bombshell.

Sniffing my shoulder, Nathalie pursed her lips. "I never noticed before, but you don't smell much like him."

"It's probably a fae thing or a Cam thing. Trust me." Dell dug her fingernails into my wrist. "They're sleeping together."

Atomic heat blasted my cheeks, but the fierce glint in Dell's eyes kept me from denying Graeson hadn't done more than spoon me and only then while he was in wolf form.

"We don't need details." Bianca showed mercy. Or so I thought before she winked at me. "Once the pack bond activates, we'll get our PPV channels back."

"You're looking at this all wrong." Dell pried my hand loose and dragged me stumbling forward. "The pack bond goes both ways, and you're alpha. Think of Cord as a set of rabbit-ear antennas for your television. You'll get the best reception of all, and Nathalie here has loose morals."

"There's nothing *loose* about my...morals." She circled her hips like a pro hula hooper. "I just like sex."

The other women groaned, but I couldn't stop my smile from spreading. As embarrassing as it was to get naked in the woods with these women, a small part of me thrilled to be included in the initiation ritual. Until Harlow and Dell barged into my life, I had no clue how much I'd missed out by not having close girlfriends to share gossip, greasy fried food, guy drama and apparently boobs.

Isaac had gone from favorite cousin to surrogate brother when I lost Lori, but it wasn't the same. We had to love each other, even when we drove one another crazy, or else Aunt Dot stood us in a corner until impending death by boredom made us repent.

This newfound ability to make friends, the rewards I reaped from putting myself out there and embracing them when they did the same, was liberating. This was what Aunt Dot had always wanted for me, to open my heart a fraction wider, though starting to care for people I might lose in a blink terrified me.

The fleeting thought of Aunt Dot and Isaac made my throat close, but I rebuilt the crumbling mental wall I used for keeping Lori's memory at bay and sealed off that throbbing hurt for a while longer.

Tonight was for Graeson. There would be time enough to wallow in guilt once Theo arrived.

"Here's how it works." Dell retrieved her jug. "This is water from Pilcher's Pond. It represents our old pack, old homes, old lives. For you it represents where your life intersected with Cord's and ours." She wiped a finger across my damp shoulders. "You've sweated out your impurities. Pouring the water over you absolves you of past sins. It symbolizes a clean start."

A clean start. What I wouldn't give if that was true. "Then what?"

"We air dry, because Dell forgot the towels." Nathalie didn't seem bothered by the idea. "After that, we dress you and take turns braiding your hair. No, really. I'm serious. It's puberty all over again."

"You don't have to go through this just for me." Their hanging dresses fluttered, ghosts of a past I wish this ritual would absolve. "You were already prepped. I'm the one holding up everything."

Stubborn doubts bred from a lifetime of being an outcast drifted to the surface of my thoughts. The females had begun their portion of the ceremony without me. Had they excluded me on purpose, or had I missed out by virtue of being absent? Would I be standing here now if Graeson hadn't fetched me, forcing the invite? These women had probably known one another all their lives. I didn't have history with them. I was new, unknown, untrusted and unwarg to boot.

"You're one of us, Cam." Dell saw right through my insecurities. "Don't make me embarrass you with naked cuddles to prove my point. You know I'm good for it."

"That's really not necessary." I eased back when she started bouncing on the balls of her feet, lest she poked out my eyes with her uninhibited jiggling. "I believe you."

"We purged ourselves earlier. How could we cleanse you if we ourselves were tainted?" Bianca rested a hand on Dell's shoulder to anchor her. "Now we'll purify you with our hands, symbolizing the absolution of all ties to our previous alpha."

Voice flat, I cringed inwardly. "Dell, you forgot to mention the part where you all take turns bathing me."

"Did I?" Dell pursed her lips. "It must have slipped my mind."

Nathalie pinched my cheeks—not the ones on my face—and cooed, "Prudes are so cute."

Tucking my thumbs in the hem of my shirt, I tugged it over my head to the raucous noise of catcalls and wolf-whistles. Flames erupted in my cheeks as Dell used my left side as a pole for dancing. Nathalie joined her while Bianca clutched her stomach as she chortled. Swaying between them, I kicked off my shoes and socks. Too winded from laughing to torment me, Dell and Nathalie strutted around Bianca until she had to cross her legs to keep from peeing.

Gulping a deep breath while they were distracted, I yanked down my panties and tossed my bra aside. Standing there with nothing but the humid breeze on my skin, I flashed back to the night in my trailer when Graeson, as a wolf, had watched me shower through half-closed lids.

Wait a minute. That happened *after* the pack bond snapped. Eyes narrowed on the gaggle of giggling females, I snorted a laugh. They were teasing me. Tendrils of belonging spread through my chest, anchoring me to these women.

Except now the seed had been planted. How many of our pack mates would tune in for a free show the night we consummated our bond? I really, really hoped Nathalie was teasing me about that part too.

"Don't look now," Dell crowed, "but the alpha is *naked*."

I dropped my head into my hands and waited for the earth to swallow me whole.

No such luck.

Dell tugged on one of my hands, Nathalie pried away the other, and they led me into the dusty creek basin. Much to my relief, they sobered once Dell fetched the water. Smiles still wreathed their faces, but reverence was there too, for me or the ceremony I wasn't sure.

With gentle and respectful touches on the non-intimate parts of my body, the women washed me and dampened my hair. When the water ran out, they spread a blanket and pushed my shoulders down until I sat. Shuffling to get into position, the three of them managed to all kneel behind me and began the task of detangling my post-workout hair and taming it into one of the intricate braids they wore. Flower petals rained down into my lap, and I picked them up and blew them off my palm.

I spaced out, lulled by the soft brush of fingers, until a delicate grunt rose behind me as Dell and Nathalie helped Bianca to her feet. The trio circled around in front of me to inspect their handiwork.

Hands clasped in front of her, Bianca's eyes went liquid. Probably hormones. "You look beautiful, Camille."

"You clean up nice," Nathalie agreed, offering me a hand up. "Let's get dressed and get this done so we can eat."

Let's eat, the official warg motto.

"Hands up." Dell approached with her arms laced through the bodice of a flowing white garment she slipped over my head. "There we go."

Unlike the others, my dress wasn't linen but super-fine silk so thin the smattering of freckles on my chest were visible through the material. That wasn't the only difference. The hem brushed my toes, and a short train pooled behind me. When Dell thrust a wildflower bouquet into my hands, the similarities between this pack binding and a human wedding gave me butterflies.

The others redressed and fussed with their hair one last time before linking arms with me. The four of us walked back to the clearing barefoot and glowing from the cold bath and the laughter. Our chortling lured the men from their carousing, and they fanned out in a loose semicircle wearing grins of their own.

Graeson emerged last, his eyes only for me, and his visual caress gave me chills.

Hair slicked back, he'd fastened the curled length with a white ribbon at his nape. His jaw was clean-shaven and as sharp as the razor responsible. Stacked with thick muscle, his bare abs quivered under my appraisal. The ivory silk pants worn low on his hips managed to be every bit as sheer as my dress.

I had seen Graeson naked, many times, and I always fought gravity to keep my focus above his navel. The subtle flicker of candlelight over his skin invented shadows that ensnared the eye, tempted my focus lower and left my breaths shallow.

Stifled laughs humiliated me for the millionth time this evening. The urge to turn and run was a twitch in my calf until Bianca released a dreamy sigh at the sight of Jensen all cleaned up and, if the tenting of his thin pants were any indication, *very* excited to see his mate.

"They're like bunnies," Nathalie grumbled. "Those pregnancy hormones must be some good shit."

"Bunnies aren't that vocal." Dell ribbed me with her elbow. "You can always tell when they're getting it on because you'll be minding your own business one minute and the next you hear *aroo aroo arooooo* and notice Bianca and Jensen are missing."

Covering a snort with my hand, I hoped the lovebirds didn't take offense, but I'm pretty sure they didn't even notice the rest of us snickering at their public display of affection.

"Alpha." With a flourish, Dell dropped into a low curtsy that sent her skirts fluttering. "May I present your mate? She didn't bite or scratch anyone during the preparations. She deserves a cookie."

"You look beautiful." Graeson leaned forward and brushed his lips over my knuckles before I lowered my hand, bumping noses with me in the process. "You're always so beautiful."

"You're not off the hook that easily." I swatted him with my bouquet. "You should have explained all of..." I swept an arm down my body, "...*this* to me."

"Why?" He dodged my next swing. "So you could apply fae logic to warg tradition and bolt before you saw there was nothing sexual or wrong about it?"

Cutting my gaze to Bianca, I raised an eyebrow as she swayed in her mate's arms while he nibbled his way across her collarbone.

"That has nothing to do with the ceremony." He cleared his throat loudly in their general direction. "They're mated and expecting. Jensen would have carried her in his arms the entire nine months if she'd let him. He's been so paranoid he doesn't want her feet touching the ground." Pride shone in Graeson's eyes as he looked at me. "You gave him a measure of peace today. That was kind of you."

"I'm glad I could help." I tapped the flowers across my palm. "You're still not forgiven."

"Challenge accepted." Smugness radiated from him. "We'll make it up to you."

We as in him and his wolf. Damn it. The wolf was so fluffy, his eyes so big and honest, that when my fingers buried in his soft white belly fur, I had trouble remembering why I was angry at the man he concealed.

Wary of the apologetic shenanigans both halves of Graeson had in mind, I noticed my bruised flowers and spruced them before the girls saw. "Tell me the truth, the whole truth, up front, and there won't be any reason to make amends."

The concept rattled around his head, and his lips pursed as if asking permission instead of begging forgiveness was a foreign idea.

For a dominant male warg, it just might be.

Contrite as a schoolboy, Graeson dusted flower petals off his chest. "Would you like me to outline the next hour for you?"

"At this point..." I scanned the clearing, gaze touching on a ceremonial dagger the length of my forearm, "...I think I'm better off not knowing."

His lips parted, ready to contradict me for asking to be kept in the dark, which was exactly what he had done and obviously still believed to be right as well as *his* right to decide on my behalf.

As a reward for giving me the option to choose to bury my head in the sand, I leaned forward and kissed the hard pectoral muscle shielding his heart. "I appreciate you letting me decide for myself."

Nostrils flared and eyes gone molten with heat and wonder, Graeson grazed his knuckles down my cheek. "That's the first time you've ever kissed me."

Licking my lips, I tasted clean sweat and tart skin. "We've kissed several times."

"No." His voice reverberated through my bones. "*I* kissed *you*. There's a difference." He leaned down, rubbed his cheek against mine and whispered in my ear, "I knew you liked me back."

Like was one word for it. There was definitely a four-letter word starting with L involved. I had trouble breathing when he stood so near, even though half the time I still wanted to strangle him in such close proximity.

"I do like you back," I rushed out before losing my nerve. "A lot. Even if I'm not great at showing it."

Blame it on the candlelight or the moon. Admitting how he affected me, here and now, ensconced with our people, felt important, as if we were laying the foundation for a future that left my mouth as dry as cotton balls.

"Aww." Dell clasped her hands together. "I foresee pups in the new year."

"Then you should blink harder." I tore off a flower head and tossed it at her. "You've got something in your eye."

"It's time." Graeson checked the moon's position in the sky. "Dell?"

Wriggling between us, she grasped my wrist and hauled me down into the portion of the creek bed they'd purified with a dusting of powder-fine salt, then she shoved on my shoulders until I sat in the crackling dirt. She positioned herself to one side of me, and Nathalie flanked the other. Bianca sat next to Dell, and Jensen joined his mate as the men followed Graeson and began filling the gaps in the circle. Once we were all seated, my fellow alpha directly across from me, the mystery began unraveling.

"Each of you made the choice to be here. Being present means you accept my dominion over you, and it means you acknowledge Ellis as my partner and equal." Gold eyes met mine, so bright his gaze burned through me. "She is my mate, and if you put me in a position to choose her or you, she will win every time. Yes, she is fae. Yes, she is different. And yes, that will alienate us from securing alliances with some packs." He raised a finger. "It will also open doors for new opportunities we will be in a unique position to seize."

Almost the exact second my throat constricted, Dell squeezed my hand in reassurance.

From the moment the gas station clerk dialed me from Isaac's phone to the percussive blast of Aunt Dot's pride and joy detonating yards away from me, my family had occupied my thoughts exclusively. No, if I was being honest, it had started the moment Charybdis painted a target on their backs because of me.

That single-mindedness had been a mistake, if an unavoidable one. Becoming alpha, shouldering the title of Graeson's mate, accepting that these people were mine to protect too, had seemed so abstract when I agreed to this. As though I had been bobbing my head at Graeson without comprehending the ramifications because my fears and worries were otherwise engaged.

Tonight there was no ignoring the magnitude of the sacrifice these people had made in leaving the security of the Chandler pack. The veil had been ripped from my eyes, my own problems shelved for later, when I had solitude to mourn, and I sat exposed to the full consequences of my union with Graeson.

The ever-present tremor in Isaac's fingers, his car keys a talisman, a promise of escape, twitched in mine.

I won't lie. I wanted to run. I wasn't this person. This woman had friends and a partner who cooked her meals and remembered the little things, like her favorite flavored water additives. She was putting down roots, if not in this place then with these people. Her family was blossoming, expanding, and even though she fit with the wargs about as much as she fit with other Gemini, they accepted her. She *belonged*.

Oh, I wanted to be her. I wanted her to be me. I wanted...all of this. The friends, the trust, the security.

And I wanted Graeson, wanted to belong to him, more than I had ever selfishly wanted anything in my life.

The wild presence in my blood sang her approval to the moon. Graeson called it—*her*—my inner she-wolf, though the phenomenon must be a recalled magical remnant. Either way, the feral possessive urge that lived inside me these days hummed with approval.

"Examine your souls," Graeson continued in a somber tone. "Search your hearts. Be certain this is the right path for you, for your family. It won't be easy, not at first, maybe not ever. Our people cling to tradition, they nurture fear and embrace superstitions where the fae are concerned." His gaze panned the circle. "Keeping your seat means you understand and accept that this pack will value our members regardless of their origins or species. Keeping your seat means you're willing to place faith in the greater world and accept nontraditional allies." A growl entered his voice. "Keeping your seat means you understand that a hand raised against Ellis is a hand raised against me. The punishment for harming a fellow pack mate will be expulsion. Blood will answer for blood."

A murmur of agreement rippled around the circle, clashing with other, grimmer mutterings, but I didn't dare meet any of their gazes. I was too afraid of what I might find staring back at me. Resentment, anger, fear, hope. The last was most terrifying.

"Everyone close your eyes," Graeson ordered. "This is your last chance to leave without facing repercussions. If you can't abide by the rules I have set, go. Return to Bessemer with my blessing."

The quiet stretched, and my nerves strung taut with the waiting. Rustling noises popped up here and there, but the scuffs were too faint for me to tell if someone—or someones—rose and left or if the shuffling was the natural impatience of predators unhappy sitting for so long while at a tactical disadvantage.

"Eyes open." Graeson's molten gaze awaited mine. "It's time."

He lifted the thirsty-looking blade from his lap and set its scabbard aside. I figured unsheathing the dagger might explain some of the murmurous sounds until a quick head count told me I had cost Graeson two members of his already small and vulnerable pack. Still a part of his six, the two deserters had been strangers to me. Honestly I had half expected Haden to make a break for it when given an out. Or maybe Jensen and Bianca now that they grasped the magnitude of what was at stake for their fledgling family. But the wargs known to me remained in their spots.

"Tonight this gathering becomes more than a sum of individuals," Graeson continued. "We become pack. We become family."

The mood in the circle as we scooted closer to banish the empty spaces was both somber with the loss of the men and excited for what was to come.

"Take the knife with your left hand. Score your right palm until blood flows. This symbolizes your willingness to bleed for your pack." He illustrated making the cut, and my gut quivered. "Mark your neighbor's left palm, a promise that their hurts are yours to share." A red line appeared across Jensen's palm. "Then pass them the knife, clasp hands and let our blood bind us."

Around the circle the dagger traveled, biting the hands of those who fed it. When my turn came, it was Dell who cut me, and deep. Jaw clenched, I made my own slice across my palm then marked Nathalie. Dell's hand slipped in mine, our essences mingling. Nathalie finished with the male beside her, and we clasped hands too. The warg blood tingled in my open wounds, feeding magic and excitement into my veins until I was drunk on the sensory overload.

Done wetting its sharp tongue, the blade returned to Graeson. Reverently he placed it inside a carved box then completed the circuit. Power, raw and wild zinged through my arms as he fed a part of himself through us all. This was a kind of earth magic I hadn't known existed, and I marveled at the rich texture of its caress.

Light flashed behind my lids, blinding me, burning his radiant visage in my mind's eye. The fierce white glow I associated with Graeson was ten times more brilliant than ever before, and it engulfed me, branded me on a cellular level.

"These are your people too now." His voice brushed my mind. *"Feed your power into the circle. Bind them to you."* A husky plea. *"Bind me to you."*

"I don't know how." I writhed in the supernova that was an alpha claiming his pack, my old self charring and my ashes scattering. *"Gemini magic is self-contained. I can't affect others with it."*

"Relax your mind. Magic is in the blood, in the mind and in the heart." A phantom kiss pressed to my forehead. *"Picture your magic as a butterfly rising up from your core. Now, will it to fly all the way around the circle and return to you."*

"Here goes nothing." Running with his analogy, I fixed the image of a butterfly in my head and imagined it rising up from my center, wings caressing my rib cage on its way to freedom. Focusing until sweat popped out on my forehead, I pictured it fluttering over the wargs' heads, christening each with its pixie-dust residue, until it landed on Graeson. *"Is it working?"*

"Yes," he rumbled, voice low and as sensual as a caress. *"I can sense you melding with the others. Now finish it."*

Biting my lip, I urged my imaginary ambassador to take wing once more, floating over the other half of the circle until that kiss of energy lit on my shoulder. As its ethereal legs touched down, a jolt shocked my eyes open, the static punch like sticking fork tines in a live outlet.

Incandescence radiated from me and Graeson in a blast that seared my flesh as light pierced my soul. White-gold and intoxicating, it baptized each warg, each link in the chain, and when it swept past me like a tsunami, silvery threads of magic glinted in my mind's eye, tethers spun from my heart.

"We did it." We had sewn the small pack together, to us. *"I can feel them."*

"You did good, Alpha." Dell butted in, chuckling in my head. *"Now you'll never be rid of me. I don't even have to mentally knock. I can just blast down your brain door."*

"A comatose alpha won't do anyone any good," Nathalie chastised.

Eyes wide, I snapped my head toward her. *"I can hear you. And Dell. At the same time."*

"You're pack now." She grinned wolfishly. *"We can conference call like nobody's business."*

"You may release hands." Graeson's booming voice in my ears startled me amid the cerebral chatter. "It's done." Rolling gracefully to his feet, he prowled toward me and hauled me upright. Tucking me against his side, he addressed the others. "Welcome, kindred, to the Lorimar Pack."

Lorimar. Lori and Marie. The two little girls whose deaths had brought us to this place, as these people, and who we would miss for always.

Hot tears rolled down my cheeks as I flung my arms around Graeson. I buried my face against his ribs before the sobs clawing up the back of my throat tore past my lips. I couldn't hold him tight enough. The harder I squeezed, the more certain I felt that I would be the one who shattered.

"Shh." He wrapped me closer and nuzzled my hair. "I didn't mean to make you cry."

Voice ruined, I sought his mind. *"You named the pack after our sisters."*

"Our pack." He drew back to stare down at me. "Is this one of those things I should have asked you about first before making a decision?"

"No." I laughed, a choked sound. "This was perfect."

The tension locking his muscles melted under my praise, and I sprinkled impulsive kisses over his face, because Graeson was trying to treat me as an equal and not a weakness he must blindly protect. Compromise didn't come easily to dominants, a truth I had learned well during my time with the Chandler pack, but he was putting in the work. This newest evidence of his devotion cracked open my soul, and I basked in the rightness of being with him. I pressed a lingering kiss over his heart, my new favorite spot, and breathed in the scent of his skin until fur rubbed against the underside of mine.

Inhaling the column of my throat, Graeson released a low growl. "Want to go for a run?"

I laughed at the mischief in his voice. "We just did."

"You heard the alphas," Dell crowed. "The race is on."

White fabric billowed in the air as the pack shucked their pants and dresses and tossed them skyward. A few darted into the trees for privacy while the rest sank to the ground and gave in to the pain beside a friend. Bone snapped and cartilage popped until wolves filled the clearing. Tails swishing, they pranced and jumped and bit playfully at one another. Only Bianca remained unchanged. She sat where I'd left her and scratched the underbelly of a massive auburn-furred beast busy kicking his hind leg in ecstasy.

A melancholy ache radiated from my chest. "I can't— Not the way you do." They peeled aside their humanity and reveled in the untamed nature of their souls. "I don't have a wolf."

"Yes, you do." Backing away, he arched his spine in the throes of change. "Let her come out to play."

Agonizing moments later, a gorgeous sterling wolf with snow white splashes of color up his forelegs climbed to his paws and shook out the residual tingles from his change. He paused at the fringe of towering pines and glanced back at me, waiting, hoping, then bolted out of sight. The others followed, except for three of us.

Picking at the neckline of my dress, I twisted around to face Jensen and Bianca. "Are you coming?"

"I can't, and he won't." Laughter rang out when he licked her chin. "I haven't felt the urge to shift since my scent changed, and he can't leave me unprotected. It goes against all of his instincts." She ruffled his fur. "Even though he can't help but answer the alpha's call by going furry."

"Will you two be all right?" The explosion earlier had me on edge. Charybdis thrived on preying on the vulnerable, and it didn't get more defenseless than a heavily pregnant woman unable to call on her wolf. Jensen was fierce, but Charybdis was no ordinary enemy. "I can stay if you want company."

"One babysitter is plenty." She huffed at the wolf licking her ear. "Go. Enjoy yourself. Nip Nathalie's tail for me."

Requiring no further encouragement, I summoned my inner she-wolf. Recalled magic blasted through my veins with the punch of an adrenaline dump. Fur pierced my skin and rippled up my arms, across my shoulders and over my neck. My jaw cracked as it elongated, and my senses heightened in a rush that left me drunk on the moon.

Nostrils flared, I inhaled the musky woods scent of wolves, *my* wolves, and chased the heady lure of my mate deep into the heart of the forest.

CHAPTER SIX

Thighs screaming with each flex of burning muscle, I jogged back to the ceremonial site to check on the lovebirds. With nips and short barks, the wolves begged me to stay and play, but their animals were fresh, just hitting their stride. Thanks to my earlier jog-a-thon, my knees were the consistency of overcooked elbow macaroni, and I couldn't feel my feet. Two legs were no match for four, and now that I was done for the night, the others could chase the horizon instead of holding back for my sake.

I pinned a sappy curl to my lips as Graeson's mind brushed mine, his approval that I had circled back to check on our most vulnerable member warming me. Spreading my awareness, I luxuriated in the ability to touch each mind in the pack. The wargs vibrated with energy and poured their emotion into the scrabble of claws on dirt. They might not know it yet, but their new alpha planned on running them until they dropped in their tracks.

Panning my thoughts toward Bianca, the better to locate her, I slammed against a mental wall that blasted me with a headache so powerful I staggered and tripped over an exposed root. "Bianca?" My temples throbbed with my pulse, but I fought the blinding pain to search for her mate. "Jensen?"

After the worst effects subsided, I pushed to my feet and leapt to the creek bed, following it around a bend and past the candlelit area where the ceremony had taken place. For a span of seconds, I thought the migraine pounding between my ears had affected my color perception, but piece by piece the whole picture came into view, and bile stung the back of my throat.

Legs crossed and expression serene, Bianca sat in a pose identical to the way I last saw her. Upon hearing my approach, she tightened her grip on the handle of the ceremonial dagger. Its tip rested on the lip of her navel, and she pressed down until bright crimson spread across the splattered fabric of her dress. Calling on the dregs of my magic, I brought my wolf aspect forward and drew on her heightened senses. A copper tang prickled my nostrils, and I understood the crusted brown stains weren't mud from wandering the creek bed. They were blood.

Her irises, usually a denim blue, shone as black as her pupils in the patchy moonlight and grew somehow darker at my approach, as though her eyes were filled with a starless night sky.

"Hey." I came to a full stop several feet away from her crossed ankles and endeavored to sound casual while my heart jackknifed against my ribs. "Maybe I should hold that for you."

"Hello again, Camille Ellis. I will keep the knife if you don't mind." Her unblinking stare pierced me. I had held a gaze hardened with the same vacant malevolence in another innocent face a few days ago. "The babe is insurance, you see."

Reaching for Bianca through the pack bond on reflex, I dunked my mind into an icy blackness that sent tendrils of cold eternity seeking through our connection. "Charybdis."

A delicate roll of her shoulders shifted the blade deeper. "As you like."

So much blood on her. Where had it all come from? "Why do you need insurance?"

"I am vulnerable when my entire awareness is present in one being, but I cannot risk bringing an avatar so near your wolves or I would lose her and endanger my current level of autonomy. This was the only way for us to meet. Therefore..." Bianca twisted the blade until the richness of her blood hit the back of my throat with every inhalation, "...I required leverage."

As much as my palm itched to drive the knife through the real Charybdis's cold heart, all the act would accomplish at this moment was ending a woman and her unborn child. I had as much faith in him revealing true vulnerabilities to me as I trusted a coiled rattlesnake not to bite.

Holding steady, I reached through the pack bond to alert Graeson then mentally swept the area once more for signs of Jensen. I found none. "How did you possess Bianca without an avatar to act as your vehicle?"

"Bianca spent a great deal of time with Emily, learning what to expect from a warg pup I imagine. A pregnant female is a vulnerable female and a valuable asset." She let her delicate shoulder rise and fall. "I laid claim to this body to, as you say, keep my options open." Her grin chilled me. "It seems I was right to mark her. Never had I dreamed she would lead me straight to you."

Harlow had initiated contact with Emily, the Chandler alpha's daughter, to trick her into performing small tasks for her. Did this mean Emily was infected too? I saw no other link between Harlow, his current avatar, Emily and Bianca. How his contagion spread gnawed at me, but I knew better than to ask a second time.

Bianca tilted her head, absorbing every detail of my disheveled appearance. "Ask me what you truly wish to know."

It was a trap. I knew it. I walked right into it anyway. "Are my aunt and cousin still alive?"

Eyes rolling back, she inhaled until her stomach rounded, then exhaled on a sensual moan. "Where would the pleasure be in telling you?"

I bit my lip, hating I had exposed the pulsing heart of my weakness.

"How you ache with their loss." Bliss wafted off her skin, and she flared her nostrils wider. "How it eats you up inside to know you failed to save them, the same as you failed to save Lori." Cruelty glinted in her eyes. "You are weak, Camille Ellis. You always have been, and you always will be. It will cost you all you love, and then, when you are broken and beg for my touch, then I might—*might*—bestow my blessing upon you."

The mention of her touch called to mind the shell that remained of Marshal Ayer after bearing the burden of such a blessing. "You're offering me a position as an avatar-in-waiting?" Did she expect me to stand in line until her magic burned out Harlow? "I'm afraid I must decline."

"How much further must I push before I break you," she mused. "It is such an individual process, one can never truly estimate the threshold until one crosses it."

Tamping down the fear and guilt, the worry and regret, I shut down my emotions the way I had trained myself to when the burden of carrying Lori's ghost in my bones weighed too heavily on me. The change in Bianca's expression was instantaneous. I had cut off her supply and slapped her back to attention. Now all I had to do was keep her focused on me and not the wolves I sensed circling us.

"What is your purpose here? Not just in this forest, but on Earth?" I deserved that much at least. "Why did you leave Faerie?"

"There is much game to be hunted here." The thing inside Bianca exhaled on a lusty sigh. "Varieties of fae exist here that Faerie has long since forgotten in her eagerness to purge her excess into this realm." She pointed a stained finger at me. "Gemini have been reduced to lore in Faerie." A laugh fluttered past her lips. "What other forgotten gems might this Earth have to offer?"

A sick feeling pooled in the pit of my gut. I doubted she meant *game* as in *animals*. She meant people. Humans. Fae. All of us.

"Earth is not your playground," I growled.

"Yet." Bianca drew herself up taller and sent her gaze searching past my shoulder. "It won't be much longer now."

"Wait." Sensing the pack's nearness, I lurched forward. "Why risk this visit? You gained nothing from it."

"Wrong." A chill permeated the word. "This visit is a gift. Treat it as such." Her knuckles whitened on the dagger's handle. "I can reach you anywhere, Camille Ellis, through anyone. I will hunt you as you have hunted me, until my vengeance costs you everything, as your ambition has cost me."

"Ellis."

A flash of bare skin drew my eye as Graeson ran naked into the clearing with the wolves panting at his heels. Faster than my lips could form a warning, Bianca reared her arm back and hurled the dagger. The cruel blade sheathed itself between his ribs. Clutching the handle with a snarl peeling back his lips, he sank to his knees, and blood flowed in rivulets down his chest.

Mind gone numb with shock—this wasn't happening, I wasn't losing him, not now, not like this—I fell back on my training. Lunging for Bianca, I captured her wrists and twisted them high and tight behind her back until her swollen belly protruded. I pinned them at her spine with a Word, laid her on her side, a position she couldn't rectify without help, and bound her ankles together too.

Charybdis couldn't have planned his moment any better if he had cracked a whip over the wolves and driven them to exhaustion himself. Fatigue overwhelmed the pack bond. Shifting back to their human skins, with human hands to help, took a lifetime. One Graeson didn't have to spare.

Threat neutralized, at least for now, I ran to him. Skidding through the loose dirt on my knees, I caught him in my arms as he toppled forward. Sticky warmth plastered the gauzy dress against my chest. The dull bump of the dagger's handle against my ribs sickened me. Gently, so gently, I guided him down to the ground on his side. The blade was serrated toward the handle, and he was pierced clean through.

"I need to examine him."

Whipping my head toward the voice, I barely restrained myself from snapping at the man's hands, which were raised in a nonthreatening pose that still managed to piss off my inner she-wolf who wasn't so inner at the moment. At some point I had fully shifted to my warg aspect, and I was salivating at the taste of violence in the air.

"He'll die unless you let me help," the man said.

A whimper got caught in my throat, and then Dell was there, wrapping me in her arms and holding me steady while the man approached. His sweat stank with fear, of me or for Graeson, I wasn't sure.

"This is Abram." Dell tightened her grip as the steady rumbling in my throat revved louder. "He's our healer, the best in the Chandler pack. Bessemer was pissed as hell to lose him."

Breathing in through my nose and out through my mouth, I hung on to sanity by my pinky nail.

There was so much blood, too much blood, and Graeson's lungs made a wet noise when he drew in air.

Competent hands made quick work of the examination. Abram finished testing the entry and exit wounds with light fingers and made a ticking noise behind his teeth. "This has to come out, and all I've got in my bag is the contents of my medicine cabinet from home. Bessemer kept the rest. My supplies, equipment, all of it."

"Can you save him?" My voice came out raw but steady.

"Yes," he said earnestly. "It won't be pretty, and I can't trust your wolf to behave herself while I work. Getting that dagger out of him will hurt, and she may not trust that I mean her mate no harm." A kind smile curved his lips. "She almost maimed me for looking at him while he's wounded. While I admire the depth of her commitment, I'd also like to keep my hands attached if you don't mind."

I tossed my head against Dell's shoulder. "I can't leave him."

"Hon, listen to Abram." She stroked my back with her fingertips. "He's treated Meemaw for years. She says he's got magic hands."

"Save him if you can." I swallowed the lump clogging my throat. "Run and don't look back if you can't."

Failure was not an option. The feral awareness growing in my middle, warped by sorrow, vowed blood would answer for blood.

"Understood." His rough hand clapped me on the back as he shared a deep look with Dell. "Get her out of here and don't let her peek until I give the all clear, okay?"

"You got it, Doc." Dell's hands bruised my arms with the strength she used to contain me while helping me to my feet, as though not quite trusting I would leave in peace. She was wise to doubt. Her iron grip was all that kept me from snapping my teeth at Abram before she turned me on my heel and marched me in the direction of the RV park. "Focus, and you can keep tabs on Graeson through the bond." She urged me past two men wobbling to their feet while more wolves struggled to find their human skins. "For now you've got to keep calm, or your panic will seep into the pack bond. If Graeson picks up on your distress, he'll fight Abram's healing to get to you. Right now you need to send him peaceful vibes, okay? Let him know you're okay. Can you do that?"

Several steps into the cool darkness of the woods, I faltered at the keening wail of a heart shattering into a million infinitesimal pieces.

"Jensen," Bianca screamed until her voice quit. *"Jensen."*

"Oh gods," I murmured. "He stayed behind with her. I couldn't locate him through the bond and then—" She'd attacked Graeson, and Jensen became the least of my worries. "We have to find him."

"Are you up for this?" Dell's fingers dug into the meat of my upper arms. "Tell me the truth."

"I can do this." I owed it to Bianca to find her mate. "I need to do this."

The hunt for Jensen lasted all of five minutes.

We found him, what was left of him, behind a moss-covered boulder. He had been ripped into glistening strips of meat with the apparent ease of a child shredding tissue paper. Teeth and claw marks, most interchangeable on such a devastating scale, left no doubt he had met his end at the jaws of a fellow warg.

Part of me mourned that I had seen so much death that more didn't gut me the way I wanted it too. The way this should have. I hated being able to analyze the scene when a normal person would have fallen to their knees weeping and retching as Dell had beside me.

"Alpha?" Haden's voice rang in my head. *"Are you all right? The bond feels...wrong."*

"Leave Bianca with Nathalie." For the sake of her baby, and her own mental health, she could never see this free of the blinding fog of Charybdis's influence. *"Bring the others, and come find us."*

We had kin to mourn and defenses to ready.

CHAPTER SEVEN

I did what I could to minimize the trauma by organizing the pack meeting on the far side of the boulder. It wasn't much, but it kept a barrier between the pack and Jensen's remains so that those unable to face the horror of his brutal murder were protected from carrying gruesome mental pictures that would haunt them.

Either my disquiet as I struggled for the appropriate words attracted the wargs to me, or they were in need of physical comfort after the events of the night. By the time I'd mentally exhausted myself with openings, the pack had drifted into my orbit. Nathalie leaned her weight against my left side and Haden brushed his right elbow against mine. The remaining three men I hadn't met milled around, heads down and shoulders hunched.

Instinct told me they were waiting for my acknowledgment. We had been tiptoeing around one another for long enough. That ended tonight. Starting with the shortest and least intimidating of the three.

"We haven't been introduced." I used the loud, clear voice Graeson adapted when addressing the pack. The slight man with his feathered bangs and sprinkling of freckles sensed my attention and lifted his head. "Please, call me Cam."

"I'm Job." His blue-gray eyes flicked to mine then back to the ground. "I'm an accountant."

"It's nice to meet you, Job." I stuck out my hand, and he hesitated before accepting. The zing of feral magic in his blood sang to mine, and I released him. "I'm glad you chose us."

A quick jerk of his head, and he eased nearer Nathalie. The tension left his shoulders, and his chin lifted a fraction. Touch was concern, approval, affection to wargs. As they huddled around me, skin to skin, it sank in that not only would Graeson and Dell—and others I considered friends—crave platonic contact, but the entire pack required physical reassurance from one another, and especially from their alphas.

"You caught a chipmunk earlier," I said to the quiet wall of muscle with his feet planted shoulder's width apart. "You didn't even slow down."

One of his shoulders rose and then fell. "I was hungry."

Shifting drained their strength at the best of times, and Graeson had ran them until their tongues lolled. Not to mention the magic of the ceremony, which had siphoned energy from them as well. Wargs required calories, lots of them, to fuel their hypermetabolism. The unexpected attack had derailed our celebration, but the food was already bought and the wolves would have to be fed soon. Even heartsick, they had no choice but to sate the cravings of their wilder halves.

Shuffling over, he stuck out his hand, fingers splayed. "I'm Moore." He grunted. "Mechanic."

Strong magic brushed my palm, and he went to stand beside Haden. That left one man apart, and he was as thin as he was tall. I counted ribs when he unfolded his arms from across his chest.

The rangiest wolf of the pack was easy to identify. "You were the one who hung back to make sure the pack didn't leave anyone behind."

"I'm Zed." He thrust out his hand, bent so far over that his forehead almost brushed his upper arm. "I run a salvage yard. Or I used to. Guess I'll be buying a new place now. At the rate Moore busts up cars, it shouldn't take long to get a parts yard fully stocked again."

Moore growled at him without heat, and Zed shuffled between me and Haden until our upper arms were plastered together from the perspiration sheening his skin. With a shuddering exhale, he leaned harder against me, his heft knocking me into Nathalie, who rested her head on my shoulder.

"Jensen is gone." A profound sadness swept through me via the bond, but not a shred of shock. Their noses had already told them all they needed to know. "We need to see to his remains." A tear leaked down my arm from Nathalie's cheek. "Bianca is an innocent in this. We can't hold her responsible for what happened here tonight."

No, that blame rested squarely at my feet.

"Bessemer warned us about the fae hunting you. Graeson explained the rest." Moore shifted his weight. "We all knew the dangers. We all have our reasons for taking the risk." His large palm eclipsed my shoulder. "This wasn't your fault."

"We never imagined this, though." Zed dragged a hand over his mouth. "God knows we never imagined this."

"The thing that did this—" Job asked under his breath. "It's the same monster that killed Marie?"

"Yes, it is." Braced for them to turn on me, for the accusations to start flying, I was stunned to silence when not one bitter word was hurled in my direction. "He's got my aunt and my cousin," I told them. "He's going after my family. After tonight, that means the pack too. He's punishing me for hunting him."

"I pledged to my alphas." Haden jostled me with his elbow as he twisted to face the others. "This doesn't change that for me or my wolf."

"Or me," Dell called.

"Or me," rippled around the cluster of warm bodies. Each of them, every single one, supported Graeson...and me.

Awkward was one word to describe standing there sandwiched between near-strangers without a stitch of clothing between them, whose inner beasts were soothed by my presence. Humbling was another. The trust they extended to me hadn't been earned. Yet. The pack bond hummed quietly in the back of my mind, utterly silent but present in a way that warmed me to my bones. Our lives were connected, our fates intertwined now, and I was done playing this game by Charybdis's rules. I was finished waiting, fed up with him striking first.

He had come after the people I loved, the people who were mine to protect. He had awakened my inner she-wolf by attacking my pack, by hurting my family. As she bared her teeth in a mental snarl, I read her intent and agreed wholeheartedly.

For these crimes, Charybdis would die with our teeth buried in his throat.

CHAPTER EIGHT

Graeson's ragged breathing was as shallow now as it had been two hours ago. Warg healing ought to have sealed the jagged wound made when Abram was forced to saw the blade back and forth in tiny increments to work the serrated edge free of Graeson's chest, but his fever-hot skin told a different story. His body was fighting, but he wasn't winning any ground that I could tell.

"Do you think magic could be involved?" I voiced my worst fear to Abram.

"It crossed my mind." He rubbed behind his ear. "It would explain a lot."

I caressed the ridge of Graeson's slick brow with my fingertip. "Would the Garzas help?"

"No." He shook his head. "They're bound to the Chandler pack, and Bessemer made certain the witches got the memo about the pack separation. They can't aid us without endangering their accord." He cut me a weary look. "Enzo called me at the clinic and informed me he could no longer supply me with some of the rarer herbs his people specialize in growing. He's good people, for a witch, but he's loyal to Miguel. We can't expect help on that front."

The Garzas were the only witches I trusted in the area. I doubted I had anything left of value to barter with them, but I'd had to ask.

"Your five minutes are up," he said gently. "Come back in thirty, and you can visit him again."

A rumble in my chest proved his caution wise. Any longer and my wolf got snarly and overprotective. Already I'd had to scour layers of skin to cleanse the overwhelming scent of Graeson's blood off me. The fresh change of clothes helped smooth my hackles too. I was back in jeans, sneakers, a fitted T-shirt, and I was ready to get down to business.

Picking up the reins as alpha, I went to check on Bianca, who I had isolated in my trailer after asking Haden to move it to an even more remote corner of the RV lot at the cost of losing the use of hookups for utilities. Charybdis had broken parts of her I didn't understand well enough to guess at how to fix them.

Jensen, her mate, the man she loved more than anything outside of the child she carried, and she had killed him while under Charybdis's toxic influence. Was there a sliver of hope for recovery from that?

"This isn't your fault." Dell leaned a shoulder against mine. "You know that, right?"

The broken record played on... "Sure." Agreeing with Dell was easier than fighting her for my portion of the blame. "Did you get the others settled for the night?"

"Yeah." She jerked her head toward the direction of my trailer. "Bianca is resting in there, and Nathalie is clearing out your bedroom to protect your things." Her gaze slid to Theo's trailer. As the home with the fewest possessions and most room to spare, it would act as home base for now. "Haden, Job, Moore and Zed are settled there." Isaac's trailer caught her eye next. "Isaac said I could stay with him, so I'm going to keep his place safe until he gets back." Her voice went scratchy at the end. "That leaves you, Graeson and Abram at Aunt Dot's place. Unless the rain they're predicting comes in, Abram doesn't want to move Graeson for a few more hours. So Moore and Job have gone into town to purchase a tarp large enough to accommodate them. We need this area contained by sunrise when the humans start waking."

"You're doing a great job." I patted her arm. "I don't know what I'd do without you."

She beamed at me with such pride, my chest swelled right alongside hers. Dell's shoulders hadn't hunched once since we left Villanow. Her gaze hadn't touched the ground in submission, except when she'd bumped heads with Graeson at the gas station. Her cocky stride had turned more than one head, and when Moore had dared put a hand on her in a proprietary manner earlier, she had slapped him. Not hard, for a shifter, but he rubbed his jaw thoughtfully after.

All in all, it was a huge and welcome change in the woman who had cowered before her previous alpha and who had once gone willingly to Moore's lap with empty eyes because a more dominant wolf had patted his thighs in expectation she would obey.

Dell was coming into her own, grabbing life by the tail, and despite the grim circumstances, I was glad to be here to see it.

"The dominance fights start at daybreak." Anticipation thrummed in her voice. "They would have started tonight if not for all this. The sooner hierarchy is established among our wolves, the sooner they can settle. Having an injured alpha has everyone on edge, and it's dangerous for us to be so near humans until we've bled off some of that aggression."

What I wanted to ask was "Haven't we bled enough already?" but the wargs knew their animals' needs better than I did. I trusted Dell. If she told me they needed this, then I believed her. "Are you fighting?"

"Yes," she said, voice hard. "Graeson protected me from Bessemer. Our ex-alpha has a thing for dominants, and it almost killed me, but it was worth tucking my tail to keep him off my back. Graeson has told me to bide my time for years." She clenched her jaw. "Well, I bided and this is the time."

"I'll be pulling for you." I kept my endorsement too quiet for sensitive wolf ears to overhear. "You seem happier now. I'd like that trend to continue."

"Me too." Movement caught her eye, and her voice trailed to a whisper. "I hope everything…"

A man dressed in tight jeans, polished boots and a sleeveless T-shirt that somehow managed to look more expensive than the last pantsuit I purchased stepped into the clearing. With his hair cut short and a bottle of chilled water in hand, he looked like a model who had been sucked through a portal from the nightclub where he had been partying—if the paper neon band around his wrist was any indication—into an enchanted forest.

"Oh my God." Dell blurred into motion, leapt the creek bed and sprung for him, wrapping her legs around his waist and burying her face at his neck. "You're back. *How* are you back?"

Gripping the undersides of her thighs so she didn't fall, the man picked his way toward me, careful his trendy boots didn't slip on dry leaves and dump him on his ass.

"Hey, coz." Ice glazed his voice. His eyes were arctic blue, and clear of Charybdis's influence. "Long time no see." Glancing down at Dell, he softened his expression a fraction. "Does she do this for everyone, or am I special?"

Hearing the unexpected snark in his voice, Dell reared back in his arms, and the color drained from her face. "You're not Isaac." Her nose wrinkled. "You smelled different, but it was close. So close." She used her warg strength to break his grip, then backed up to me. "You must be Theo."

"I am." He cocked his head. "Who are you? One of Isaac's girls?"

Arms linking around her middle, she blinked fast. "No."

"This is Dell." I hooked my arm around her waist, and Theo's eyebrows climbed his forehead as my open affection with her stunned him. Had I needed more proof he was untainted, he had just given it to me in spades. "She and Isaac are…" *complicated*, "…friends."

"An honest mistake." He raised his hands in a placating gesture. "You can't throw a stone without hitting one of his castoffs."

My jaw popped from the pressure of grinding my teeth. "Ah, there's the cousin I remember."

Casual cruelty was as much his style as the artfully tousled hair on his head. How Isaac stomached him, I had no clue. Five minutes with him, and already eager claws pricked the tips of my fingers. "Dell, I'm taking him to Aunt Dot's trailer to talk."

"Yes, Alpha." She straightened her spine and nodded to Theo. "It's nice meeting more of Cam's people, even if you are her asshole cousin and not above groping the ass of a woman you've never met."

"You jumped into my arms and put your gorgeous ass in my hands," he protested. "What was I supposed to do?"

"Not take advantage. You knew that welcome wasn't meant for you, and I'm certain you could guess who it was meant for. Yet you didn't put me down or correct my misconception." She spun on her heel and, tapping her temple, started walking. "Call if you need me."

A sigh lodged in my throat as I led Theo into his mother's trailer, hating I was about to be alone with him and my suffocating guilt.

The door had been left unlocked so Abram could use the facilities he needed. The clutter of his belongings resting on the kitchen counter and the general chaos in Aunt Dot's bedroom told me he was in the process of moving into his temporary quarters and preparing to transition Graeson in too.

Picking my way through the living room, I stumbled face-first into the wall when a boot hit my spine. My cheek smashed into the curved metal, and stars exploded in my vision. Theo gripped my shirt and yanked me around, slamming my shoulders against a family photo mounted near a window and bracing his forearm across my windpipe. "What the hell have you and your inferiority complex gotten us into this time?"

"Not..." I sucked in oxygen through my bared teeth, "...my fault."

The waver in my tone was all the invitation he needed to pounce on my insecurities.

"You chose to enlist in the marshal's program, Cammie. No one twisted your arm. In fact, I remember Mom begging you *not* to sign on the dotted line. You accepted a promotion to the Earthen Conclave knowing it meant you—and your family—would be put under a microscope. You're the one who chose to invite the magistrates' agendas into our lives." Disgust soured his scent. "As if that wasn't bad enough, you dragged my mother and brother into hostile warg territory. Your decisions are what brought us here. You're the one living out your Tarzan and Jane fantasies while Mom and Izzy are gods know where." He pressed down until I gagged. "This is *all* your fault."

Wild magic sang in my blood, and pelt brushed beneath my skin. "Let go of me."

Anger I understood. I deserved it. Resentment, well, that was our relationship in a nutshell. Every charge he'd laid at my feet was true, except the Tarzan and Jane bit, but my insides were chewed up just as much, and my she-wolf would gladly rend a pound of flesh from his hide to assuage my guilt right about now.

"Still can't control your shifts for shit." A humorless huff passed his lips. "Shut it down, or I'll shut it down for you."

Tawny pelt dappled with black rosettes sprouted from his left elbow to his fingertips. Hand thickening to form a massive feline paw, he flexed pale, sickle-shaped claws.

"Cam?" Dell's mental voice sounded cautious.

"I'm fine." Dell wasn't the only one turning over a new leaf. Theo wasn't bullying me into submission ever again. *"Just a family squabble."*

A rush of prickling energy electrified my skin as the change swept over me. Silvery fur with black tips sprouted. Muscles thickened. Bones in my jaw snapped loud in the confined space. Heightened senses made my head swim. The delicious scent of fear pervaded my nose, and I salivated.

"I am alpha here," I rumbled through my elongated muzzle, the guttural words rising from the well of recalled magic my she-wolf drank deep from these days. "Submit or die."

Reminding me yet again why he was my least-favorite cousin, Theo swung his meaty paw at my head. Had his claws landed, he would have ripped off half my face. Back teeth aching with the need to sink into his flesh, I launched myself at him, wrapping my arms around his waist and tackling him to the linoleum. Shocked air burst from his lungs on impact, and his rock-hard skull bounced off the floor with a satisfying *thud*. Saliva pooling in my mouth, I unhinged my jaws and took the oh-so-fragile skin of his throat between the sharp points of my teeth. Salt from his skin left a tang on my tongue, and the coppery taste of his blood from the pinpricks of pressure I'd applied set my stomach rumbling.

Theo's hands shot up beside his head, knuckles brushing the floor in a capitulating gesture. His claws retracted, and the paw receded until I counted ten fingers in my periphery.

Reluctant to surrender my prey, I held him pinned until my inner predator accepted his surrender and faded to a wary tingle in the back of my mind. Bone snapped as my face realigned, and fur tickled as it shed my arms. Sitting back on my heels, I became myself once more.

"What was that thing?" Theo slowly massaged the bloody column of his throat as though seeking reassurance I hadn't ripped out anything vital. "I've never seen anything like it."

"That's my wolf." Claiming her out loud for the first time felt right. "And she doesn't like you."

"Your...wolf?" The acrid scent of fear mixed with an undefinable emotion permeated the space. "You're really alpha here?"

"Co-alpha." Much as Aisha had done, I took my title from my mate. "Go for anyone else's throat like you did mine, and they'll rip it out for you with my blessing."

Rolling off Theo, I stood and extended my hand down to him. Cautiously, he accepted the offer. As comfortable with the brush of Aunt Dot's and Isaac's magic as my own, Theo's grip still brushed a familiar signature up my arm. I hauled him onto his feet, twisted him sideways then shoved him into an oversized recliner that dominated Aunt Dot's living room. The plush material bogged him down, and his shell-shocked expression struck me as almost comical. He eyeballed me as if he didn't know who I was anymore.

That made two of us.

"Mom said you were getting serious about a warg." He toyed with the paper bracelet on his wrist. "I didn't believe her. I figured she'd binged on that supernatural soap opera of hers again and was projecting."

"Graeson and I are serious," I assured him. "We're mated."

"Mated." The band tore, and he stared at it in surprise. "Your eyes shine gold when you mention him."

"My warg aspect is evolving." I touched my cheek. "Isaac thinks because I've gone so long without Lori's blood that taking in the warg magic, using a few as donors, has kick-started a second *becoming*."

"Does that mean you can't...?" His gaze dipped to his lap, mouth set in a tight line as he started tearing the strip into pieces. "Is Lori gone?"

"I'm not sure." A pang arrowed through my heart that I might have lost her. Again. "I don't reset often, and I haven't had reason to since Isaac mentioned his theory."

Bracing his elbows on his knees, Theo stared at me through eyes so like Isaac's it made my chest tighten, and linked his fingers in front of his lips. "Tell me everything."

Pinpointing the exact moment things went south was as simple as remembering my first trip to Villanow, Georgia. Before Marie Graeson's death, Charybdis had been an amalgamation of clues held together with supposition. After Marie, he became a tangible horror brought to life by the starkness of her brother's grief.

I told Theo what I could, lips throbbing with pain as I skirted truths I had sworn to keep secret, and then I sat back while he digested all I'd said.

"Leopards don't change their spots." He nudged tattered scraps of paper across his thigh with an absent fingertip. "The killer fixated on you after the kelpie died, right? Why? You're not his type, unless you count your ability to imitate Lori. Even his methodology doesn't match his previous MO."

"We don't know how much of his MO is his own preference versus that of his avatar. He's like a chameleon in that regard. He seems to amplify the natural inclinations of his host." Or maybe not. The kelpie fit the profile. Ayer and Harlow did too. They had acted against their will, but the flavor of their transgressions mirrored the current host personality. All except for Bianca. Murdering her mate and threatening her unborn child? I didn't need a friendship bracelet to know those actions were totally out of character for her. "Our working theory at the time was the kelpie's murder spree was an attempt to create a circle around the state of Tennessee."

"A circle of that size..." Confetti sprinkled the floor when he jerked upright. "There's not a fae on Earth who could wield enough magic to activate it. Not alone."

That might have been true. Once. Stinging lips warned me against explaining how Charybdis had escaped Faerie through a portal created by the Morrigan. "He wouldn't have to be all-powerful." Just very, very clever and willing to spill enough blood to grease the wheels of his scheme. "Not as long as the spell was self-sustaining."

"True." Perhaps surprised to agree with me, his eyebrows arched. "I can't decide if it was worse when I thought he was a powerhouse of brute energy or when you convinced me of his ruthless intelligence."

Strength we could overcome with enough force. Wits applied with vicious precision, now that was dangerous.

Mulling over that unsettling revelation, Theo cocked his head. "What happened to the spell? The circle, I mean? Can it still be activated, or has it been defused?"

"The kelpie was the only link between the deaths. Without it as a binder, a focus for the negative energy, the spell dissipated. The circle was never completed." All that preparation, all those lives lost, and for nothing. "Charybdis holds me accountable for that."

"You made it personal." A grimace twisted his expression. "At least as far as he's concerned."

Admitting the case had felt personal all along—first because of Lori and then because of Marie—got stuck in my throat.

"He's returning the favor tenfold." I released a humorless laugh. "Let me show you something."

Grateful I had changed earlier, I dug my phone from the hip pocket of my jeans and pulled up a set of images before passing it across the table. The folder contained pictures of each item I had found on the steps of my trailer while in Villanow in addition to the items Graeson had rescued from the water sprite's cavern. "Do these mean anything to you?"

"Hmm." He angled the screen to flash the geode. "You and Lori had an entire bag of those one summer and wouldn't share. Lori sat on Mom's porch and cracked them open with a freaking hammer right under the window to Isaac's and my bedroom."

I smiled at the memory. I wasn't the only one Lori had lovingly tormented.

"How would Charybdis know about this?" His forehead wrinkled. "These memories are vintage. Did you talk to Cord or Dell about your childhood? Is there any way Charybdis could have, I don't know, overheard?"

"I hit the high points." Or were those low points? Yes. Definitely that. "Small details like this? No. I haven't thought about this stuff in years, let alone talked to anyone about it." I shifted in my seat. "Besides, he's not into eavesdropping. That's not how he gathers his intel. He likes taking it direct from the source."

"That means he must have had access to someone who knew that information, right? That means Mom, Isaac, you and me. Or..." he frowned, "...your folks."

"Exactly." I rubbed the sore spot over my breastbone. "All of us were accounted for prior to this. Aunt Dot, Isaac and I stuck together, and he kept tabs on you. The only ones off the grid are my parents." By their own choice. "I haven't heard from them in years, and I haven't tried contacting them either. They're the most vulnerable, which is why I'm calling in favors to locate them."

"I have contacts I can tap too. I'll send out the first batch of queries before bed." He swiped his thumb over the screen. "All of these are memories from our Tennessee summers. We have a lot of good ones from there." His brow puckered, and he glanced up at me. "I figured that's why you asked for the transfer."

That Theo had gotten his wires crossed wasn't surprising. He visited every few months, but his life was separate from ours. Decisions we made had no bearing on him one way or the other except as a new destination when he bought plane tickets.

"The spot came available, and Vause mentioned it." Despite all the good memories, Aunt Dot broke tradition the summer after my family dissolved. The next June the four of us ditched the mountains and began exploring the rock formations in and around Goblin Valley State Park in Utah. "Aunt Dot perked up at the idea. She'd been missing the mountains, I think. After I saw how much it meant to her, yeah, Vause pushed the papers through for me."

"What's her take on this?" He bent to pick up his mess. "Have you contacted her for help locating Mom and Izzy?"

"No." I ducked my head, ashamed that I had ever put my job before my family's safety. "She's missing."

"Missing?" Theo sat up slowly. "Magistrates don't go missing."

"I spoke with her Unseelie counterpart, Magistrate Martindale. Vause disappeared from behind her locked office door. Security at outposts with assigned magistrates is tight." No one got near them without a background check, an appointment and a vigorous pat-down. "Whoever took her killed one of her guards in the process, and those guys are hardcore."

Theo loosed a low whistle. "Is this related to Charybdis?"

"Your guess is as good as mine." The truth was I hadn't put much thought into what it meant that she had been taken. She had professional ties to me but not personal ones. On the surface it didn't seem related. "Vause was taken within hours of when Aunt Dot and Isaac disappeared." Yet Charybdis hadn't bragged on his coup. Why was that? Unless he was innocent for once. But if he wasn't to blame, then who was? Who else would dare take on a magistrate? "I don't see how Charybdis would have had time to make the trip to Maine and then back to Georgia in that timeframe."

"I don't believe in coincidence." Theo shoved the trash in his pocket and crossed his legs. "Sounds to me like you've got him running scared. Why else would he risk so much? Attacking a magistrate? That's asking for a marshal to put a few rounds in you." His restless foot started wiggling. "She must have known something. Maybe she got a tip? He could be scrambling to cover his tracks."

"None of his actions make sense unless I confront him." The very nature of his gift birthed an obvious hunger for connection, though he broke everyone he touched. Perhaps because of that, he craved the temporary fixes even more. "He's getting something out of the hunt. We think he chose ritual sacrifice as a means of powering his circle because he's familiar with collecting that type of energy. Right now he's happy prolonging the chase.

Otherwise why taunt me by lashing out at the people closest to me?"

"That would explain why he started with your friend— Harlow?—and escalated from there." Theo uncrossed his legs and sat forward. "A magic user would fashion a circle out of familiar magic to make it easier to manipulate. There I agree with you."

"He was patient with the girls," I recalled softly. "His timeline was so precise. It made him predictable." Glancing around the familiar trailer gutted me. The whole place felt empty without Aunt Dot's warmth making it a home. "This time he made a wild grab. Several really. He's lashing out faster, acting erratic."

"Did you ever figure out his endgame from before? Why he wanted the circle? Could his previous timeline be tied to a critical event?" Theo held my gaze, absent of scorn. "Is it possible he's getting sloppy because he's desperate to meet the original deadline?"

The soundness of his observations impressed me, and I repaid him the compliment of sizing him up in much the same way I had noticed him appraising me earlier.

How much of our mutual animosity was habit? How much of our reciprocal dislike was the product of childhood pettiness and teenage angst? How much was grief and time to blame for the rift so deep between us that he had started a new life away from his mom and brother in order to be absent from mine?

No definitive answers popped into mind, and that bothered me.

I didn't have so much family that I could afford to give up on what little I had left.

"Ellis."

I bolted to my feet and skidded through the living room on my way out the door.

"I'm coming."

"Cammie?" Theo trailed after me. "What happened? What's wrong?"

The hum of the pack bond, the joyous rallying of each individual voice as it recognized Graeson's presence, drowned out my cousin. I ran straight to the makeshift tent and shoved aside the heavy plastic tarp. Groggy hazel eyes locked with mine and hauled me to my mate's side as though our hearts were magnetized.

Hot tears rolled down my cheeks and splashed on his forehead. *I thought I lost you.*

"I told you, sweetheart," he rasped through a tight voice, "you won't get rid of me that easy."

"Alpha?" Abram intruded on the moment I chose to rain kisses on Graeson's face and neck. "This guy says he's with you?"

Theo. That fast I had forgotten about him. "He's my cousin. My other cousin. Theo."

"Don't crowd her," Abram warned him. "Our alpha has claws when it comes to her mate."

Rocking forward as though he had been shoved, Theo caught his balance several yards from Graeson's pallet. A stern-faced Zed stood guard near the entrance flap, his frame as slight as the saplings used as tent posts, and his fingers tapped out a quick cadence on his thigh as he sized up my cousin.

Blood draining from his face, Theo absorbed the scene before him. The hodgepodge shelter, the bloody cloths, the dagger with brown crust flaking off the handle. Antiseptic gave the air an astringent quality, and I sneezed, but not before I noticed a shadow flicker across the material near the rear flap. My money was on Dell pulling sentry duty.

"This is Cord Graeson?" The hot glide of Theo's voice through the quiet startled my attention back to him. "Good gods. What happened here tonight? Why didn't you tell me?"

Meeting his gaze, aware I was pulling the hair-trigger on our ceasefire, I still told him the truth. "I didn't trust you."

Theo bit the inside of his cheek and nodded once. He left without saying another word, and I huffed out a tired sigh at blowing our temporary truce right out of the water.

CHAPTER NINE

"So that was Theo." Arms pinned straight at his sides by cloth restraints to prevent him from scratching his wounds in his sleep, Graeson flexed his fingers until I put my hand in his. "He smells more hurt than angry." A frown struck his face as his nostrils flared. "Why do I smell your blood?"

Cocking an eyebrow at the patient, I humored him. "We fought, like always."

"He drew blood." The dangerous observation rumbled through his healing chest.

"I drew more." My cheeks tingled. "I introduced him to my wolf."

A smile split Graeson's lips. "I hate I missed it."

"I do too." I opened my mouth, but the words dried up, and I clicked my teeth together.

As usual, he didn't need me to speak to hear what I left unsaid. "Ellis, you aren't to blame for what happened to Jensen or to Bianca." He twitched his wrist until I glanced at him. "Or to me."

"Charybdis took Harlow because she was my friend. He followed me to Villanow and took my family right from under my nose. He followed me here, killed a pack member and shattered Bianca. He almost killed you, because you're mine. All of this is because of me." I made a fist and rapped on my breastbone. *"Me."*

Gold saturated his eyes, his alpha glare in full force. "What he does is out of your control."

"That doesn't change the basic truth of the situation. When a person is the cause of a problem," I argued, "it is by definition their fault. He targeted my friend, my family, my pack and my mate." Guilt surged hot and sour up my throat. "Those actions hurt me, and he knows it. He craves it. He won't stop coming after me until I have nothing else to lose."

"Don't say it." His hand crushed mine in an effort to anchor me by his side. "Don't even think it."

I braced for a fresh wave of hurt, because I had to put it out there since it had clearly crossed both our minds. "You would all be safer without me."

"I can't—" Jaw flexing, he tried again. "I can't do this without you. We're a team." His fingers dug painfully into my wrist. "I should have asked before naming you alpha, I know that, but I was afraid you'd say no." He noted the red marks on my skin and eased his grip. "I was scared you wouldn't want this." His mouth tipped down at the edges. "That you wouldn't want me."

"How could you think that?" It boggled the mind. "You're the most confident man I know."

"Not where you're concerned." His chin dipped. "I can want you, crave a life with you, shift the pawns until the queen is within my grasp, but I can't make the final move. That's yours, and it terrifies me."

"I'm what the big, bad wolf is afraid of?" I nudged his lip upward with my finger, forming a half-smile that didn't stick. "I'm flattered."

"Ellis—"

"No, give me a minute. Just listen. Let me get this out, okay?" I found somewhere else to look, because his reaction held the power to break me. "I'm messed up. I don't fit in. Anywhere. I haven't in so long I don't remember how belonging feels." I frowned, realizing that was no longer true. "Or I didn't. Not until I met you." His fingers stroked my arm, but I kept staring at his chest, at that spot that made my lips tingle when I kissed it, at the blood seeping under the bandage wrapping his ribs.

"You're bossy, opinionated, bark too many orders, think you know everything—"

His hand dropped to his sides. "Is this supposed to flatter me back?"

"—but you're also the kindest and most thoughtful man I've ever met," I continued, choosing to ignore his outburst. "You know me, the real me, and you're still here. You're still trying every day to win a heart I'm pretty sure has belonged to you for a lot longer than I just realized." I laughed self-consciously. "Maybe you're the one I should have asked before I..."

His core tensed, breath held. "Before?"

I braced my forehead in the curve of his neck so I could breathe him, so I didn't have to look him in the eye. "I fell in like with you."

"I'm beginning to speak Ellisese fluently." He tilted his head so his cheek rested against my hair. "That's as good as an *I love you.*"

I didn't say he was wrong, and when I pulled back, it was to see the brackets around his mouth deepen until his face struggled to contain his smile.

"Camille," Abram called through the tent flap. "Visitation is over. He still needs his rest."

The sobering reminder of our present circumstances dimmed the light in his eyes, but it failed to extinguish the slow burn in my chest and southernmost regions when his fingertips brushed my hip.

I was a coward, too chicken to show him my true heart. But down where dusty childhood hopes and faded grownup dreams lay fallow in the barren field caged behind my ribs, the seeds for love had sprouted. The ground there had been dry and cracked, and Graeson had toiled to break that hard outer crust to access the fertile soil beneath, but every sincere word and each thoughtful gesture nurtured the roots and sent them tunneling ever deeper into my soul, until there was no way to weed those seeking tendrils without ripping out the heart of me.

"He's awake," I protested. "Can't I stay a while longer?"

"No, ma'am." Abram popped his head inside, nose wrinkling as he took in the bandages stained with Graeson's blood when they hadn't been prior to my arrival. "He needs his rest, and the herbs I've given him will knock him out again soon. Besides, you two are too newly mated to be left unsupervised. Between the bloodlust and, well, lust, your pheromones are tricking Cord's body into priming itself for action he's not getting." His eyebrows winged higher as he stared hard at the hand straining against the restraints to massage my hip. "I rest my case."

"Regaining consciousness is a good sign." I turned a more critical eye on Graeson. "That means he's healing, right?"

"Cord is young and strong." Abram raised his hands in a placating gesture. "He'll make a full recovery. He needs a few days of rest, that's all."

I stood and bent over Graeson, pressing a lingering kiss to his forehead. "Behave for the doctor." I tapped the end of his nose. "I'll see you in thirty minutes if you're a good boy."

Smile going soft at the edges, he caved to a fierce yawn and let his eyes close. "Not if I see you first."

Abram chuckled softly and waved me toward him, away from the patient whose drugs had obviously kicked in if he thought that was a witty comeback. Gripping my arm, he led me a few yards from the tent. "A word of caution." He jerked his chin toward Graeson. "This pack is small, and these wolves are loyal to Graeson, but there are more than a couple dominants in the bunch. Injured alphas don't stay alphas for long."

"You said he was going to make a full recovery from this," I hissed.

"He will, and I'm not trying to frighten you." He patted my shoulder. "You aren't a warg, and you aren't used to the posturing alphas do to keep their packs healthy. That's why I haven't been hard on you for wanting to spend so much time with Cord, even though it makes the other wolves antsy."

"That's crap." I shrugged off his hand. "No one would make a peep if Jensen was in that tent and Bianca was tending him."

"They aren't alphas." He sighed and tucked his hands into his pockets. "The pack needs to see you spending less time with Cord, not because you don't care, but because you're confident he will recover and soon. They need to see you're not concerned, that they have no reason to be worried either. It will settle them." He leaned closer. "Dominance fights start in a few hours, and the last thing you want is for one of these wolves to get it in their heads they're alpha material."

Magic tingled in my veins. "A move against Graeson is a move against me."

"You can't interfere with a dominance fight unless you want him disqualified." He shook his head. "He would lose alpha either way in the shape he's in now." Voice pitched low, Abram hammered home his point. "There was magic in that blade. Fae origin is my guess. The others don't need to know that, not right now, not with everything that's happened tonight. Not when there will be blood spilling here soon."

I bit my lip until I tasted pennies but nodded that I understood.

Abram raised his hand like he might try patting my shoulder again, but the aborted gesture turned into a wave as he left me alone with my thoughts and returned to Graeson since being a healer gave him a pass to stake out the tent all he wanted.

Huffing out an irritated breath, I tamped down my jealousy and focused on his advice.

Right now, I had the goodwill of the pack. According to Moore, each member had their reasons for leaving the Chandler pack. Whatever they were had made aligning with a rogue dominant and his fae mate look good by comparison. I had known those things, of course, but

Abram's somber delivery made me think the reason we had an excess of dominant wolves was because these wargs were on Bessemer's shitlist too.

It made sense to me. In retrospect, knowing what I knew about Graeson's tendencies to nurture the ones who needed him most while also having a skewed perception of who those people might be, that he would choose other dominants causing friction to take under his wing in an attempt to hold them all together.

The six wargs who left Georgia to follow Graeson had proven they were willing to skirt an alpha's laws. They had also proven they were willing to take the punishment for their actions. Did that absolve their initial rebellion? Was their behavior a product of an instinctual loyalty to Graeson they were helpless to defy as their wolves aligned themselves with a more dominant alpha? Or were their actions the misguided but well-meant byproduct of wargs who thought they knew best, like Graeson?

The former would explain why Bessemer let the others go without a whiff of confrontation—even the heavily pregnant Bianca. Had the tradeoff for peace been worth the sacrifice of a pup? Granted, with Bianca being a half-blood, Bessemer might have bet on the child being born unable to shift.

A cold lump settled in my gut as Abram's confidence gnawed on my overburdened conscience, and I groaned until the noise turned into a frustrated growl.

All this time I'd assumed that Graeson handpicked the people who came with us. That he'd offered the likely ones a choice and those brave enough had taken him up on his offer. Not once had I considered that he might have cobbled together the misfits and troublemakers and offered them refuge with us to spare them from life under Bessemer's rule.

The stubborn man with a heart too big for his own good might have excised the cancerous tumor in the Chandler pack only to absorb the infection into ours.

For once I took comfort in an absolute truth: Graeson did nothing without a reason. These were the wolves he wanted. Broken, dangerous, twisted or otherwise, this was the pack he had pieced together. He had presented me with the fully assembled jigsaw, sealed with Mod Podge and suitable for framing.

Now I had to trust that Graeson was more than an intriguing set of tattoos, and that he hadn't bitten off more than our wolves could chew.

Borrowing my she-wolf's keen nose, I trailed the sour notes of bitterness and regret straight to Theo. I found him slumped in Aunt Dot's recliner, toying with a short remote, one of five, taken from the ruler-straight line up on a side table at his elbow.

"Hey." I reclaimed my spot in the kitchen to avoid crowding him. I was learning it wasn't wise to corner wounded animals. "I should have told you we'd had trouble."

"You think?" He plucked at the rubberized buttons with his fingertips. "What happened?"

"We lost a wolf tonight." Recalling Jensen's pride at learning his child would shift made my heart ache. "A pregnant female shifted and killed her mate while under Charybdis's influence." Glossing over the details of Jensen's death did nothing to stop the images from flashing through my mind. "She's currently on lockdown in my trailer."

"And your wolf?"

A week ago I would have snapped that Graeson wasn't my wolf, but I had since grown a possessive streak. "Graeson was attacked by the same woman. She magicked a ceremonial blade with a nasty spell and used him as a pincushion. It stunted his accelerated healing abilities, but our pack doctor says he'll make a full recovery in a couple of days."

"A ceremonial blade," Theo mused. "Makes sense. There's bound to be latent power buzzing around in there with all the blood it's tasted, right? Assuming you're right about how Charybdis harvests energy, he might have warped those magical remnants to fuel his spell."

"I hadn't considered that." The ceremony had been one of joy, for us, but I didn't know the dagger's origins. I wasn't sure it didn't come with baggage that might overlay ours. "We've been working on the assumption he requires negative energy, but maybe there are several flavors and that's just his favorite."

"Happiness and joy are powerful but fleeting." His jaw flexed. "Grief and regret are just as potent, and those feelings tend to linger, fester. Mix in a healthy dose of thirst for vengeance and guilt, and you've created an emotional Molotov cocktail."

I cocked my head in his direction. "I don't remember you being this smart."

"No one does." He snorted. "You can't outshine a supernova, right?"

"You mean Isaac." Sibling rivalry between the brothers remained alive and well it seemed.

"I don't mind that he's the favorite." I made a choking noise, and he backtracked. "I don't mind it much. Anymore." He shrugged. "Living away from the caravan, in places where I'm not measured by the Isaac Standard, helps."

"I can understand that." Since he was being candid with me, I returned the favor. "That's one of the aspects of my job that most appeals to me. Out there, I could be anyone. I'm a fixer who blows into town, handles business and then leaves. No strings. No pitying stares. Total anonymity. In and out and on to the next thing."

"We're a pair, huh?" He laughed, but sadness tinged it. "I always thought you and Isaac should have been twins. Lori and me, we were the hellions. Always in trouble.

Always looking for our next fix. You and Isaac, you guys were the Gemini ideal. You were both so freaking perfect I had to fling mud at your prim little dresses sometimes to piss you off, rile you up, prove to myself you were real." His chuckle as I went board-stiff with shock rang with genuine amusement. "Maybe that did used to be us. Maybe now we've got more in common than I thought."

"Maybe you're right." His openness inspired me to bare a corner of my own soul. "I should have been upfront with you. You deserved to know about the troubles we're having. I'm doing the best I can, and it's not good enough."

"You're protecting your...mate." He seemed to struggle there at the end. "I get that. We've never been close, and this is all new to you. I get why you'd hold back. It's fine, Cammie. I mean it."

"Maybe we should have gone after each other with claws bared years ago," I joked. Mostly.

"Mom would have been horrified." His chuckle tapered to a sigh. "When I tell her this story, you understand that I'll be the one who kicked your butt, right?"

"Of course." Pressure between my ears made my head pound.

"You might want to see this," Nathalie's voice swept through my mind.

That sounded ominous. *"Are you still at my trailer?"*

"Yep."

"I'll be right there." I pushed to my feet. "I have to go check on the woman I was telling you about."

"The one who killed her mate?" Theo stood too. "I'll go with you." He hesitated. "If you don't mind."

Olive branch extended and accepted.

"I'd like that." I grabbed an elastic band out of my pocket and twisted my hair into a high ponytail. "You should see what we're up against."

Quiet reigned in the camp. Unable to stop my gaze from tagging the tent where Graeson rested, I managed to walk past without slowing down. Abram sat on a cinderblock at the flap, and he smiled when it became clear my walk wasn't a social call. At least not for them.

Warg hearing being what it was, I didn't bother knocking. Nathalie would have heard me coming even if my weight hadn't rocked the trailer when I climbed the steps.

"Is Bianca all right?" I peered over her shoulder toward the bedroom. "What's wrong?"

"It's not her." She held out her hand, and a familiar phone sat on her palm. "It's this."

"That's Izzy's phone." Theo crowded the door behind me. "What are you doing with it?"

"I found it in a box on the counter." Nathalie bristled as she passed it to me. "It rang and rang and rang until I got tired of hearing it and came to investigate."

Arms crossed over his chest, he stared down his nose at her. "What did you find while you were snooping that was worth dragging Cammie out here?"

Temporary allies we might be, but apparently Theo wasn't pulling punches with anyone else.

Vibrating with anger, Nathalie snarled, "Enzo Garza called."

Theo's brow creased at the name. "Who?"

Gut roiling, I clutched the cell like a lifeline. "How did he get Isaac's number?"

"No clue." She shrugged. "He asked for Dell, so maybe she gave it to him."

Considering how Isaac was glued to his phone and Dell didn't own one, I could see her giving out his number as her emergency contact.

"What did he have to say?" After Abram admitting to being cut off, I assumed the rest of us would be too.

"Hang on." She grabbed one of my notepads off the kitchen table. "I wrote it down so I wouldn't mess this up." She passed it over to me. "Enzo said a client paid for a divination that went sideways and thought we might be interested in Miguel's prediction."

Afraid to read the words until I knew, I asked, "How much did this information cost us?"

"Nothing." A deep line formed between her eyebrows. "He said this was a favor for Dell."

The witch, who worked for the Chandler pack along with his brother, Miguel, had a sweet spot for my friend. But free information? Dell's meemaw once tipped scalding coffee down her chest chortling at the idea of a witch giving anything away without cost, but that was before Bessemer exiled Dell from the Chandler pack. This might very well be the first of many breadcrumbs Enzo dropped in the hopes it lured her back to him.

As invested as Dell was in Isaac, I could have told Enzo he had no chance with her, but after meeting him, I got the feeling he already knew.

"Here we go." I braced for the prophecy. "The one you seek is marked by the Huntsman's thumb," I read out loud. "Soon the Wild Hunt will ride. Soon the damned will be claimed. Soon the screams of thousands will ripen the air."

"The Wild Hunt?" Theo took the notepad and skimmed the note. "That makes no sense. The Wild Hunt is confined to Faerie, and Faerie is cut off from Earth. There's no way for the hunt to cross realms. Besides, the Huntsman hasn't unleashed his hounds on this world in ages." He tossed the pad onto the counter, and it skidded. "I think this Enzo guy got his wires crossed. He can't be that skilled at divination if he's giving away free samples."

"The Garza brothers are the real deal," I assured him. "Enzo has a soft spot for Dell. I doubt seriously his brother has any idea he's passed on this information."

Theo made a thoughtful sound but didn't elaborate.

"I appreciate you letting me know." I tapped Isaac's phone against my chin, drawn from my musing by the shuddering exhales coming from the bedroom. "How is Bianca?"

"She cries and sleeps." Nathalie rubbed the crease between her eyebrows. "I cleaned her up, and it doesn't make sense. Her hands and body were soaked with blood, which I can see if she tried to help Jensen, but there was none near her mouth." She swallowed hard. "I saw the bite marks. Someone gnawed on his bones. Bianca wasn't in her right mind. Why clean her lips but not her hands?"

"You don't think she killed him." Doubt thickened my voice.

"No." She rubbed her hands up and down her arms. "I don't."

"I hope for her sake that you're right." I pocketed Isaac's phone in case Enzo got the urge to be helpful a second time. "Though if Bianca is innocent, that means Charybdis has another person under his thrall. Someone with sharp teeth and inhuman strength. Possibly another warg."

Our run through the woods had been frantic. Any one of the others could have branched off and circled back as I had, found Jensen and killed him. As much as I wanted to believe we would have felt a pang through the pack bond, we hadn't registered Jensen's death. He hadn't cried out to us for help. Neither had Bianca.

Recalling that icy blackness surrounding Bianca's thoughts, I expected that answered the question. Charybdis had strangled the bond and taken his victims in silence.

"Get word to Haden." I needed to get back to my laptop. This kind of information had to be shared, and I was hoping Thierry might have some insight for me into the Faerie angle. "Have him tell the others—in person—that the pack bond might be compromised."

A flicker of panic tightened Nathalie's features, and instinct guided me to rest my hand on her arm.

"Moore will be swinging by in a half hour." Relaxing a fraction under my touch, she thrust her shoulders back. "I'll get him to babysit while I spread the word."

"I'll be in Aunt Dot's trailer if anyone needs me." I showed Theo out the door. "Let's try to keep the mental chatter down to a minimum. We don't want to tip our hands." Though if Charybdis had his foot in the door, it didn't matter how quiet we kept our brain radios. "Stay a few more hours, and then I want a new guard posted, okay? Ask Job or Moore."

Zed was new to me, but Dell trusted him to have her back while she watched Graeson's, and that was all the endorsement I required. I wanted him right where she had him. Protecting my mate.

Mouth tight, Nathalie expelled a sharp breath. "I think that would be best."

Avoiding the path that led past the tent, I hustled back to Aunt Dot's trailer before the temptation to visit Graeson took root. Theo followed me without comment and sank back into Aunt Dot's recliner with a phablet he removed from his pants pocket. While he handled his business, I set about mine. I hauled the overnight bag I'd packed off the bench in the kitchen and removed my laptop. I settled in my usual spot from the mornings when I joined Aunt Dot and Isaac for breakfast, and sent Thierry an email with the Garzas' prophecy and an update on the night's events.

I was tapping my fingers on the touchpad when my phone started ringing. "Ellis."

"Comeaux here." The marshal sounded tired, but we all did these days. "We put a rush on those results."

My grip tightened on the shell. "And?"

"I wish I had better news." A sigh blasted the microphone. "We found nothing suspect. The techs ran their tests based on your samples in the conclave database. All biological and magical materials appear to belong to you and your family with one exception, but the anomaly might very well be explained away by your mating to Mr. Graeson. We can't know for certain unless he's willing to submit a hair sample."

"There was warg DNA found at the scene?" I massaged my forehead. "Never mind. Of course there was. Isaac gave Dell and me a ride home from the airport in his truck."

"She was human at the time?"

"Yes." Fanged-out wargs were hardly TSA-approved passengers. "What exactly did you find?"

"Four black hairs." A tapping sound filled the background. "The driver's side window was open, and the hairs were discovered on the plastic lip near the rubber seal."

"Hairs could have been transferred from our clothes." My aspect had black-tipped fur. The fur could be mine. "Wargs shed. A lot. Matching a warg to the sample would be difficult, especially since we've cut ties with the Chandler pack, and there's a good chance the fur came from one of them."

Aisha, of course, popped into mind, but she had been chased out of town after her mate banished her. Not to mention the fact Isaac had witnessed our first meeting and the bloody aftermath of it. He might have hesitated where Harlow was concerned, but he wouldn't have trusted Aisha enough to allow her to lean in his window.

"Speaking of the Chandler pack," I interjected, "did you happen to get a call from Bessemer for assistance?"

"No." Frustration stung across the line. "Should I have?"

"We found my aunt's truck. Someone parked it on Chandler land and cast a fire spell on it. The explosion caused a few injuries, nothing serious, but that type of magic is self-contained. The woods weren't in any danger from the sprites munching on the metal." Thank the gods. In a dry summer, that type of massive fire could have devoured the entire forest. "I doubted Bessemer would reach out since he was certain the trouble would follow us when we left." And it had.

"Did you find any...?" He cleared his throat. Remains. He wanted to ask if there were any remains.

"No," I rasped. "The fire was too involved to get close."

"I'm sorry to hear that."

I nodded like he could see it while my throat squeezed tight. Aunt Dot was alive. She had to be. I would accept nothing less.

"I'll write up an incident report." The low buzz of a weather radio reporting hummed in the background. "There should be a corroborative record in case it's needed in the future." I listened to the warning about a severe thunderstorm punctuated by beeps while he made his notes, but the conversation never recovered. "Sounds like we've hit a dead end." He made a clicking sound behind his teeth. "Our techs got nothing. Any evidence the humans missed was sterilized by the erasure spell."

"Back to square one." I closed my eyes. "I'm glad you kept me in the loop."

"I'll give you a call if we turn up anything else."

"I'd appreciate it."

We made more awkward goodbye noises, and the call ended.

The freebie prophecy might have been one step forward, but the lack of evidence had set us two steps back.

CHAPTER TEN

I jolted awake on a gasp, heart pounding from the tendrils of a fading nightmare. Dark waters. Sharp teeth. Crimson waves. Shivering, I scrubbed at the drool crusting my chin and fingered the indents pocking my cheek from where I'd slumped over my keyboard. Unsure what had jarred me from my sleep, but too familiar with my grim dreams to believe I could have escaped one alone, I scanned the darkened living room.

A smile quirked my lips when I spotted the figure slumped in Aunt Dot's chair. Theo must have drifted off too. Rubbing my eyes, I straightened my spine with a wince and stretched until several vertebrae popped in rapid succession.

Wiggling my mouse, I woke my laptop and checked for a response from Thierry. I found one, but the subject line coaxed a growl out of me. The message was an autoresponder. She was out of the office and would be for the next few days. So no help from that quadrant for a while.

I knew what I ought to do, what I needed to do. Go to Butler, Tennessee. I had to follow the clues Charybdis had planted to their end. But Graeson... I couldn't abandon him while he was vulnerable.

A sharp howl pierced the night and set my scalp prickling. I reached for the pack bond, and it flooded my head with images of gore and the flush of excitement.

Quietly as possible, I let myself outside and located the pack. The wolves formed a tight circle near the dried creek bed. In the center, two wolves battled, blood spraying the thirsty soil. My fingertips burned, the tips of my claws eager to pierce my skin. I smelled copper and tasted elation as the wolves jockeyed for position, frantic to enter the ring and have their mettle tested.

Flesh gone tight, I fought off my she-wolf's attempt to rise and dominate. Pinching the pack bond closed, I backed away as a snarling beast who might have once been blonde before the crimson soaked her fur howled her victory and beckoned her next contender.

I wandered aimlessly until I found myself back on the walking track. I made it two steps before I sensed him. "Graeson." Abram's warnings forgotten, I rushed to his side and looped my arm around his waist. "What are you doing out here? Are you crazy? Do you want to be attacked?"

He grunted. "That's why Doc pushed me to my feet. The others need to see I'm healing."

This close, with his skin sweaty from the effort to get this far, I smelled the bitter tang of fae magic as it seeped from his pores. He wore a loose T-shirt and cut-off shorts made from old sweatpants.

"I twisted my ankle on a root," I lied in a clear, steady voice. "I was going to sit on one of these benches for a minute before heading back. Would you mind keeping me company?"

Graeson laughed softly and winced for it. "Whatever my mate requires."

My nape prickled with the sensation of being watched, but screw it. Graeson was hurting, and he needed to rest or all his show of strength would accomplish was prove he was still as weak as a kitten. I could protect him, but it would diminish him, and we couldn't risk that. Not until the pack had time to settle.

We sat on the cool plank bench and listened to the snarling and snapping echo through the early morning.

"We need to talk." He took my hand and placed it on his thigh.

"I don't like how you said that."

"You're leaving," he said on a soft breath. "Your thoughts keep running on a loop through my head, and I want to be angry, but you're making too good of an argument."

"I'm sorry." I winced. "I didn't realize I was projecting."

"Your mind was hazy when I touched it earlier." He smiled crookedly. "You must have been sleeping. That's probably why your worries slipped through the cracks."

"Is that why you're really here?" I pegged him with a frown. "Tell me you didn't get out of bed for me."

"The ground is hard and wet." He smirked. "Trust me. It's no hardship to get off that pallet."

"I'm being serious. You are not allowed to endanger yourself for me. Especially when I can't be there to make sure you don't do something stupid." I amped up my scowl at his confused expression. "I'm worried about you, okay? It's eating me alive. Abram said I can't show it, and I get that predators attack weakness, but you're also human, and I—"

Faster than I could finish rambling, Graeson pressed his lips to mine. His tongue swept across the seam of my mouth, and I parted to grant him access. A moan rose up my throat, and I dug my fingernails into his thigh until he withdrew with a satisfied hiss.

"I like that you worry about me." He grinned at the crescent-shaped marks on his upper legs. "I like when you mark me up too." His amusement slipped. "But Abram is right. We have to be strong for our people, and that means we have a hard choice to make."

A lifetime of insecurity bubbled to the surface, and I couldn't breathe through the hurt. "It sounds like you're getting rid of me."

"Ellis, you're mine." He cupped my face. "I know you don't trust that yet, but I'm going to keep saying it until you do. You are *mine*. The decisions we make for our pack, for your family, are not a reflection of us. We are solid. We are fine. These troubles will pass. One day soon I'll get to show you exactly how much you're loved." His thumbs slid down my throat, fanned across my collarbones, and my breath caught on his promise. "But until then, we have work to do."

The pack bond hummed to life, and the rush of devotion he fed to me filled me up from my toes to my crown. "Okay." I shuddered when his hands slid down the crease in my arms, trailing along the sides of my breasts. "What did you have in mind?"

"You're making a trip to Butler where you're going to follow up on the clues Harlow left." Blinking out of his haze, he eased his hands down my sides and tugged me closer. "And I'm going to stay here and get us organized."

I leaned against him, careful of his injury. "Sending away your mate at a time like this seems dangerous to me."

"It is and it isn't." He rested his chin on top of my head. "I'll make the rounds this morning, convince everyone I'm okay, and then we'll announce your trip. That I'm willing to let you go is a sign of strength, and the others will understand that what you're doing isn't just for your family, but for our pack too."

"I still don't like this."

He rumbled out a laugh. "I'll be fine. Do you really think anyone could get through Dell?"

"Wait." I drew up straight. "You're not sending her with me? I don't get a babysitter this time?"

"I'm afraid not." He shook his head. "She's going to be my beta by sundown, and in a healthy pack, that means her position is here with me." His lips pursed. "I'm trusting that Theo can protect you." He bit the inside of his cheek then amended, "I'm trusting that he can watch your back."

I narrowed my eyes at him. "Who are you and what have you done with the real Cord Graeson?"

"I want us to work." He went serious. "You're a strong, independent woman, and I can't keep you in a bubble and not expect it to burst one day."

My vision went hazy, and I blinked rapidly. "What if Charybdis attacks while I'm gone?"

"I don't think he will." Deep lines bracketed his mouth. "All of this is a show. Why put on a performance if you don't have a front-row seat?"

I worried my lip with my teeth. "He knows if he hurts you or the others that I'll come running."

"It's worth the risk." Resolve deepened his voice. "We have to break this cycle before it breaks us."

"Since your mind is made up, and I know how stubborn you are, I'll start researching flights." I stood and raked my gaze over him one last time. "Are you sure this is what you want?"

"No. It's not what I want." He took my hands. "I want you to stay with me, glued to my side so I can protect you. This is...what I think you need. This is me being straight with you even though I wish I could rewind the last fifteen minutes and wipe this conversation from your mind."

"Now that sounds more like the overbearing Graeson I know and love."

"Love," he all but purred as he rose to his feet, yanking me closer. "Maybe I should get stabbed more often."

Barely restraining myself from jabbing him in the chest, I flattened my palms on his abs. "Don't even tease about that."

A pleased-as-punch grin hovered on his lips. "Just promise me one thing?"

I let him link our fingers and reveled in the warmth of his grip. "I can do that."

"Be careful." His mouth crashed into mine once more, so hard our teeth clacked. "Come home to me."

"I can do that too." I smiled, lighter now that the decision to go had been made for me. Maybe having a bossy warg around would come in handy from time to time, not that I would ever admit that out loud. "Do you want me to walk you back?"

He was already shaking his head. "You go ahead. I'll give you a head start."

Lips tingling from his kisses, I left my injured mate alone on the dark strip of pavement, an act that curdled my gut. Marrying a fae might have been easier, the learning curve shorter, but a flickering memory of the faded plastic flavor additive bottle he carried in his pocket had my lips curving in a goofy smile.

This thing between us just might work after all.

CHAPTER ELEVEN

Theo and I made our exit before the last dominance battle ended thanks to a perfectly timed flight leaving from the local airport. I didn't get to say goodbye to Graeson. I spotted him walking, his stride fluid and gait easy, with a bruised and battered Moore, and decided a quick mental touch would have to suffice.

Over the years, I had experienced many types and several degrees of loss. Lori vanished in the blink of an eye, her death a rock skipped across the smooth surface of my life, its ripples echoing to this day. The severing of ties to my parents had been more gradual. I felt them withdraw, little by little, until one day they dropped me off for a weekend visit with Aunt Dot and postponed my pick up in weekly increments until I was eighteen. Isaac and Aunt Dot's disappearance stung, a raw nerve exposed by the uncertainty of their situation. But stepping into the cab Theo had called and watching the campground grow smaller in the rearview mirror, that scooped out my heart and made me feel like I'd left a piece of my soul under a plastic tarp in the woods.

I must have bought a ticket at the counter, and I got on the plane at some point, but the first moment of clarity I experienced after putting Chattanooga behind me was stepping into the lobby at Tri-Cities Regional Airport. Theo set to work securing a rental car, but I was a million miles away. Not until we arrived in the town of Butler, and I stepped out of the car, did the fog vanish.

"I've been here before," I murmured as nostalgia teased at hazy memories. An old plywood sign stood across the street, its faded paint a welcome message. Block letters across the bottom spelled out their motto. I read it out loud. "The town that wouldn't drown."

"We used to pass through here on the way to Cherokee National Forest." Theo nodded at the ancient general store. "Mom used to buy us all Cokes in glass bottles from there. We always grabbed rock candy and those old pencils with bark still on them."

Rock candy. One of Harlow's clues.

Vertigo swept through me, as if all the answers I sought whirled tornado-quick around me, the debris clicking together like puzzle pieces that formed brief glimpses of the total devastation before swirling apart.

I crossed to the store in a daze and pushed inside under a tinkling bell strung over the door. A gust of air smelling of fudge and leather hit me in the face. No one greeted me, and it lent an eerie quality to an already bizarre experience. Wandering the aisles, I spotted strange and unusual tourist-trap trinkets that echoed with the memory of childhood summers. How I would beg for redneck pencils or try to convince Dad he needed a corncob pipe when he didn't even smoke.

When I turned down the last aisle, a glare on the picture window caught my eye. Beyond it, Theo leaned against the car, legs crossed in front of him while he tapped away on his phone's screen. Behind him huddled a two-pump gas station that used to be painted green and gold but now boasted the red-and-white logo of a national brand. An elderly man sat on a rumpled shirt out front, his head tilted back and his mouth wide open as he dozed in the shade of the portico. A brown bag sat between his feet, and a short row of six inch tall hammers lined the wall beside him.

Leaving the general store behind, I crossed the street and approached the man. A torn cardboard scrap read:

Crack your own geodes. Two for ten dollars. Hammers five dollars each.

Geodes. Another clue.

I had been right to come here. Maybe. At the very least I had been right that Charybdis wanted me here.

This close I smelled alcohol on the man's breath and backed away before I disturbed him. I returned to Theo, who remained consumed by the screen in front of him.

"Well?" He glanced up from whatever he was doing and quirked an eyebrow at me. "Did you find anything?"

Ghosts from our past, but that's not what he meant. "This is too perfect." I leaned against the car beside him. "Charybdis was here. He had to be. How else could he know those items from my childhood would still be relevant?"

"Tourist towns don't change much," he argued. "It could have been a gamble on his part."

"Maybe." It didn't feel that way, though.

Twisting around to glance behind us, Theo frowned. "What's up with the old man?"

"This is where Dad bought those geodes." Hard to believe the same guy was still peddling them all these years later. "I don't see much point in questioning him. He seems pretty out of it."

"Smells like he stays that way." Theo fanned his nose. "I can't imagine he does much business."

"He does well enough if he's still here." I eyed his darkened screen. "Any luck with your contacts?"

"None yet." He brought it to life. "From what I can tell, your folks went off-grid in the Gemini community about five years ago. No one's heard from them. I located one person with recent contact. About six months ago, your mom showed up at Pix Yourself, an herbalist shop run by pixies in South Carolina. She ordered three dozen tubes of a cream used to treat diaper rash and bedsores and a dozen bottles of that peppery-mint shampoo she used to hoard."

My ears rang as the clues kept stacking higher and higher, a compass point still spinning, but I got the feeling this town, this area, was its true north.

"Do they have an address for her?" I battled the sense of vertigo. "Any contact information?"

"None." He scrolled down the message screen. "Your mom places the same order annually. She holds it by name only, pays cash, picks it up alone and in person." He blew out a frustrated breath. "Clotilde, the shop owner, mentioned the truck was the same the last two years. Both times she noticed the Tennessee license plate. Before that, it was a different vehicle, different plates each time."

"A truck sounds right for a personal vehicle." They were a favorite among Geminis for a reason. When you towed your home everywhere you went, you needed power to make the ride as smooth as possible. "The others must have been rentals."

"Why let her guard down? You don't erase yourself unless you don't want to be tracked." He gazed across the street. "None of this explains why they vanished themselves in the first place." His phone buzzed, and he dismissed it without checking. "I wish Mom were here to ask. She got postcards and the occasional phone call at least. She might have had some idea of where or why they were hiding."

Fresh guilt hammered at me. Since becoming an agent with the Earthen Conclave, I'd had ample opportunities and resources to hunt them down. I hadn't been tempted, not once. They had abandoned me, and I had been more than happy to return the favor.

"I wonder where Dad is?" The cream bothered me. More kids were out of the question. Mom was past her childbearing years. But bedsores? That could mean any number of things considering my parents weren't spring chickens. One of them might have had an accident and required prolonged bedrest. It might not be serious. It didn't have to be life-threatening or life-altering. But suddenly not knowing how my folks had fared over the years ate at me. "Mom would tell us, right? If Dad... If something was wrong... She would call, wouldn't she?"

"Yeah." His gaze dipped to the ground. "I'm sure she would."

Even without my heightened warg senses, I could hear the lie.

"Come on." I shoved off the car and started back toward the gas station, the side entrance this time. "We need maps."

"I have my phone." He tilted it back and forth. "We don't need paper."

Tech boys and their toys. "Do you want me drawing on your phone with a marker?"

"What would you...?" Horror made his eyes go round. "I have a *stylus*."

"Forget it." Like Isaac, Theo didn't share my hang up with paper. When I needed the big picture brought into focus, I wanted a tangible object to really *see* what I was looking at. "I'll give you two some privacy." I left Theo cradling his cell like a babe to his breast and raided the store for snacks and maps of the area.

Charybdis had sent Ayer here. Why? What was the connection between her and me and this place? There was only one way to find out. We had to search every store and every square inch of the surrounding wilderness until we stumbled across whatever Charybdis meant us to find.

"Afternoon, ma'am." A young man with ruddy cheeks manned the register. "Is this all for you?"

"Yes." Arms loaded with maps and junk food, I dumped it all on the counter. "This is it."

He rang me up, I paid my bill and returned to the car.

"Did you find what you needed?" Theo asked, inching away from me, like I might tackle his phone with a Sharpie.

"Yes." I spread out my loot and began skimming the maps. I stood there long enough my stomach growled a friendly warning I hadn't eaten in too many hours to count. Shifting so often required serious calories, and I had to feed my wolf to keep her strong. I had snacks to take the edge off, but what I craved was meat. "We should grab something to eat then work our way through the stores." I kept eyeballing Carden's Bluff on the map, rolling the name around in my head. It rang familiar. A past campsite perhaps? "I'm going to ask the attendant a question."

"Mmm-kay." The aforementioned stylus was out, and he was flicking it like an orchestral conductor across the screen.

I pushed inside, map in hand, and pulled up short as the teen raised full-black eyes to mine.

"Camille Ellis," he said in a whisper-soft voice. "You might be smarter than you look after all."

"You set up the dominos." I kept an aisle of candy bars between us. "Are you frightened now that they're falling?"

"Afraid? Me?" His borrowed voice cracked on a laugh. "Of you?"

"I'm right here." I spread my arms. "Why don't we settle this right now?"

"You always rush the sweetest parts." He shook his head. "I could have had you at any time. You would have given yourself to me had I asked. You would now. I see it in your face, the desperation to bargain with me as though I could be bought." He straightened a lighter display beside the register. "There is no delight in being honorable. There is no flavor in sacrifice. There is no savor in redemption." He bared his human teeth. "I *hunger* as all the old ones do. I want that which will sustain me, that which will fill the ache in my middle, that which I have never tasted."

"Where is my family?"

"You won't find them here." A sly grin twisted his features. "Sorry to disappoint."

"No offense, but I don't trust you." I studied his avatar, the two-year service pin on his vest. "You took that man knowing I would follow the breadcrumbs Harlow left to this place."

"Or perhaps Marshal Ayer brushed fingers with him collecting her change when she passed through." He straightened his T-shirt. "Perhaps this Sean Taylor is an accidental pawn."

"Is that all it takes?" I cocked my head. "A touch?"

Amusement danced at the corners of his mouth, but he didn't answer.

"You kept tabs on this boy." Sarcasm dripped from my words. "You leapt into him the second I got in range. That's as much of an accident as the sun setting."

"Touché." He leaned his elbows on the counter. "I was hasty last night. I harmed your wolf, and it angered you in a way I hadn't anticipated."

"He's my mate." Hardly breaking news since Charybdis had access to Bianca's memories.

"The thought of losing him wrecked you." He wet his lips as if tasting the panic wafting off my skin. "More than even the loss of your family."

Startled, I barked, "No." Even though I wasn't sure it was true.

"Yes." He tilted his head, studying me at his leisure. "You strategized when Harlow vanished. You allowed an investigation to take its natural course when your aunt and cousin vanished. Your parents, well, there's so much resentment and childish hurt there." A visible shiver racked him. "Gods how much you feel. Is it a product of living among humans I wonder? Fae in my world are cold, hard, like frost-crusted diamonds. Here you're flesh and blood, real." He licked his lips. "Delicious."

"Why did you bring me here?" I pressed. "What do you want me to see?"

The salacious grin melted from the cashier's face. He blinked rapidly, eyes lightening until the only black remaining was contained in his pupils, and he startled to notice me. "Did you forget something?"

Just like that, Charybdis was gone.

How could I outsmart an ancient fae who could go anywhere, do anything, be anyone? How did he manage it? The surveillance video Thierry shared with me clearly showed a man stepping from the portal. He vanished. Into thin air. So was the man an avatar Charybdis used for traveling through the portal? No. That made no sense. No physical body dropped on screen, and the angle was wrong for it to happen off-camera. Maybe the magic involved had ripped him from his host. Maybe the portal had been keyed to recognize him and wearing someone else's skin wasn't an option. Maybe he required a body native to this realm to inhabit. Or maybe I was talking myself in circles, because the truth was *we just don't know*.

"I forgot this earlier." I grabbed a packet of gum from the nearest rack and slapped a dollar on the counter on my way out, too shaken to risk touching him. "Keep the change."

Outside, I strode toward the rental and climbed in the passenger seat. Theo joined me with an arched eyebrow.

"Charybdis knows we're here." I glanced back at the store and found the clerk staring at me through the glass. He gave an awkward wave. "I think... He's been waiting on me."

Eliminating the stores in town took us about three hours. We spent longer finding a decent hotel than we did crossing off each shop. There were no more visits from Charybdis, but he had done what he intended and shaken me.

My phone chimed an email indication, and I fumbled the device out of my pocket. I had hoped for a response from Thierry. What I got was a one-line note from Comeaux.

Your mother got a speeding ticket nine months ago in Hampton, Tennessee.

A quick Googling told me that was the town next door. Curiouser and curiouser.

Finished with the businesses on the left side of the road, I stood on the sidewalk to wait until Theo emerged. He did, at last, with a huge plastic bag of food dangling from his fingertips. He jogged across the street and lifted his arm. "Dinner," he explained. "Our hotel doesn't do room service."

Warmed that he had thought of me, I paid him a smile for his kindness. "Did you have any luck?"

"No." He tied the bag's handles in a knot, an old habit of his. "From what I can tell, the only places that are still held by the original owners from our childhood are the general store and the gas station."

Disappointing, but I had figured as much. "That's what the clerks told me too."

"It's going to start getting dark soon. I'd rather we had a locked door between us and Charybdis by then." He tilted his head back, searching the sky. "I vote we go back to the hotel, eat and pull out those archaic maps of yours."

"We can start clearing the campgrounds tomorrow," I agreed. "I'm familiar with his scent. I think I can track him."

Unless he used an erasure spell, but I didn't mention that. I got the feeling despite his protests to the contrary, Charybdis wanted to be found. Whatever trap he'd readied, he was prepared when he left me the trinkets. His actions seemed desperate as he burned the candle at both ends to spur me into action.

On the way back to the hotel, I filled Theo in about the text from Comeaux. "Charybdis threatened my parents the first time we spoke. After today, I can't deny there's a reason he chose this place." My feet ached with every step thanks to a blister I had earned today. "I think they're here. It makes sense, right? This whole area is full of memories for me. My parents loved it up in the mountains. What better place to fall off the grid than this?"

"Marshal Ayer came here before you got involved in the case," he pointed out. "How could he have known about you then? About what you would cost him? It seems to me if he had, he would have come for you first so you couldn't ruin his circle before he finished setting it."

"Good point." We reached the hotel, stepped into the elevator, and I leaned against the railing. "We're missing something."

"If you ask me, we're missing a lot of somethings." He snorted. "Still, it's a possibility your folks could be nearby. You're right that they had strong ties to the state, and they knew you guys were living in Three Way. Maybe they wanted to be off the grid but still have a safety net?" He tapped his phone's screen in quick succession. "That would put you on opposite ends of the state, about seven hours apart. You could make that trip in a day if worse came to worst."

"All these years," I murmured. "They could have been so close, and yet never reached out to us."

Theo clapped a hand on my shoulder. "Losing a family member is hard."

"Losing your sister and your parents in the span of six months is harder."

He didn't have a response to that. We didn't talk much at all as we set up to work in my room. We ate, studied the maps and planned out our routes for the next two days. More than that and I would have to reevaluate. Leaving Graeson behind while he was vulnerable made the pack's anti-phone stance all the more frustrating. His absence was a constant ache throbbing on the edges of my mind. Separation from the others made me antsy. No pack bond meant I was locked in my own head, and the lack of ambient feedback starved me for a level of connectivity impossible to replicate on my own.

Sleep, when it came, tugged me under like a riptide. For once I was glad to be carried away.

A metallic taste in my mouth roused me out of a familiar nightmare where I bobbed in an endless ocean while silvery fish with blunt teeth chomped on my toes. Curling my legs under me, I massaged my feet to reassure myself I hadn't lost any little piggies. Halfway back to sleep, the bitter taste intensified, and its meaning lifted the hairs on my nape.

Glamour.

I was tasting fae glamour so viscous air felt like pudding in my lungs, and any slim hope it might have been Theo making a late-night visit evaporated.

I eased upright and slid off the mattress. No sooner had I tiptoed across the room and pressed my back to the paneling beside the door did the knob twist. I held my breath as a slice of light from the hallway cut across the room and bisected the pillow where I had been sleeping.

All I could see from this vantage was a black leather glove, fingers splayed against the veneer as it nudged the crack wider. The ornate tattoo binding his wrists would have given him away as fae even if his scent hadn't. I summoned my wolf without thought, the two of us fitting seamlessly together as we stalked our prey.

Silent as a whisper, he eased inside, his pale eyes dialing wide when he spotted me leaning there, watching him. Before he snapped out of his surprise, I slammed my elbow into his gut. He bent forward on a grunt of pain, and I fisted his hair, using my grip to fling him over my shoulder. He hit the floor on his back and coughed in shock while I shut the door quietly and locked it. The iron tang of blood from a scratch on his temple, courtesy of the sharp edge of the heavy wooden bedframe, whet my appetite.

Down, girl.

"Magistrate Vause sent me to fetch you," he grunted.

"Is that right?" My jaw had gone tender as the wolf fought to surface, and my words slurred. "Prove it."

"I'm going to get my phone out of my back pocket." He rolled his hips and pulled out a slim, black cell then punched in a speed-dial combination. "Magistrate, yes, I am with Agent Ellis now." He extended his arm toward me. "Talk to her. Get your proof."

Warily I accepted the call. "Magistrate Vause?"

"You attempted to contact me." Her clipped tone and cool delivery were as familiar as Aunt Dot's hugs. "Consider this your callback."

"I tried your private number. Magistrate Martindale answered. He seems to believe you vanished and that foul play was involved." I slid my attention back to the deadly fae lying on the floor. "He mentioned one of your guards was killed."

"Yes." An uncharacteristic low note imbued the word. On another woman, I would have named it remorse, but Vause regretted nothing in my experience. "He attempted to kill me, and we couldn't allow that to stand."

"Why would he do a thing like that?" I drawled, making it clear I could imagine several reasons.

"He was taken as a host." Deftly, she deflected my sarcasm. "Oisin had been with me since he was forty. He died at eighty-nine. A mere babe."

Familiar with her habit of slipping away without notifying her Unseelie counterpart of her itinerary, I pinched the bridge of my nose. "Is it safe for you to be on your own?"

"I was attacked in my office, by one of my own people." Her haughty scoff further reassured me she was, in fact, Vause. "Is it safe for me anywhere? Now, what was the reason you called? Understand I won't be reconsidering your leave, so I'll save you the breath for asking."

I was so far past worrying over my job and performance record I couldn't spot them in my rearview mirror if I squinted.

"Charybdis has taken my aunt and cousin." I ground my teeth to keep from snapping at her. "He's threatened my parents and attacked members of my pack. I called to ask for your help."

"Can you stop making that noise?" She managed to sound offended by my growl. "It's quite distracting and sure to draw unwanted attention."

I throttled back the rumble in my chest. "Better now?"

"Marginally," she allowed. "I am sympathetic to your plight, but I'm not certain how much I can help you. I have my own oaths to uphold and my own safety to consider."

"How did you know where to find me?"

Silent moments ticked past, and I imagined Vause deciding which version of the truth to share.

"For the good of the organization, the conclave keeps meticulous records on our employees and their families."

I bit my lip and managed an "Mmm-hmm" that sounded a few degrees less murderous than the roiling in my gut.

"I expected you to reach out to your parents," she said at last. "Their last-known whereabouts were in the Butler area."

"I see." There. That sounded civil. "Are you saying the conclave lost track of them? My own resources have confirmed they're keeping a low profile."

More silence lapsed. This time it was deafening.

"Your parents were kept under surveillance from the time you entered marshal academy until a few short months ago."

"Why?"

"You're an anomaly. A mature Gemini without a twin. We were curious how your skills would manifest over time, and I must admit, I was wrong about Cord Graeson's influence on you. Thanks to your connection to him and his wargs, we've gained valuable insight into the workings of Gemini physiology."

My back hit the wall. It was all that propped me upright. "You're saying I'm a science experiment. That you've been tracking my family, Graeson, the wargs, all of them. Do you honestly not get what a huge invasion of privacy that is?"

Not to mention how pointless it was to surveil my parents when we had no relationship. Unless she thought their particular combination of DNA was the cause for my survival.

"You signed the paperwork," she reminded me. "You gave us freedom to complete a thorough background search, among other things."

"A background search is not the same as ongoing surveillance," I gritted out. "Why waste the resources? I'm not that interesting. Gemini avoid the conclave. It's not like cataloguing me will help your recruiting efforts."

Employment with the conclave had been the first stepping stone on my path to atonement. I joined because I was broken and lost, and they promised me meaningful work and a place to belong.

"I made an oath, Camille."

The simple, unadorned statement gave me chills. "What can you tell me?"

"A rotating detail was assigned to monitor your parents." The *click-click-click* of a retractable pen button being pressed filled the line. "When the last marshal scheduled to report for his six-week shift failed to arrive, I sent agents to their last-known address." *Click-click-click.* "The marshal was found dead, and your mother and father were gone. No evidence could be obtained from the scene due to a series of cascading erasure spells set off at the time of his death."

"Erasure spells?" I thumped my head against the wall, sifting through everything I knew about Charybdis, about my parents, but it did nothing to jog my brain. Piecing the timeline together, I finally hit on a connection. "Wait." I pushed off the wall. "Marshal Ayer had receipts in her pockets from a trip to Butler."

"I won't ask how you came by that information since it would require me to dismiss you from the Earthen Conclave."

That was not a no. It bolstered me to make an investigative leap. "Ayer killed the other agent."

"Yes."

"Is she aware of what she did?" Our time with Harlow had been too brief to determine how much she retained of what she'd done. "Is that why she turned herself over to the mental hospital?"

"Marshal Ayer was catatonic when she was discovered at your parents' home. The marshal responding thought she was a victim too, a survivor, at first, until she attacked him. She had been there for so many days prior to discovery, she was half-starved, and the temptation of a fresh blood supply proved too much for her. She had to be restrained and sedated at the scene."

"I want that address," I found myself saying, even though I wasn't sure I wanted it at all.

"I expected as much. I gave Fionn permission to share it with you." Her chair groaned as she readjusted. "Regardless of how cognizant Ayer was of her actions, I made the decision to admit her to Edelweiss so that she couldn't be used against us again."

A sense of foreboding slithered through me that perhaps what Mai and I had done was far riskier than we had imagined at the time.

"What she knows or does not know is uncertain at this point. She's being kept sedated to prevent Charybdis from revisiting that host."

I drew myself upright. "Sedation prevents Charybdis from reentering a host?"

"We believe so, yes. Even after contamination, he seems to require consciousness to seize control of his victims."

Meaning this might be the solution for taking down Harlow the next time we met. Or, gods forbid, any family and pack mates he might have infected.

The guard who had kept his composure all this time raised his head off the floor. In one lithe movement, he sprang to his feet and prowled closer. "The time for questions has come to an end."

Shoved into the spotlight, I wracked my brain for the most pressing questions. "How is Charybdis taking hosts?"

"Oisin and Fionn never left my side on days when I was scheduled for meetings. Not all fae are as respectful of their magistrates as they should be. That day Fionn remained in my chambers while Oisin positioned himself at the outer door. Before he attacked, he frisked a man who came bearing a package for me. One we have since determined to have been stolen off a mail cart on one of the lower floors. The delivery was a ruse. The man in question was nonresponsive when Fionn questioned him, much as Marshal Ayer was." A weary sigh sifted through her. "I believe that was the point of contact."

Twisting my bottom lip between my fingers, I pinched until it hurt to jumpstart my sleep-addled brain. "You're saying Charybdis infects people by touch."

Thinking back to the clerk at the gas station, even farther back to when he took control of Bianca, he had almost admitted as much, hadn't he?

"That is the theory the evidence supports." The pen clicked again. "Camille, I know it goes against your nature, but I must advise you that, should you encounter a host, you must kill it before it touches you. Otherwise you'll never cut out all the rot."

Too late, I almost admitted while my gut plummeted into the soles of my feet. I hadn't touched Harlow, but Graeson had. Not that it mattered since I had tackled both Ayer and Bianca. That meant we were both at risk of infection.

"I can't kill his hosts," I growled. "They're innocent people."

"Who will harm other innocents until they are stopped. Consider your pack's wellbeing if you care so little for you own. Until Charybdis is dead, your wargess can't be left unsupervised. Certainly not while she's pregnant. The temptation would prove too great for Charybdis to resist. He would have her kill the babe to feed off the agony—hers, the pack's...yours. As attuned to the pack bond as he would be in her body, he could harvest the pain easily."

Of all the wargs in our pack, he had targeted the softest and most fragile of us all.

"You're a new pack. The babe represents a new hope. Wolfborn pups are rare, and you've already confirmed that's what hers will be." Confident in her information, the depth of her knowledge of us astounded me. "By harming her, he wounds the entire pack. By taking her mind, he's infected your pack bond. It's a conduit for him now."

"Can he feed off the emotions of those who are connected to her?" Another idea chilled me. "Can he infect another mind while joined with it through hers?"

"Both are distinct possibilities."

"That's why you had your guard killed." Despite her obvious attachment to him, Vause hadn't hesitated to put him down when it came to his death or hers. "You couldn't afford the risk."

"One touch, and he could have taken me. Imagine the damage he could have wrought if he controlled a magistrate. I can't be compromised. He has already killed to learn what I know, but what he's gained is but a drop in an ocean of secrets. Things I would—and have—killed to protect." Reading into my silence, she softened her tone. "Fionn would have killed me had he failed to prevent my contamination. It is the only way. Harden your heart to it now. This can only end one way, and that is in death."

Harlow had survived Charybdis the longest. But Aunt Dot? Isaac? Mom and Dad? How did I earmark any one of them as an acceptable loss? I couldn't. Even though my parents had broken my heart, they were still my family.

As long as we were all alive, there was still hope we might reconcile in the future. Death was permanent.

"You don't trust me—" she began.

I couldn't stop the scoff burning my nose. "I can't imagine why."

"This union of yours with Cord Graeson is not an alliance I would have chosen for you, but I respect that you do have genuine affection for him, and him for you." The other shoe hovered for a full minute. And then it dropped. "That doesn't change the fact you must not return to him. Stay as far away from the pack and that poisonous bond as you can."

Why further proof of her prejudice surprised me, I have no idea. "Graeson is the one person who has never lied to me, and you're asking me to repay him by walking away."

"Marshal Ayer was one of the guards for your parents, as I've mentioned." The clicking pen returned with a vengeance. "We have reason to believe that first contact between Marshal Ayer and Charybdis when he stepped out of the portal in Wink is the reason why he targeted you."

The shift in her narrative threw me enough I didn't question the connection.

"As your recruiter, all reports on your family were to be given to me in person. Marshal Ayer had ended her six-week commitment and was required to check in with me prior to returning to her family. I was attending a mandatory meeting in Wink and granted her permission to visit me there despite the risk of discovery." Her voice tightened. "I was in a meeting with the other magistrates when the portal breach occurred. Charybdis caught her on her way to my temporary quarters, and her knowledge gave him access to every piece of information we had on you and your family, and I'm sorrier for that than you can ever know."

The room whirled. My ears rang. Air solidified in my lungs.

Happenstance? Serendipity? Fate?

That was her answer?

How many times had I combed over crime scenes or sat in on autopsies only to be present when the poignant answer to "why her?" was inevitably *wrong place, wrong time*? How often did the killer have no previous knowledge of the victim? Or swore he had subdued his dark urges until they combusted and devoured the nearest person?

The simplicity of that answer, the implication that any person, no matter how moral or just, could lose it all in a blink of unprovoked malice, had never satisfied. It sure as hell didn't now.

A sharp *crack* perked my ears. I stared dumbly at the phone as it spun across the floor. A heartbeat later, my knees buckled and I joined it.

"Agent Ellis, are you all right?"

The guard's question was drowned in the white noise rushing through my head. I had been so fixated on the why, I hadn't absorbed the how. How Charybdis snared my attention in the first place. How he tailored his methodology to fit his target. How he hooked me, right from the start.

Charybdis had been in Ayer's head. Possibly even Mom's or Dad's. He might as well have been in mine the way he had selected my worst fears and pitted them against me. Adding his own gruesome signature, he all but recreated Lori's death with each victim the kelpie had taken.

All those girls were dead...because of me.

Marie's blood was on my hands.

I drew my legs against my chest, wrapped my arms around them and dropped my forehead to my knees. I had come so close to having it all—a mate, a home, a future. All of that was gone, snatched from my outstretched arms in the span of seconds it had taken me to lose Lori, my parents, my family.

Graeson would hate me when he figured out I had cost him his sister.

I had cost him everything.

The honor of being chosen as his mate, the pride at being an alpha, left a cold place in my chest as those accomplishments withered. I would lose the place I had been carving out among the wargs, and my warg aspect would shrivel and die along with those dreams. A ragged howl tore through my chest, but I clamped my mouth shut over it. The she-wolf wasn't real. She was just as much a figment of my imagination as the idea I could ever deserve to belong with a man like Graeson.

Rocking back and forth, I kept my jaw locked and swallowed convulsively to hold the acid at bay.

Vause's guard squatted in front of me, a safe distance away. I watched him through the crack of my legs as he signed off with the magistrate and pocketed his phone. Lips mashed into a firm line, he scanned the ceiling as if hoping for divine intervention. None came. None ever did. I could have told him that.

"I must go." He went down on one knee. "I have left the magistrate alone for as long as I dare."

Flicking my wrist, I shooed him on his way, hoping he would be quick about it so I could get my head on straight before guilt pumped my stomach contents.

"Forgive me." He struck so fast his hand blurred. "I have my orders."

The downy blanket of oblivion beckoned, and I curled into its embrace. The hard edges of the world went soft and muzzy until I could breathe again. There was no shame here, only acceptance and warmth. The swaddling blackness enveloped me, and the rest fell away.

CHAPTER TWELVE

Waking up on the carpet in my hotel room, muscles sore and hip aching, was not a great start to what promised to be a long day. I gritted my teeth, rolled over and pushed to my feet. An itch brought my hand to my cheek, where I found a ragged sheaf of notebook paper adhered to my skin. Using the bathroom mirror to guide me in its removal, I flipped it over and read the information written in elegant script. The words pierced my grogginess and made my heart pound faster.

I sent Theo a text to meet me at the Waffle Iron, the restaurant we had scouted for breakfast, then changed into fresh clothes and ran my fingers through my hair. I grabbed my phone, wallet and the paper and headed across the street.

Turns out I hadn't sent him a wakeup call. He was digging into a stack of pancakes when I shoved through the doors. I strolled right up to his table and slapped the scrap of paper down beside his plate before collapsing on the bench seat across from him.

"You've got a smudge." He rubbed a finger under his eye. "Right there."

"Doesn't matter." I stole his glass of water, tossing it back with one hand while the other tapped the note. "That's my parents' last-known address."

"How did you get that?" The fork slid from his hand and clattered to his plate. "I've had people digging for days, and they all came up empty."

His club connections must keep him plugged into the Gemini community, but we were few and far between. There was a whole supernatural world out there, and sometimes it took organizations like the conclave, with their questionable morals, to deliver. That didn't mean I had to like it.

"I had a visitor last night." I gave him a quick rundown of my night, from Fionn's arrival to waking this morning sprawled across the carpet where he'd left me.

Theo listened, fingers drumming the table, reminding me so much of Isaac when the urge to run struck him it hurt. He barely waited for me to finish before he shot his hand in the air and called, "Check."

We paid and exited before my stomach got a chance to rumble at the scent of the bacon I didn't get the chance to eat.

Theo programmed the address into his phone's GPS app then passed the note to me for safekeeping. I clutched it until the paper crumpled, but I couldn't let go. This was it. I was about to see the place my parents had called home. I was about to see their new life firsthand, and I wasn't sure if I hoped things looked the same as I remembered or if different would be simpler. Like if they had cut ties to everything it might be easier for me to stomach instead of life going on as usual for them, except without me in it.

The drive passed in quiet except for the robotic directions voiced at regular intervals.

"Are you sure this is right?" Theo threw the car into park in the driveway of a modest brick home positioned in the center of an older subdivision. The grass was overgrown, but there wasn't a weed to be found, so the lawn had been cared for until recently. "This is so...permanent."

I checked the paper for the hundredth time since discovering it, then matched the address to the mailbox. "This is the address Vause gave me."

We stepped onto the sidewalk and approached the door side by side.

"The gate leading into the backyard is open." He jerked his chin. "That gives us privacy from the humans."

Nodding, I crossed the stepping-stone path that curved around the side of the house. Theo joined me, and I shut the gate and latched it to prevent any well-meaning neighbors from interfering. A set of French doors led out onto a tidy patio outfitted with a grill, patio furniture, the whole nine yards.

I checked the doors and the two rear windows. All were locked. There were no handy spare keys left under rocks or under mats, either. The conclave didn't skimp when it came to cleaning up messes in human-populated areas. I didn't know what to expect once we got inside, except I could guarantee all the surfaces would be sanitized and anything fae would have been removed.

The easiest way in was to break the panel of glass near the handle so we could reach inside and open the door. I reared back my elbow, ready to do the honors, but Theo caught my forearm.

"Let's keep this quiet, okay?" He glanced left to right. "We don't know how nosy the neighbors are here." He gripped the handle and held on tight, the metal heating until it glowed. Theo pulled out a warped chunk of locking mechanism and dropped it on the dirt. "There. Wasn't that better?"

His recalls weren't as impressive as Isaac's, but he did okay. Better than me. I almost asked what superheated creature he had used as a donor but decided it wasn't my business who had been warming his bed lately.

"After you." He swung one half of the patio doors open and stepped aside. "Be careful until we figure out if they set any spells after they left. We don't want to walk into something nasty."

Crossing that threshold left me shaken, but in a good way. As alien as the brick box acting as a home base for Gemini struck me, the interior reminded me of stepping inside my parents' Airstream. The walls were covered with metallic paper. I ran my hand along the nearest panel, and my fingers bumped where someone had taken the time to hammer silver upholstery nails into the wall. The same pictures once screwed into the curved walls of the trailer hung from drywall in frames. The furniture was the same or similar, larger without a size restriction.

Theo turned a slow circle. "Have we entered *The Twilight Zone?*"

"It sure looks that way." The living room flowed into an open-concept kitchen. Touches of the familiar adorned every surface in the most bizarre mix of past and present I could have ever imagined. "The bedrooms must be this way. I'm going to clear them."

I examined a tidy half bath in the hall then entered the master bedroom. I touched the quilt at the foot of the bed, the one my maternal grandmother had handstitched as a wedding gift shortly before she and her twin passed. The en suite bathroom held no mysteries, and I left the oddly sterile rooms to explore the rest of the home.

The second bedroom had been converted into a storage room with metal shelves holding all sorts of medical supplies. Incontinence pads, tubing, syringes and alcohol wipes, clean sheets, bedding protection and plastic-looking underwear.

"Theo," I called, my voice wavering. "Come look at this."

What I really meant was *Don't make me face this alone.*

The sharp ache shredding my chest intensified, and I wished so hard for Graeson that my wolf pushed a whine up the back of my throat. More than his sound advice, I missed him. His strength. His warmth. I didn't want to face this by myself. Theo was family, but he and I had never bared our souls the way Graeson and I had despite knowing each other our whole lives. My jagged heart wanted its matching half, the one guaranteed to fit and make whatever we uncovered bearable.

"It will be okay." Theo's hand landed on my shoulder and squeezed. "Whatever this means, it's going to be all right."

Throat tight, I nodded and entered the hall to face down the last room. Quick as I could, before I lost my nerve, I shoved open the door. Ice incased my feet, anchoring me to the threshold. My knees locked, and I had to grip the doorframe to keep myself upright.

Rose walls, blush carpet. Stuffed animals and prissy dolls. Tattered books and bins full of toys that had been hand-me-downs from my parents. The entire room was a shrine to Lori and her favorite color.

"I don't understand." Again and again, my gaze was drawn away from the tiny details on the fringes of the room to where a full-sized hospital bed dominated the center of the space. "What does this mean?"

A few machines sat on built-in shelves to either side of the bed. There were nooks where more units must have been prior to Ayer's massacre.

Theo examined the machines, the setup, and anchored his hands on his hips. "There are units missing, but what's left is..." He raked his hands through his hair. "This wasn't about convalescence. This room was setup for long-term care." His lips pinched. "We're talking life support here for a person with little or no cognitive awareness."

"How do you know?" I croaked.

"I've seen these before." He tapped small gems set into the silver railings near the head of the bed. A few had been pried out with claws or a tool, but most had shattered in the process. "There's a clan of lesser dryads in Orlando who use them. When a tree is old and dying, or infected with pests, they'll carve out notches in the trunk and embed bespelled gemstones to put the spirit in stasis so they don't suffer the pain of a slow death."

I made a circuit around the room, fingers brushing over old friends and familiar belongings. I stopped at the closet, half-expecting more supplies but discovering a treasure-trove of frilly nightgowns. The size was small, but adult. The colors were vibrant, the patterns varied but full of childish whimsy.

"This doesn't mean anything," I said as much to myself as Theo.

Prying myself from the cheerful clothes, I shut the door and leaned against it. If only shutting out the scramble of my thoughts was so simple. Across from me, Theo sat in a rocker I hadn't noticed tucked on the far side of the bed. He held a yellowed, dog-eared copy of *Bunnicula* in his hands.

"There must be an explanation." He stared ahead, voice empty. "Lori is dead."

His voice rose at the end, making it a question, asking me to back him up on what we accepted as truth and fact.

"She's gone." The bedrock shoring up my life wobbled perilously. "I don't know what this means yet, but it can't mean that."

Mom and Dad had abandoned me. I got that. I had moved on. Mostly. They cut me out of their lives, and I understood. I was a near-exact replica of what they had lost. They would look at me and see what might have been. I could forgive them that weakness thanks to Aunt Dot's unconditional love.

But this...

This made my gut pitch with the possibilities. Lori was dead. *Dead.* Right? She was my twin. My sister. I would know if she was alive. Deep down, I would have known she wasn't really gone. That's how twin bonds worked, wasn't it? That connection was the reason no twin outlived their sibling for long. I was a freak. All my life I had been the oddity, the outsider, the lone Gemini in a culture of pairs. Except... What if I wasn't?

My parents wouldn't keep something this huge from me. From us all. Would they? Did I know my parents well enough to make that call? Was any eight-year-old's perception of their mother and father close to the reality of them? And what about Aunt Dot? She was an adult—

my mother's twin. She would have known. If this was what it looked like, then she must have been aware of their charade. My parents would have needed help that night, and after. No. It wasn't possible. It couldn't be. That would mean Aunt Dot had lied to me every day by not telling me for years. Every breakfast, a lie. Every good-night kiss, a lie. Every time she told me she loved me, the worst kind of lie.

Head shaking, I backed out into the hall. "I can't do this."

I ran through the house, the ghosts of my past breathing down my neck, without a backward glance.

The drive back to the hotel was heavy with things left unsaid. Escaping into the parking lot gave me room to breathe, but the reprieve was short-lived. I strode inside and made a beeline for the elevator.

"Ms. Ellis?"

I glanced over my shoulder to find the desk clerk trailing me. "Yes?"

"You received a message while you were out." He shoved a piece of notebook paper at me. "The caller requested I place this in your hand myself."

After taking another look at his neat-as-a-pin attire, I noticed the badge affixed to his shirt that identified him as a manager. "I appreciate it."

"Here at the Comforting Inn, we take great pride in our guests' satisfaction. Our goal is to ensure that every stay is as perfect as we can make it." He pointed at the web address running along the bottom of the page. "If you don't mind, could you visit our website and take a brief survey? It helps spread the word about our excellent customer service and allows us to continue to excel at—"

"Yes." I spun on my heel. "I'll do that."

I jabbed the button for the elevator and studied the message. The area code was familiar, but I had contacts all over the country. When glaring at the ten digits failed to jog my memory, I scanned the bottom of the page and the hotel's information. I tripped over their phone number, compared it to the handwritten message and sure enough, the area codes matched.

Who would be calling me from a local number? Only one way to find out. I retrieved my phone and dialed.

"Hello?" a soft voice answered on a rush of breath. "Cammie?"

A thousand childhood memories blasted to the forefront of my mind. *"Mom?"*

"Yes, baby, it's me."

"I—" I stumbled into the hall when the doors opened, and sat on a bench underneath a mural. "I thought you were taken. Your guard was killed. Vause told me. Where did you—? Why are you calling now?" I slumped against the wallpaper. "What's going on?"

"Our neighbor, a rock troll by the name of Seamus, spotted someone at our house." Her tone gentled. "We asked him to call if that ever happened. We had to know if we were being hunted, and it made sense the first place a tracker would start was at home."

"So you haven't been kidnapped?" A man shot me a strange look as he passed. "You're okay?"

"We're all fine." She hesitated. "You went inside the house."

My fingernails pierced my leg through the fabric of my jeans. "Theo and I did, yes."

"Then you know."

"I don't know anything anymore," I admitted.

"I didn't want you to find out about your sister that way."

A filament of anger snapped free of the ball of guilt roiling in my gut, and I growled, "It seems to me I was never supposed to find out about her at all."

She didn't contradict me.

"I'm glad you called," I gritted out. "I was worried."

"We need to talk," she said in her best mom voice. "In person."

The possibility Charybdis was yanking my mother's strings occurred to me, but I wanted to see for myself, with my own eyes, that she was safe and undamaged. Then I could call the conclave and arrange protection for them. Even with my job in jeopardy, they would do that much for me. I hoped.

I met her demand with one of my own. "I want to see her."

I would never believe this was real if I didn't. My parents had run before, and they might run again. This might be the only chance I got to figure out exactly how massive their betrayal was before they vanished from my life again, possibly for good this time.

"I expected you would." She made her peace with my requirement. "Here's the address. Make sure you aren't followed."

I wrote it down and ended the call. I was still sitting there, staring at my phone like it might sprout fangs and bite me, when Theo swaggered into the hall with a young woman on his arm.

"Are you serious?" I cocked an eyebrow at him. "This is how you handle what we just saw?"

"Who are you?" Baring rows of needlelike teeth, the woman snapped her jaws at me. "He's mine. I saw him first."

"I doubt that." I snorted, amazed to find an ounce of humor left in me. "I've known him all my life, so I'm pretty sure that means I saw him first." I flicked my wrist and rose. "By all means, Theo, do what you've got to do. Whatever that is you're doing." I jabbed the elevator's down button. "I'll catch you later."

"Where the hell do you think you're going?" He peeled the woman away from his side and grabbed my upper arm. "You're in no shape to be out there alone."

"I'm going to meet Mom." I broke his grip and stepped into the empty booth. "You coming or not?"

Casting a final glance at his date, who pouted prettily despite the dental nightmare in her mouth, he gusted out a sigh and adjusted his crotch. "I guess not."

After blowing her a kiss, he stepped into the elevator with me. The door closed in her face, and her frustrated roar shook my eardrums. I scrunched up my nose and glanced at my cousin. "Really?"

"She's a rarity." He shrugged. "I was curious."

And hurting as much as I was.

We all had our coping mechanisms. I wasn't about to shame his when mine was often equally as self-destructive. What a pair we made. He and I were more alike than I had ever imagined.

CHAPTER THIRTEEN

The address Mom gave me took all of thirty minutes to reach. Part of me expected her to return to her Gemini roots now that the going had gotten tough, but no. She had chosen what I assumed was a rental home in yet another cookie-cutter subdivision. The gleaming pickup in the yard was the same as the one the pixie had described, a throwback to the lifestyle they had abandoned, and that one detail hammered home this surreal moment.

"Are you ready?"

I started at the sound of Theo's voice and whipped my head toward him. "Yes?"

"It's going to be okay." He patted my thigh. "Whatever's in there..." his throat worked, "...you'll be okay."

Pasting on a smile, I nodded. "Yeah."

Not buying it for a minute, he pressed me. "It's better to know, right?"

"Yes." It came out stronger that time. "I want the truth."

Or the lies would haunt me as surely as Lori's ghost had all these years.

We exited the vehicle and took the tidy path up to the front door. Fingers trembling, I kept missing the doorbell. I ended up smacking it with the heel of my palm, which caused Theo's lips to tic upward.

The door swung open on a breath of air smelling of herbs and growing things. The woman who stood in the doorway was a tad shorter than me, a little blonder than me, and more beautiful than I remembered. Her blue eyes—clear of Charybdis's soulless influence—filled with moisture that leaked over her cheeks, and she blinked to clear her vision.

"Step lively, now. Get in here." She peered over our shoulders down the empty street, her gaze lingering on the windows of her neighbors' homes. Her paranoia reassured me that she was in control of herself, at least for now. "We don't have much time."

We hustled inside, and she shut the door and sealed it with a charm so powerful I sneezed as the magic activated.

"We can't be too careful," she said with an apologetic smile. "Please, follow me into the kitchen." She opened cabinets and pulled out four glasses. "Can I get you something? Tea? Lemonade? Water?"

"Where did you get the magic?" I kept to the tiled entryway. "I doubt Aunt Dot could manage the spell you just activated."

"Your aunt hasn't lived through what we have." A line puckered her brow. "My sister isn't the only Cahill with witch friends and enough power to ignite a multitiered ward."

"Maybe if you'd stuck around," Theo drawled, "we would know what you were capable of."

I don't think I had ever loved my least-favorite cousin as much as I did in that moment.

"I heard voices," a masculine baritone rumbled. "Is she here?"

Dad rounded the corner and joined us in the hall outside the kitchen. "Cammie," he whispered, throwing his arms wide and not waiting for me to decide to step into them. He scooped me up and crushed me to his chest, his arms just as strong as I remembered from all the great big bear hugs of my childhood. "I'm so glad to see you." He set me down and wiped his cheeks dry. "You're so beautiful—and tall. The pictures Dot sent didn't do you justice." He laughed. "You're as lovely as your mother and as tall as me. Gods be praised, what a blessed sight."

"And you brought Theo?" He stuck out his arm, fingers splayed. "I would have expected Isaac. It's good to see you kids put the past behind you."

"The past never stays in the past, does it?" Theo made no move to accept the forearm clasp Dad offered. "I'm sure Isaac would be here if he hadn't been taken by the same fae who attacked you." He placed a hand over his heart in mock sympathy when Mom gasped. "I'm sorry. You didn't know? Maybe if you had reached out to tell us what had happened to you, we could have avoided meeting here like this."

"Theo." I touched his forearm, grateful his lashing out meant I got to play good cop to his bad cop. "We've come this far. We might as well hear them out."

Dad shoved his hands in his pockets and ducked into the kitchen. Mom was right behind him, so we let them guide us to the table and took our seats while she poured sweet tea into familiar glasses neither of us wanted to lift.

Mom sat across from me and fidgeted with the tassels on the edge of her placemat. "You have questions, I'm sure."

Ice water flowed through my veins. "You told me Lori died."

My parents exchanged a glance saturated with dread and an emotion perilously close to...relief.

"The Lori you knew did die that night," Dad answered, anguish thick in his expression. "Your sister..."

"We revived her." Mom's voice warbled. "It was too late. Lori suffered massive brain damage."

I leaned back in my chair, fingers worrying the drops of condensation on my glass. "Is she...?"

"A dryad acquaintance of ours enchanted a few items, most of which we had to leave at the house after the attack. They keep her free of any pain she might be feeling and resting easy." She picked at the strings until one came off in her hand. "She never woke up, not really.

She doesn't speak or blink. Her body is alive, but her mind—her soul—they left us that night."

"When the rogue agent came after us, we packed the necessities and made arrangements for what we couldn't carry to be brought here to this bolt-hole." He indicated boxes of medical supplies left open on the counter. "Lori depends on a tube in her throat to help her breathe. She's fed through a separate tube in her stomach. There's also the catheter to consider." His laugh was tired, bitter. "Mundane medical supplies are easy enough to come by, but we rely on magic to keep her as comfortable and as safe as possible. This breach, or whatever it was, with the conclave has forced us to make do, and that's not a thing I can abide much longer."

"How did the conclave get involved?" I had heard Vause's side of the story, but I wanted theirs.

"The conclave performed an intensive background search on you before you were allowed to enter the marshal academy. She found us within weeks; she even came out to visit with us and your sister." Mom set her jaw. "She refused to allow you to join unless we accepted their offer of 'help'. She knew we had no one else to turn to, so she pressed us hard. Eventually we agreed with Magistrate Vause and allowed her to place an agent with basic medical training on the premises in case Lori went into distress."

"Vause was protecting her investment." That sounded about right. Her knowing about my sister made a lot more sense than her posting guards with my parents when we had no interaction, and any genetic information could have been gathered with a swab to the inside of their cheek. "She didn't tell me she knew, but it doesn't surprise me."

Not much Vause did shocked me. She was a magistrate, a law unto herself, and she had proven too many times she was willing to bend me until I broke. This time, she just might get the satisfaction of hearing me snap.

"We had already cost you so much." Dad shared a look with Mom. "We refused to be the cause of you not getting the career you wanted. Even if it meant climbing in bed with the conclave."

"It wasn't all bad." Mom noticed my frown. "The agents assigned were very polite and knowledgeable, eager to help and willing to get their hands dirty." Her lips tipped upward at the corners. "They gave us a glimpse of the person you might have become."

"That's why you left Cammie with us?" Theo spoke up for the first time since entering the kitchen. "To hide all this from her?"

"We had no choice." Color leached from Mom's cheeks. "The danger was too great if she stayed."

A frown puckered my brow. "What do you mean?"

"Gemini die in pairs for a reason, baby." Mom reached for my hand, thought better of it and tucked hers under the table. "Twins have a special bond. Even human twins share a psychic bond, a sense of awareness of the other. In Geminis, it's more than sixth sense, it's a survival mechanism. No Gemini can survive without the psychic feedback from their other half."

Meaning I had never been a survivor. I was just defective in a different way than I had been led to believe.

"We look to our twins for our reset," Dad elaborated. "We share blood and magic with them on a regular basis. The truth is that each pair is an equal in their relationship. Siblings are linked mentally, magically and physically. Cut that off, and a Gemini is crippled. The magic goes out, seeking a receptor, and is expended instead of bouncing back to you. Slowly your body will drain itself trying to latch on to a circuit that doesn't exist. Eventually you will die. It's only a matter of how long it takes."

No one had told me this in as many words. Had they been worried it would frighten me? Or that I might figure this out? Even now I had goose bumps thinking of how close I had come to death. Before I thought there was a sliver of hope, that stubbornness counted, but all the battles I had imagined fighting for survival had been petty skirmishes instead.

"That doesn't explain why you dumped her on Mom." Theo's jaw flexed. "Nothing you've said so far excuses that."

"The connection keeps us all alive, but it can also do us harm." Mom tucked a loose curl behind her ear. "A connection with a twin fighting a long-term illness is dangerous. Their magic will seek out the healthy energies of their twin in an effort to heal themselves, draining their sibling until they both weaken and die."

I risked a glance up at Mom's face. "So you thought if you put enough distance between us that I would last longer?" Had I not been looking at her, I would have missed her nod. "That's why you left me with Aunt Dot."

"Yes." A brittle smile broke across her mouth. "We tested our theory, first a week or so at a time and then for longer periods. Staying with Dot, and away from us, kept you healthy. You got sick within hours of coming home."

"We had to make a decision." Dad squared his shoulders. "The hardest one of our lives." He took Mom's hand and held it to his chest, over his heart. "We let you go so that you could survive."

"You could have visited, written, called. Something."

"The risk was too great. No one else knew about Lori. We couldn't ask another Gemini for help, or word would travel back to you eventually. We didn't have friends we could trust with her care, and we couldn't bring her with us without getting you sick." Dad shook his head. "We made the right choice, the hard choice, and cut ourselves off from you. We would rather have your hatred than have to watch both our girls wither in front of us."

Throat tight, I took a drink of tea before I could speak again. "I don't hate you."

Hope sparked in both their faces, and it drove a sharp spike of regret through me. This visit was a balm to old wounds, but it wasn't a solution. It wasn't a happy ending. It was a short visit, and then it was right back to us living separate lives.

"We wouldn't blame you if you do," Mom murmured. "You don't have to spare our feelings."

"I've had a good life." I cut a glance at Theo. "Aunt Dot raised me right, and I had cousins that might as well have been my brothers for company." Gods knew Theo had tormented me in ways only a true sibling could. He had picked up right where Lori left off. "I wish you had trusted me with the truth. I understand why you did what you did, and I'll make peace with it eventually. Even if you had waited until I turned eighteen, I deserved to know about Lori—about why you cut yourselves out of my life— but you didn't step forward then either, and that's what hurts most."

Heads bowed, my parents held on to each other as if I were a storm they had to weather. Hurting them hurt me too. All of us were scarred up and broken by Lori's... I wasn't sure what to even call it anymore.

Somewhere in the house a timer dinged, and Dad got to his feet. "Sorry, I was working on something for Lori when you arrived. I'll be right back."

"Wait." I stood when he did, and Theo rose beside me. "I'd like to see her."

"Okay." He reached for Mom's hand and drew her to her feet. "This way."

This house was smaller than their last and much less tidy without the conclave cleanup crew wiping up after them. This place was lived in. Open medical supply boxes littered all the counters. Bags of chips and snacks awaited Dad in his favorite spots. Books covered every surface, the topics varied. Mom read three or four at a time, always in different genres. I spotted a cookbook, a science fiction novel, a contemporary romance and a guide to motorcycle repair.

My parents stopped in front of the last door in the hallway, and Dad wrapped his large hand around the small brass knob. His chest rose and fell, gathering courage was my guess. His other hand flattened against the raised panels. With a twist and a push, he opened the door in the total silence all parents were capable of when checking on sleeping children.

This room wasn't the comforting bastion of childhood memories the other had been. The plain white walls and khaki-colored carpet lent a sterile quality to a room that already lacked personality. A new hospital bed occupied the center space, and machines were arranged around the head of the bed. Subtle beeping, the hiss of oxygen and whir of electronics combined to create ambient noise.

I jumped when Theo clasped my shoulder. I glanced at him, but he wasn't looking at me. His gaze was fixated where mine had yet to roam. Coward that I was, I allowed myself to waste a few extra moments searching the room with a bland eye before focusing on the reason I was here.

The scene from *Snow White* came to mind, the one where she rested in her glass coffin, dead but not. Bespelled. Frozen in time. Perfect. Except no true love's kiss could dissolve the tubes keeping Lori suspended in this moment.

Crossing to her took an eternity. And when I reached her side, I had to try several times before I covered one of her hands, both folded over her middle, with mine. Her skin was soft and warm, her hair parted in the middle and French braided so that each twist trailed down the pillow under her head and almost down to her hips. Our faces and builds were so identical that I could have been staring down at myself.

"Hi, Lore," I whispered. "I've missed you so much."

"Give them a minute alone." Theo entered my periphery. "We'll be outside when you're done."

"What about you?" I caught him by the wrist. "Don't you want to visit with her?"

"Yes." His throat worked. "But I can wait my turn."

Once alone with my sister, I started talking. I didn't stop until I had given her highlights of all the years she had missed. I told her about the academy, about the pack...about Graeson. When I ran out of topics, I pulled a chair near the bed and told her how much I had missed her, how much better all those events would have been with her around to enjoy them with me, how sorry I was that I hadn't been faster or stronger or stood up to her in the first place to protect her from her adventurous nature.

A knock at the door tugged me from my thoughts. Theo slipped inside without waiting for me to answer and rested his hands on the silver railing of Lori's bed. "Your parents think you should take a break. You've been in here for two hours, and they say touching her for long periods of time will weaken you faster."

Two hours? Nodding, I pushed to my feet. Or I tried to. I didn't make it all the way before wobbling knees sank me back down onto the cushion. I raised my arms and watched tremors ripple through my hands. I stared at Lori, peaceful and unaware, and forced my legs under me.

Theo's lips thinned. "Can you make it on your own?"

"Yeah." Voice gravelly, I tried again. "I can get back to the kitchen."

"Call if you need me."

He turned his back on me, and I left before I overheard what he said to Lori. They had been best friends, closer in some ways than she and I had been. Both of them had larger-than-life personalities and an unquenchable thirst for mischief. Isaac and I were the sticks in the mud. Theo and Lori... They had been an unstoppable duo. Isaac and I had envied them. I was old enough to admit that now, though I doubted Isaac ever would because his brother would never let him live down the admission. What I wouldn't give for Lori to give me the same hard time just once more.

I found my parents in the kitchen, Mom with a book and Dad with a screwdriver in one hand and a circuit board in the other. They both dropped what they were doing and raked their gazes over me, assessing the damage that small contact with Lori had done.

"Let's go outside." Mom slid a coupon between the pages of the chapter where she left off reading, grabbed a bottle of greenish water from the fridge, and led me through sliding glass doors onto a patio on the opposite end of the house from Lori. "You'll feel better out here." She unscrewed the cap and passed the bottle to me. "Drink that. It will help. It's how I cope being away from Dot for long periods of time."

I did as she instructed and gagged on the first sip. "That's horrible."

"The alternative is worse." She gestured toward one of the chairs tucked under a patio table. "Sit. Rest."

I didn't have much choice since my legs had given up on supporting me. "What will you do now?"

"We're going to stand and fight." Dad joined us and shut the door behind him. "We can't leave Dot and Isaac in the hands of this crazed fae."

I choked for a different reason. "I won't endanger you like that."

"You don't have a choice." Mom crossed to Dad and leaned against him. "I can find Dot." She tugged a familiar necklace from under the neckline of her shirt. "Our parents had these made for us when we were kids. Back then connecting with family wasn't as easy as pulling out a cell phone and making a call. Letters were slow to be forwarded. They followed a few towns behind, so meeting on the fly was impossible. This helped." She twirled the simple tiger's-eye pendant between her fingers, and I noticed it wasn't so plain after all. A thick metal needle inset its core, and it wobbled as she moved. "Dot is its true north. I can use this to lead us to her."

"I'll take it." I held out my hand. "You should stay here with Dad and Lori."

"The magic only works between twins." She shook her head. "You can't use it. It would only lead you back here."

"You're okay with this?" I asked Dad.

"We haven't been there for you or the rest of the family in a long time." He kissed the top of Mom's head. "We

can't walk away from this, and we can't leave Lori alone."
His gaze found mine, strong and steady. "We've talked
about this, and we trust you to keep your mom safe."

I braced my elbows on the table and dropped my face
into my hands. "Charybdis threatened you both. His
avatar, Marshal Ayer, was here. So he knows about Lori."
I rubbed my forehead. "I would be delivering Mom right
into his hands."

"We can find Dot and—" Mom argued.

"It's not that simple." I explained how Charybdis
operated, how his hosts worked, and my parents fell
silent. "Even if we get to them, they run the risk of being
tainted, and we run the risk of being infected." I dropped
my hands and sat back in my chair. "How do you capture
a fae who's incorporeal like that? Without harming his
avatar?"

"Fae who require an avatar integrate fully with their
host." Mom was slow to add, "To kill the fae, you would
have to kill the body he occupied."

"Except he's proven he can hop from person to person
as it suits him. There's some proximity involved. He must
use his current avatar to get in range of his new host."
That was how he took Bianca. He used an avatar, most
likely Harlow, to get close enough to possess her. "There's
no way to know who he has under his control. We can't
kill everyone and hope we take him down in the process.
There are too many innocents involved."

Dad mulled over the problem. "It sounds like we need
to isolate him."

"Isolation works." The fewer bodies in a given area, the
less chance he had of leaping into a host in time to escape.
"I don't see us luring Charybdis into an obvious trap. He's
smart. There's no way he'll go into an area at our request
without a backup host or an escape plan."

The sliding doors parted, and Theo emerged wearing a
thoughtful expression that made me curious about how
much he had overheard since he had obviously been
listening.

"So eliminate the variables," he said, taking the chair beside mine.

"Wow." I snorted. "The answer was right in front of me this whole time. How did I not see that?"

"We have something he wants." He tapped my hand where it rested on the tabletop. "Bait, coz. We have bait."

"He could have taken me at any time, yet he hasn't." I shook my head. "He's not going to end his game early just because I'm tired of playing."

"He will if we rescue Mom and Isaac. Your parents are safe, I'm safe. The pack is safe, and Graeson knows how to protect them." His smile grew. "Take away his leverage, and what has he got? Nothing."

"A fae with nothing to lose is a dangerous fae." I considered it. "Who makes the sleep charms for Lori?"

"A dryad your dad gave computer lessons to back when they first got popular." Mom rubbed her thumb over a gold ring she wore with empty settings. "We send her precious stones, and she stores magic in them. The charms can then amplify any emotion or sensation. We chose calming energies to keep Lori comfortable."

I turned to Dad. "Do you have any spares on hand?"

"A few, but not enough I can afford to give up even one." He reached for Mom's hand. "We can get more. It would take a day or two."

"Do that." A plan began forming that just might get us all out of this in one piece. "I'll pay whatever fees are involved for the raw materials and the casting."

At least when it came to simple charms, witches tended to accept cash just fine.

My jaw stretched on a yawn, and Mom shot me a worried frown. "You should get back to your hotel. You'll need your rest if this is going to work."

"I think that's best." I stood on aching legs that twinged with every step. "I don't feel so hot right now."

Dad circled the table and wrapped his arm around my waist. "Lean on me, Cammie-Lammie." He held me tucked against his side. "I've got you."

It was a group effort to get me outside and into the car. Dad kissed my forehead and shut the door. I was asleep before the car stopped rocking.

CHAPTER FOURTEEN

"What the hell is wrong with her?"

Wincing at the noise, I shifted onto my other side and curled up tighter in my seat.

"You need to calm down." Glass muffled Theo's response. "This is not what she needs right now."

"Either move out of my way," a dark voice promised, "or I will move you out of my way."

The car door opened behind me, and hot air rushed over my back. A warm hand, rough with calluses smoothed down the length of my arm. *"Ellis?"*

Sunshine poured into my head, bright and pure and tinged with rich emotion that buoyed my spirit. My eyes cracked open, and I couldn't stop my grin from spreading. I also couldn't reach back through the bond. The connection was thin, wobbly. "Graeson."

"Hey, sweetheart." His knuckles caressed my cheek. "How are you feeling?"

"Tired." I leaned into his touch. "Better now that you're here." I lurched upright. "What *are* you doing here?" My gaze tagged his chest, and my hand rose to cover the site of his wound. "How are you?"

"I was going crazy without you." He reached in and helped me out of the car. "And I'm fine. Doc says I'm at ninety-five percent and rising."

"What about the pack?" I wrapped an arm around him to gain my balance. "Who's watching them while you're gone?"

"We're all here." His smile gentled. "Once I told them where I was going, I couldn't have paid them to stay put."

Tears sprang to my eyes, and I hid them against his shirt. "I missed you."

"I'm glad to hear it." He nuzzled the top of my head. "I kept trying to reach you through the pack bond, and it was sending my wolf into a frenzy hitting that blank space. Even though my head knew it was impossible to span across great distances, my heart wouldn't give up."

Breathing in his mix of scents, pine and wood smoke and man, I relaxed for the first time since leaving him. "Where are the others?"

"In an RV park across town, nothing fancy. It's jammed with humans, but we'll make do."

"Do you two want to take this reunion inside?" Theo grumped. "You're causing a scene."

The sidewalks were empty from what I could tell, but his scowl cut deep. Apparently he hadn't forgiven me for not confiding in him about Graeson, or maybe he was just pissed at Graeson for existing, and seeing the alpha in all his glory had reminded him of that fact.

"Let's go up to my room," I said, not caring how suggestive it sounded. "I can explain there."

The trip, short as it was, exhausted me. The chilling truth of my parents' warnings was evident in every heavy step it took me to reach the bed and drop onto the mattress.

"I'll swing by later." Theo rapped on the doorjamb. "You kids behave."

"You're going out?" His twitching fingers told me he was already miles away. "Are you sure that's safe?"

"I need to get some air." He rolled his head on his neck. "After today…yeah…I need a breather."

Air not being what he meant. "Okay." I leaned forward as Graeson stuffed pillows behind my shoulders. "Watch your back."

"Enjoy yourselves." He smirked and began closing the door. "I know I will."

Graeson checked that the door was shut and locked it before pulling the task chair from under the desk to the side of the bed. He dropped into it and examined me toes to hairline. "If you were a warg, I would think this was separation sickness. It can happen in pups and juveniles when they leave the pack for the first time. After going their whole lives with that connection, losing it can be traumatic."

"It kind of is," I admitted, and filled him in on all that he had missed.

"Put that way, I can understand why they did what they did. Even if I don't agree with how they went about doing it." He laced his fingers with mine. "Seeing you this way proves they were right to worry."

"The funny thing is, I really do feel better now that you're here." I rolled onto my side so I faced him. "It's not just some mushy romantic thing, it's the truth."

He made a thoughtful sound in the back of his throat. "I can sense the pack from here, but I know what to look for. It's possible you're tapping into the bond through me." A frown cut his face. "I tried reaching you earlier, in the parking lot, and I hit a wall."

"It's been a while since I took blood." I rubbed my thumb over the spur hidden under my fingernail. "Do you think that could be it?"

"It might be." He noticed my hand and traced the edge of the nail with his fingertip. "I hoped that binding you to us would mean you didn't need to take blood to remain connected."

"I'm a Gemini," I said softly. "We have to exchange blood regularly, even with our siblings, to maintain our reset. Otherwise, we end up with one like mine that was crafted from memory and not a true reflection of its current state."

"Then you'll take blood as often as you need it." He made it a decree befitting his station. "The other pack members can volunteer or not. It's your choice." A pleased rumble vibrated his chest. "I wouldn't mind being your only donor."

I laughed at his possessiveness. "I'm still not sure how I created my own warg aspect. She ought to be a direct reflection of yours or Aisha's or Dell's wolves, but she isn't. I've never taken blood from several people of the same species at all, let alone in such a short timeframe, until I returned to Villanow. Maybe that's the reason why she carries different attributes from each of you."

"So you'll have to continue taking from me and Dell if you want to maintain the aspect as she is." I nodded, and he grunted. "I can live with that."

"I'm glad you're so accommodating."

"Starting now." He offered me his hand. "I want you back in my head where you belong."

"Ah. Now that's more like it." Bossy to a fault. "For a minute there, I thought you'd lost your touch."

Considering my mate was equal parts bark and bite, I did as he asked. This time. My fingernail wobbled, and my spur emerged. I clasped hands with him and pierced his skin. The rich flavor of his blood hit the back of my throat, and the pack bond crackled up my arm and sizzled in my head the same as if I'd gripped a live wire. I jerked forward, coughing as the energy suffused my cells and urgent voices banged on the door of my mind. Graeson grasped me by the shoulders and held me steady until I got my breathing under control.

"Cam?" a hopeful voice prodded me. *"Is that really you? Are you back?"*

"Hey, Dell." I laughed out loud. *"I'm back. You didn't miss me, did you?"*

"Cord has been nuts without you. I mean certifiable. As beta, I made the executive decision to get you two back together before the dominance fights got more out of hand and he ended up battling it out for omega status just to take the edge off since he's fought everyone else."

"You're beta *now?"* I clasped my hands in front of me, earning an odd look from Graeson. *"That's great. I'm so*

proud of you. There isn't a better warg for the job." Then I slitted my eyes toward the alpha beside me and asked out loud, "Dominance fights?"

"Dell," he growled inside my head.

I was never going to get used to conference calling warg style.

"Gotta go," she squeaked in an un-beta-like fashion, and her presence faded.

"Wasn't this separation meant to prove you were a healthy and capable alpha?" I slid my legs over the side of the bed, no longer the least bit tired. "Yet it sounds to me as though you started picking fights as soon as I left. If you were going to beat them into submission," I joked, because he had been forced to harm his people before, "you should have come with me in the first place."

"I'm not saying Doc was wrong but—"

"He was wrong," I supplied helpfully.

"You're fae, and allowances should be made for that." He wrapped his hands around my calves. "You can't be expected to know or follow all of pack law, not where it conflicts with your morals and your instincts."

"Mmm-hmm." I didn't struggle when he used his grip to haul me closer to the edge of the bed. "That's very big of you, considering how I'm not the one who broke down and chased after you not even twenty-four hours later."

A faint slash of red burned in his cheeks, and I cupped his face between my hands to show how much his devotion meant to me.

"I missed you," he grumbled. "You leaving was like cutting off an arm. I had these phantom twinges, but the limb was no longer there. It drove me insane." He thumped his chest. "My wolf was foaming at the mouth. You know how much he loves you."

I raised my leg and traced the inseam of his jeans with my big toe. "Is he the only one?"

"You know I love you." A baffled expression settled over him. "I'd shrink you down and carry you around in my pocket if I knew a witch handy enough to pull off the spell."

"I do know." He had pursued me too hard for it to be otherwise. "I just like hearing you say it."

After the day I'd had, I needed that reaffirmation that someone out there loved me and would stand by me no matter what. Not to minimize the sacrifices my parents had made, but being loved that much from afar was almost as bad as not being loved at all. The heart couldn't tell the difference, that much was for sure.

He scooted his chair closer, until his knees hit the mattress, and tugged me onto his lap. Smug grin wreathing his face, he kicked back until I had to straddle him or fall on the floor.

"Graeson." I clutched his shoulders to keep my balance. "What are you doing?"

He craned his neck, wrapped his arms around my waist and caged me against him while his lips burned a hot trail up my throat, across my jawline to my ear. "I love you, Camille Ellis."

I melted against him, nuzzling my face against his neck, and whispered, "I love you too, Cord Graeson."

The words had barely left my lips before he gripped me around the rib cage and lifted me away from him, the better to see my face. "No, you don't get to hide that from me. Not the first time. I want to hear it again. I want to see you speak the words."

A flush heated my cheeks, and it took every ounce of gumption I had to meet his molten-gold eyes when I said, "I love you, Cord Graeson."

Scooping me against his chest, he stood and folded my legs around his waist while he spun us around the room. I laughed until tears leaked from the corners of my eyes, a release I sorely needed, and held on while he danced us through the tiny living room before returning to the bed.

"Hop down," he ordered, when I made no move to let go. "You need your rest."

"No." I tightened my legs around him as I linked my arms behind his neck. "What I need is you."

"Are you sure?" His eyes widened a fraction, and his throat bobbed. "You had a rough day, and I don't want you to regret this in the morning."

"The roughest days are still ahead." I ran my fingers through his hair. "I have a lot of regrets, but this—being with you—could never be one." I leaned in and dropped a slow kiss on his lips. "We've been mates in name only for too long." I shimmied my hips against him, and his answering growl vibrated my chest. "I'm ready to own my title."

His mouth crashed into mine, bruising in its intensity, and I whimpered. Lightheaded, I didn't register him setting me down on the mattress until my shoes thudded to the floor and cool air brushed the soles of my feet. His nimble fingers shimmied my pants down my thighs. He peeled off my T-shirt and flung it over his head, ringing one of the lamps fixed to the wall. All that stood between me and Graeson were my panties and bra...except...he hadn't undressed himself yet.

"Stop right there." I threw one hand up to postpone his advance. "Don't even think about climbing in with me while your clothes are on."

He glanced down at himself. "You've seen me naked a *lot*." He gestured toward me splayed on the bed. "You naked, now that's something special."

"I've seen you naked when you were shifting." I sat up and braced on my palms. "That doesn't count."

Furrows creased his brow as he flipped the button on his jeans and lowered his zipper. He tugged his shirt over his head and tossed it aside then stood there as if I had stumped him.

Fighting the urge to reach for him, I fisted the sheets. "You haven't gone shy on me, have you?"

A cocky grin broke across his mouth. "No." But its edges softened. "I've never been with someone who wasn't a warg." He ducked his chin. "It's nice that you want to see me, that you haven't…"

"Sneaked a peek?" I laughed so loud I clapped a hand over my mouth. "I never claimed that."

"That's not what I meant. You're not half as subtle as you think you are, and I don't mind it." His answering chuckle liquefied my girly bits. "I mean I like seeing you like this. That you haven't shared this part of yourself with the rest of the pack." He shrugged. "It's just for me."

As much as I hated to correct him… "Actually, thanks to the purification ceremony, the girls have already seen the free show." He made a dismissive gesture, and I got it. "Oh. That's not what you meant. You don't want the guys seeing me naked. That's a double standard, you know, and that's not okay. The women get to see you naked every day. Sometimes several times a day."

"I'm a warg." He hooked his thumbs in the band of his jeans. "It's my culture. You not sharing the sight of your beautiful body with anyone but me, that's your culture." He shoved his pants down and kicked out of them. "And I like that. It's another of those compromises we discussed earlier. I'm fully willing to embrace it and respect that about you."

My answering snort tapered to a whimper. I might have admired his backside to my heart's content, but I had done a decent job of avoiding eye contact with the free-range trouser-snake I had once wished a bad case of poison ivy on. Until now.

"Am I allowed on the bed now?" He angled his head. "Don't think I haven't noticed the wolf doesn't have to ask permission first." I patted the mattress, and he joined me. "Let me help you with that." My bra slid down my arms with a flick of his wrists. "There. That's better."

My stomach fluttered, but in that uncanny way of his, Graeson set to soothing me. His kisses were soft and gentle, even if they held a hint of teeth. Soon I was pliant in his arms, and totally naked if the panties twirling around his finger was any indication.

"You're good," I admitted as they went sailing.

"I've had a lifetime of practice getting naked." He nipped my collarbone as he settled between my thighs. "I'm happy to share my wealth of knowledge with you."

Laughter kept me in the moment, and when grief and hurt and worry tickled the back of my mind, when that little voice said I was being greedy, selfish, to want this, I banished those thoughts before they took root. Tonight was for me and Graeson. The rest could wait until morning.

"Been dreaming of this." Graeson lowered his head to my breast, and my toes curled at the sensation of his warm mouth on my flush skin. "You're beautiful. You know that?"

I threaded my fingers through his hair and tugged. We could play later. Right now, I craved him. His light filling the cracks in my heart, his gentle touches soothing my worries. I ached to belong to him, body and soul. Longed to take his scent until no one would doubt he was mine.

That last part might have been my wolf talking...

I angled his head back until his glazed eyes focused on me. "I want you."

Pressing lingering goodbye kisses on his two new friends, he traced my seam with his fingertip and growled at the moisture he found there. I was ready for him. I tilted my hips to tell him so. Fisting his length, he guided himself inside me, and we both groaned at the sensation.

His hips set a rhythm mine fought to match, and I raked my shifted nails down his back, marking him. The bite of pain had him arching into me, and I leaned up to press a kiss over his pounding heart. He covered me, his large body dwarfing mine, and reached between us. His expert fingers flicked over my sensitive nub, and pleasure exploded from my core. I drifted back to earth as he rasped my name, his lips caressing my ear as he came.

I clutched him to me, our heartbeats pounding and breaths sawing from our lungs. He didn't seem to mind. I should have learned from his wolf that Graeson was a cuddler.

A twinge of remorse had me seeking the muscular planes of his back with my palms, but his supernatural healing had wiped away all traces of the damage I had done. I liked to think he would have pink lines for a while longer at least. A smile tugged on my lips. I'd have to work harder next time.

"What's with that grin?" he panted, face buried in my neck.

I froze. "You can't see my face."

"I felt a bolt of smugness zap me through the bond." His lips curved against my skin. "I also caught something about marking me up better next time."

"I thought I was blocking better than that," I grumbled.

"Touching you breaks down the barrier." He chuckled. "And I was listening very hard."

I shoved his shoulder, rocking us both. "Clearly I need more practice." Graeson rolled his hips, and my eyes widened. "I didn't mean right now."

"Hmm?" He trailed stinging bites from my jawline to my collarbone. "Did you say something?"

My lips parted as his hand slid down my abdomen, and I gasped as his clever fingers found their mark. He flicked his thumb, his sharp teeth worrying my sensitive neck, and I went boneless. "I...um..."

And that was the last coherent thought he left me all night.

CHAPTER FIFTEEN

Graeson and I were enjoying breakfast at the Waffle Iron when Theo arrived. He slid into the booth beside me and stole a strip of bacon off my plate. Graeson, who sat across from us, narrowed his eyes but withheld the growl I sensed lurking in his thoughts.

"Good morning, tail-waggers." Theo crunched thoughtfully. "You're looking stronger this morning, coz."

Heat threatened my cheeks, but I kept my expression neutral. "And you're acting like the cat who caught the canary."

"This is my souvenir from last night." He opened his hand underneath the table, exposing a circular membrane in the center of his palm. "Watch this." His fingers twitched, and the flap of skin parted to reveal at least a dozen rows of serrated teeth. "I recorded it for Isaac." He concealed his new weapon before it could be noticed. "He'll want to experience it for himself."

My mouth dropped open, about to ask what that mean, hoping it didn't mean they shared women, but I crammed a strip of bacon in there instead. *Not my circus, not my twin monkeys.*

No wonder he hadn't stopped by my room again last night. He'd been too busy playing with his newly acquired talent.

"I spoke with Mom this morning." I took a sip of orange juice, fresh-squeezed, because yes, Graeson had asked before ordering. The man carried a grudge against concentrate you wouldn't believe. "She's going to meet us here in a half hour, and we're going to see what this pendant of hers can do."

"Do you want reinforcements?" Graeson brushed my mind.

"I would leave you behind if you let me. The fewer people involved, the less risk to those I love."

"I respect that you're trying to protect me, and as co-alpha, I veto that plan." He sipped his juice. *"We're in this together."*

I had figured as much. *"What about the pack?"*

"Dell will be fine on her own for a couple of days."

"And if she's not?" I raised my eyebrows. *"We have no idea where this journey will take us."*

"The thing I've realized about being alpha is..." he reached for my hand, *"...it's damn hard work."*

Our fingers interlaced, and his presence strengthened in me. *"Are you saying you'd let someone else take the reins?"*

"No." He sighed out loud. *"It's a nice dream to have, though."*

Meaning despite our differences, and the state of the pack, he was confident he could hold his rule with Dell as his second. That she had finally come into her own swelled my chest with happiness. She deserved the rank to match her heart.

Theo waved his disturbing mouth-hand in front of my face. "Are you two doing that thing where you talk to each other in your heads and exclude other people at the table who are sitting right in front of you from the conversation?"

Graeson and I answered him at the same time. "Yes."

"I thought so," he grumped.

The waitress came to take his order, and the next thirty minutes passed with only the scrape of utensils on plates and the clang of glassware to interrupt the silence hanging thicker than burned waffle smoke in the air.

Mom arrived right on time, and alone. I understood now why she drove solo, and for a fae used to traveling in large groups, it had to be an uncomfortable necessity for her. Her smile faltered when she noticed Graeson, whom I hadn't mentioned the day before.

"I hope you slept well." Theo's flat gaze settled on her. "Cammie didn't sleep much last night, if you know what I mean."

"Theo," I warned him.

"This is Cord Graeson," he said, voice thready with old anger. "He's a warg. That means you guys will soon have grandpups to abandon. Won't that be nice?"

"Theo, you're entitled to your anger. Ellis is too." Graeson stepped in front of Theo, cutting him off from Mom. "Now is not the time to be petty or spiteful. Save it for later. Right now our focus has to be on finding your mother and brother before Charybdis realizes we have Mrs. Ellis here to help."

Jaw flexing, Theo ducked his head. "You're right."

With my cousin cowed, Graeson faced Mom and extended his hand. "I'm Cord Graeson, Alpha of the Lorimar pack."

The opening he left me, to claim him or not, lasted less than a second.

"He's my mate." I tucked myself against his side. "He's going with us today in case we need another set of hands."

"Your mate?" Tears sheened her eyes. "That's wonderful. I'm so happy for you." She brought him in for a brief hug. "Both of you."

"I should have told you yesterday." I owed her that much of an apology.

"After everything we dumped in your lap?" She patted my cheek. "We're lucky you remembered your own name by the time we were through." A timid smile crooked her lips. "You look healthier today. I worried spending so much time with Lori would...but you're fine." She exhaled as though she had carried that worry around with her since we parted. "I'm relieved you recovered so quickly."

"The pep in my step is all thanks to him." I patted Graeson's chest, realized how that sounded and blushed ten shades of red. "I meant to say that the pack bond helped me recover. Having him near helped me regain my strength."

Mom's shoulders relaxed a fraction. Maybe she was thinking the same thing I was, that if the pack bond could sustain me, then visitation with Lori was a real possibility. One I wanted to pursue when this was all over.

Remembering my manners, I asked, "Have you eaten breakfast?"

"I ate at home." She flicked a ladybug off her shoulder. I hoped it meant good luck. "Your dad has cared for Lori by himself for up to three days, but that's stretching his limits. There are some things that just go easier with two people."

"I understand." Three days. We could work with that. "I don't think we have to worry too much."

"Why?" Grasping the implication, she pressed a palm flush with her chest. "He's here?"

"He popped into a gas station attendant when I first arrived." I glanced down the street where one pump remained visible at the far end. "He can't be far." I frowned. "Or he has a string of hosts in place, linking him to this town."

"How does he...?" She rolled her hand.

"Touch, we think." I ignored the vise clamping tighter around my heart, the one reminding me Graeson had touched Harlow, I had touched Bianca, and we had both touched Theo. Not to mention my hug from Dad yesterday, which circled around to Mom... For all I knew we were all infected, primed and waiting for Charybdis to spring yet another trap. "I don't know the distance requirements or how many hosts he can keep control of at once."

"We don't have a choice but to act, so I say it doesn't matter." She squared her shoulders. "I'm not walking away when I can help. I've done that too much in my life."

Graeson squeezed my hand, and I got the message. He supported Mom's stance, that she was as much in search of atonement as I had been all these years.

"Mom gets shotgun," I told the others. "Who wants to drive?"

"I will," Theo volunteered. "I want us to get there in one piece."

It occurred to me then that he hadn't let me drive, not once. I let it slide that he was calling my skills into question, because the last time he rode with me I had managed to cream a stop sign. I had been sixteen at the time, but Gemini memories stretched long.

"That leaves you and me in the back." Graeson pulled on my hand, and we started walking. *"I'll try to behave."*

I appreciated the distraction, but facts were facts. *"I don't believe that for a minute."*

His mental laughter warmed me all the way to the car.

Factor in all the wrong turns we made attempting to follow the pendant's needle via available roads, we still made excellent time. After discovering Harlow hidden in plain sight at Pilcher's Pond, I had few doubts Charybdis hadn't done the same with Isaac and Aunt Dot. He wanted them found. I believed that. Why else leave the clues and wait for me to connect the dots? He was leading me around by the nose, and the only advantage we had was Mom.

"Is this it?" Theo slid the car into park off the shoulder of the road and peered through the windshield at a dilapidated log cabin at the end of the driveway. "Can you tell if they're in there?"

Mom clutched her pendant, eyes closed, and nodded. "This close I can feel Dot without the amplifier."

The entire trip had taken about an hour and a half. I estimated the distance from town, as a crow flies, to be half that.

"What's the plan?" Graeson rumbled beside me.

"I don't have one," I admitted, leaning forward to get a better look. "I don't sense any glamour. What we're seeing is really what's there." I opened my door and stepped out, because why not? If he was waiting in the cabin, then he could see us from the window. Pulling on recalled magic, I completed a partial shift to make use of my wolf's senses. "There's no magic in play out here. I can feel a vibration coming from the house itself, but the property is clear. I think we can approach safely."

The others joined me on the rocky soil. Together we approached the house, searching for signs of life. I stepped onto the porch, elongating my nails as I went, and caught a shimmer out of the corner of my eye. Theo was assuming an aspect too, but I couldn't risk taking my eyes off the house long enough to parse out what form he had chosen. Mom clutched her pendant and gave off no magic. Living as she had, below the radar, she probably had none to recall.

My fingertips brushed the doorknob, and the metal shot a bolt of agony zinging through me before it opened. "He spelled it." I shook out my hand. "I can't tell if it was rigged to send him a warning or if it activated defenses already in place." Prickles coasted up my arms. "I should have considered the reason the property read as clean was because the magic was latent."

Genius that I was, I had activated it with a touch.

Graeson came to stand beside me, and the others joined us on the creaking planks. "Do you smell that?"

Now that he mentioned it, I couldn't stop my nose from itching. "Fresh. Damp. Earthy."

We puzzled over it for a second, but Theo's curse brought our attention zooming to the far edge of the property. The earth shook, and the house groaned behind us. A smattering of rocks that might have once been part of the landscaping rolled free of their sunken depressions and clashed in deafening cracks. The mound rose taller and taller until a form began taking shape.

"Oh shit," Theo said eloquently.

Graeson rubbed his jaw. "Couldn't have said it better myself."

"A megalith," Mom gasped. "I haven't seen one of those in decades." She darted a frantic glance around the area. "They live in family groups. There could be three or even a dozen more, depending on the size of the mound. Entire sections of the Smokies are made of them."

They must have lived undisturbed for a long while to be buried so deep in the soil, to be so lichen-spotted and weathered by years of exposure. I had no idea how rock creatures reproduced, but they would have had plenty of time, space and resources for it here on this forgotten tract of land.

"How do we fight that?" Theo's hands began glowing red, the skin blackening and splitting to reveal a lava flow for veins. "Are they being controlled?"

"I doubt it very much." Mom wrung her hands. "They're simple creatures, peaceful for the most part. They defend their lands and young aggressively."

"Of course they do." I touched Graeson's arm. "Distract them for me?"

"There could be worse inside." His scowl deepened. "I don't like the idea of you going in alone."

"I'll go with her." Mom paled, but her chin lifted. "I haven't used a donor in years. The conflicting energies caused Lori distress, and we had to sell the RV to buy a proper house for her, so we quit cold turkey." Meaning she could no longer rely on the wards to siphon her borrowed magic. "I have no magic to recall. I'm no use to you out here."

Without her magic, she was little better than a human. At least if she stuck with me, I could keep tabs on her.

Theo's lip curled. "Now might be the time to revisit that policy."

Easing between them, I faced my cousin. "Let's keep juicing her up as a last alternative, okay?"

With reluctance, Mom agreed to take blood if we needed the backup.

"Get moving, Ellis." Graeson rotated his torso, limbering up for the fight to come. "We can keep them distracted for a few minutes, but the quicker you get out the better."

"Be careful." I rose on my tiptoes and kissed him. "You too, Theo."

"Aww." Theo mimed wiping a tear. "You do care."

I rolled my eyes and took Mom by the hand. "You heard the man. Let's go."

Light poured in through the broken windows, making it easy to see inside the cabin once we jiggled the swollen door open. The floor had bowed, but the walls and roof appeared sturdy enough. This place had been crafted to endure. We made a quick circuit of the space, which was one open room, but I sensed no magic and uncovered no clues.

"The pendant indicates she should be right here." Mom knelt and began fingering each dusty plank, prying at the boards with her nails. "I don't understand." She sat back on her ankles when she found nothing loose. "It's never been wrong."

Casting my gaze around the room, I was debating shifting my fingers to claws and drawing on my warg aspect's strength to rip out the floor when the whole house trembled. I ran to the window, desperate to spot the guys, but they waited where we had left them. Three more giant rock men stood in the clearing, their bodies forming pebble by pebble, which meant they weren't to blame for the earthquake.

My gut sank into my toes. There must be more of them. "They're under the house." I hauled Mom to her feet, primed to run if the floor buckled. "Oh crap." Lightning·

quick, it hit me. "Aunt Dot and Isaac are under there too. That's what the pendant was trying to tell us."

Her eyes rounded, and her fingers shook in mine. "Can we get them out?"

"Now would be a great time for rocks to learn how to bleed." Stone skin would really come in handy right about now. Too bad monoliths couldn't be donors. "Keep an eye on the guys through that window, but stay out of sight. I don't want the monoliths focused on us. Not yet."

Potent magic rippled over my body, aided by Graeson's blood, and the now-familiar popping noises of my warg aspect rising filled the quiet room. Sensory information flooded me. Musty boards, damp from the rain. The hum of termites in the walls. The graveled rumble of waking giants under our feet. That last part was the worst.

I dropped to my knees, made a fist and punched a hole in the rotting boards. Through the gap, I saw the earth churning, pebbles rolling this way and that. A stone eye paused to blink at me as it tumbled past, then continued on its way. Sweat dampened my shirt as I stuck my head under the house to search for hints as to where my aunt and cousin might be. "I don't see any sign of them." A six-inch ridge of concrete near the outer edge of the foundation caught my eye. "There's a cellar. Come on."

We shoved through the back door and circled around the rear of the house, trying to keep hidden from the monoliths focused on Graeson and Theo out front. The cellar doors were bolted with silver chains fresh from a hardware store. The lock gleamed. It was new too. What had appeared to be concrete from a distance was aging plaster. The doors of the cellar were two flaps of corrugated metal similar to what had been used on the roof.

"Stand back." I flung out my arm, and Mom retreated a few steps. "Here goes nothing."

I didn't waste time on the chains. I couldn't break them, even with warg strength. They were too thick. I leapt onto the doors, which groaned in protest. A heartbeat later, they failed under my weight, and I went crashing to the bottom of the cellar. I landed on my hands and knees, and the metal sliced open my palms as rust flakes rained down around me.

Thank the gods the underground storage area was as large as the house. I had taken a calculated risk that might have meant me plummeting to my death—or Aunt Dot or Isaac's. Considering imminent death was upon us thanks to the pissed-off monoliths, I figured the worst that could happen is the three of us crossed that finish line a little quicker.

"Cammie?" Mom called. "Are you all right?"

"I'm fine." Mostly. Nothing that a drop of Graeson's blood wouldn't heal in the next few minutes. "I see a partition in the rear. Give me a minute."

My tumble had attracted the attention of several mid-sized stones, which burrowed into the dirt and set off another earthshaking event. I got the distinct feeling they were tattling on me. Careful not to step on one of them, I picked my way to the plaster wall that sealed off a good six feet of space. I felt my way around it but found no door or hatch. Another spasm rocked me, and the fragile plaster split. The sour odor seeping from the cracks had me turning my head and coughing against my shoulder.

"Aunt Dot?" I pounded on the wall. "Isaac?"

No answer.

I sank my furred fingers into the cracks and pried chunks of wall free. Soon it became clear that where the seam had ruptured was fresh plaster. It crumbled into my hands while the walls to either side remained unmoved. The smell overwhelmed me, and my gut twisted while the worst-case scenarios ran rampant.

"Hey," a scratchy voice whispered.

"Isaac?" I tore into the wall with renewed vigor. "Hold on. I've almost got an opening large enough for you to fit through." My shoulders ached and nails bled with the effort. "Is Aunt Dot with you?" The darkness of their tiny room was absolute. "Is she okay?"

"Harlow did something to her," Isaac rasped. "Mom hasn't moved or spoken since she put us down here."

A twinge rippled through my chest at the sound of Harlow's name. She was a good kid, and Charybdis was ruining her.

"Don't worry. It will be okay. I brought the cavalry. Mom, Theo and Graeson are here." I sat back when the path was cleared. "Can you walk? Or do you need assistance?"

"I think I can manage." He scooted closer to the hole and stuck his head out, breathing deep of the fresh air. "I can't leave Mom."

Worrying my lip between my teeth, I settled on the only course of action that made sense. "I can't carry her alone, and you're too weak to help." I turned toward the light and the shadow Mom cast. "I'm going to have to get Graeson."

Another tremor shook the earth, and he scowled at a bouncing rock. "What's going on up there?"

"This whole property is a monolith den. It's one giant landmine, and I stomped on the trigger." I pushed to my feet. "I get the impression they haven't been woken in a long time. It's taking a while for them to get mobile." Thunder crashed overhead, and my stomach tightened. "We don't have long before they come looking for us. They'll crush the house and bury the cellar if that's what it takes to protect their home."

He winced and adjusted himself. "You better hurry."

Hurry I did. Back at the opening, a coil of rope bopped me on the head before I got a chance to call out to Mom. She peered over the edge, spotted me rubbing my scalp and called, "Sorry, baby. I didn't realize you were back yet."

"No problem." If we survived this, I could always pop some ibuprofen later. "Is it anchored?"

"Yes." She gripped a knot and held tight. "I'll keep it steady for you."

Jogging was about the only exercise I got, so my upper body strength was slim. I had to call on my warg aspect to climb out of there, and Mom gasped and stumbled back, falling on her butt in the dirt when she processed the extent of my transformation.

"H-how is this possible?" She stood and approached me with caution. "Wargs are born, not made."

I worked my jaw to shake off the transformation before answering. "Isaac thinks my reset is resetting."

"Remarkable." Her lips parted. "You truly are a special girl, Cammie."

No, I wasn't, but parents weren't great at seeing the reality of their kids, only the mirage of childhood sweetness they cast over them to soften the sharp edges forged in adulthood.

"Hold your ground, and keep an eye out for movement. I have to get Graeson." The sounds of battle carried from the front yard, and I winced. "Aunt Dot is bespelled, and Isaac is weak. I have to get help."

"They're down there?" She dropped to her knees at the edge. "I thought when you came back alone…"

"I found them." I patted her shoulder. "They're safe." *For now*, I added silently.

"I'll keep watch." She drew a pocketknife and flicked the gleaming blade open. "You go get your mate."

Respect for Mom buoyed my spirit, and I jogged to the corner of the house. Wary of alerting the lumbering monoliths to our location, although the ones under the house must already sense intruders, I flattened my spine against the building and reached for Graeson's mind, praying the distraction didn't cost him.

"I need to borrow your muscles." I peered around the corner to pinpoint his location but came up empty. *"Aunt Dot is unconscious, and Isaac is in a bad way. I'm not strong enough to help. I'm going to have to tag you out."*

"No, you're not." His mental snort had me gritting my teeth. *"I have another option."*

"What—?" Howls cut short my question. *"The pack is here?"*

"Haden and Moore are here." Smugness radiated through the bond. *"I figured better safe than sorry."* A slight hesitation had me worried, but he added, *"Is this one of those things I should have told you ahead of time?"*

Shaking my head where he couldn't see it, I had to accept this was classic Cord Graeson, and I couldn't fault him for it. Not when it might be the very thing that saved my family. *"You're the strategist in this relationship. I trust you to make the right call for our people."*

"In that case, stay where you are."

I smothered a snort. *"I never saw that coming."*

"I'll bow out when they arrive. Four legs are faster than two. They can keep up the distraction while we get your aunt and cousin to safety."

"Come around back. There's a cellar. That's where we'll be."

"See you soon."

"The sooner, the better." Shoving off the logs, I returned to Mom and filled her in on the situation. "Now we wait."

"Now we work. See that?" She gestured toward a small stone building up the incline. "It's an old pump house. That's where I found the rope. There's another coil and a few tools if we need them."

"Good thinking." I touched her shoulder. "I'll grab what we need and be right back."

While she resumed the sentry position, I clambered up the slope. The door swung open under my hand, and I popped my head inside. The rope coiled on a railroad spike driven into the wall. I slid my arm into the opening and hiked it up onto my shoulder. Most of the tools were rusted from lying on the ground, which was damp earth. No floor in here. I tested a few, and they snapped under pressure, the metal or wood or both too rotted to be useful. Backing out the door, I was struck by how solid and heavy it was. Despite the years of exposure, it hadn't warped, and the bottom hadn't decayed. I latched it closed and returned to Mom, who had fashioned a loop and was tying a mariner's knot where it joined the rope I had used earlier.

She lifted her work for my inspection. "If Isaac is as weak as you think, we can have him step in this and hold on while we haul him out of there."

Small as the knot was, I had doubts. "Will the knot hold?"

"I grew up on the road in the days before the whole clan could afford RVs." She scoffed. "I can tie knots for tents, laundry lines, horse halters and boats all day long, little girl."

Fair enough. "What about Aunt Dot?"

A calculating gleam lit her eyes. "Did you notice the pump house door?"

"I did." Seeing where this was going, I cut her off at the pass. "It's solid, almost petrified. I bet it weighs a ton."

"Your mate is a warg," she said, as if that explained all the mysteries of the universe.

"That doesn't make him indestructible." A flash of his chest, soaked in blood, the knife protruding, stole my breath. "I'll see if I can find a substitute."

A quick scan of the area netted no suitable alternative for what Mom had in mind. There was only one reason she could want the door—so we could use it as a litter. I returned to the pump house and studied the hinges.

"What are you doing?" Graeson panted near my ear.

I soaked him in with thirsty eyes, but he was fine. Not a scratch on him. "I need this door."

"Okay." He ushered me aside and ripped it off the hinges. "Now what?"

I stared at him, dumbstruck. "Should you be doing that in your condition?"

"I told you, I was at ninety-five percent. One hundred percent after last night." He leaned forward and kissed the tip of my nose. "I won't break."

Instead of saying what beat in my heart, that where Charybdis and his schemes were concerned, we were all breakable, I jerked my chin. "Let's get this down to the cellar."

Mom was staring off in the distance, the snarls and growls of the wolves ringing out as the second wave tagged in for their turn. She startled when I touched her arm, and I wondered if the wolves frightened her. How could they? Compared to the monoliths, the wargs were like...fluffy puppies.

"I'll go down and show you what we're up against." I grasped the rope and climbed to the bottom, then scurried out of the way. Graeson landed in a crouch beside me seconds later. "Show-off."

He grunted and followed me to the half-demolished plaster wall. Isaac had climbed out and now sat on the churning earth, sweat beading his forehead. I searched the opening and spotted a nest of gray curls. Isaac must have spent his time dragging Aunt Dot nearer the fresh oxygen too. Gods knew that miserable hole where they had been reeked from their confinement.

As keen as his senses were, Graeson didn't so much as wrinkle his nose. With a straight face, he hauled Isaac to his feet and slung an arm around his waist. "We'll get you out first and then come back for your mom."

Isaac put up a fight but was too weak to do more than annoy Graeson enough to swing him up into a fireman's carry and walk him to the rope. He trussed Isaac up like a Thanksgiving turkey, then climbed the rope to help Mom haul him out of the cellar.

While they labored with Isaac, I examined Aunt Dot. I touched her skin and found it cool, her expression peaceful. Her utter stillness funneled my thoughts toward how Lori had appeared frozen in time too. I snapped out of it as an idea occurred to me.

A dull thump told me Graeson had landed back in the cellar. "I've got an idea." I waited for him to join me. "Help me get her out in the open."

He climbed inside the small room and lifted her in his arms. I hadn't meant for him to carry her alone, but I stood back and let the man work. He settled her on the ground, head cocked as he listened to the crash and boom of rock colliding so near the house the floorboards groaned overhead.

"I want to check her pockets." I tore the hem of my T-shirt and ripped off a handkerchief-sized hunk of fabric. If my suspicions were correct, the last thing I needed to do was go in barehanded. "Here goes nothing."

I patted her down the way I would a suspect and was about to turn her onto her side when I found a zipper running down the seam of the sporty capris she wore. I pressed my hand to the outside and located a hard bump the size of my thumbnail. After pulling down the zipper, I reached into the compartment, careful to keep my fingers covered, and pulled out a shining pink stone. Quartz most likely, and definitely bespelled. Its magic seeped through the fabric, and my lids fluttered.

Shock radiated up my arm, and my eyes flipped wide open.

Graeson had knocked the gemstone from my hand.

"Ellis." He shook my shoulder. "Snap out of it."

I opened my mouth to respond as the house groaned overhead. Planks buckled and snapped, spearing the cellar floor with their ragged points. Rocks pelted the dirt floor as a stone calf thicker than my waist crashed through the debris. A slice of sky opened up above us, illuminating the furious rock man who was systematically tearing out the walls of the house over our heads. A roar that sounded like smashing boulders rang in our ears.

The monoliths were done playing tag with the wargs. They were hunting us.

"Cam?" a weak voice snagged my attention.

"Hold on." Graeson gathered a woozy Aunt Dot to him and cut me a look. *"Move."*

The stone glinted in the far corner, close enough I could slide over and grab it. Magic that potent might come in handy, especially since my parents had finite resources and we had limited time. We might not be able to wait on the dryad to enchant more stones before we implemented the next phase of our plan. Not after this.

"Pick up your feet, woman." Graeson stepped in front of me. "Or I will shift, and I will bite you."

Curling my lip, I shoved to a standing position. He was right. I was acting foolish, desperate, and desperate people made mistakes that cost them their lives.

I sprinted toward the cellar opening and untangled the rope, thankful we wouldn't need the door after all. Together we bundled up Aunt Dot. Again Graeson climbed up to help Mom pull her to level ground. As I waited for my turn, shifting from foot to foot, my gaze kept sliding back to where the gem rested covered in dirt.

The monolith waded through the rotten flooring like the ancient oak planks were pudding and stomped a clear path right toward me as its wrecking spree continued. Certain it hadn't seen me yet, that it was just demolishing its way around the house, I tensed to make a run for it.

That gem dropped into Harlow's pocket could knock her out long enough for me to get her to safety. It was a guarantee I couldn't resist. Muscles tensed, I sprang forward as a frantic whine brought my head up. There was no voice, but a barrage of images slammed into me.

Theo rammed his fist into the gut of a monolith. Its stone navel wept magma, its furious bellow a battle cry as it swung a massive forearm toward Theo, knocking him off his feet and sending him flying.

I didn't wait for the rope. I shifted my hands and dug my nails into cracks in the plaster, hauling myself higher until Graeson cursed and lifted me out the rest of the way. "Theo—"

He set his jaw. "I'm on it."

"We have to get them to the car." Assuming it hadn't been crushed yet. I turned to Isaac. "Can you walk?"

Isaac wobbled to his feet with a sharp nod. Aunt Dot made it to her knees before collapsing. Calling on every drop of magic left in me, I assumed my warg aspect. "Geth her on mah back," I lisped through fangs. Her weight settled against me, and I set off at a clip toward the rental. Mom kept pace with Isaac, and I watched them from the corner of my eye.

Thank the gods, the car was untouched except for the cracked rear windshield. A lumpy rock the size of my fist twitched near the trunk. I stepped over it and sidled up to the passenger door, where I raked deep furrows in the paint with my claws while attempting to open it. "Cheth for keths."

"The fob is in the cup holder," Mom confirmed, sliding behind the wheel and cranking the engine. "Sounds like everything is as it should be."

With Isaac's help, I managed to get Aunt Dot off my back. I sandwiched her between the car and my hips so she wouldn't face plant and then twisted around to get her settled in the backseat. Magic poured off me, as slick as sweat, and my aspect faded.

"Hold her upright," I ordered, shoving Isaac in beside his mother. "I'm going back for Graeson." And Theo.

"No need." Graeson arrived with Theo in his arms. He placed him gently on the backseat, ignoring Isaac's frantic questions. Chaining my wrist with his hand, he yanked me aside as two muddy wargs, foaming at the mouth from exertion, leapt into the backseat, sprawling across laps as best they could. "Moore broke a leg and Haden has a crushed rib," he explained before I could ask why they didn't run for the safety of the trees instead. He slammed the door behind them, dragged me to the front passenger seat, sat and folded me onto his lap then forced the door shut. "We're clear."

A frustrated roar echoed by several granite throats told us the monoliths had spotted us.

Tires spun and dirt sprayed the air behind us as Mom stomped on the accelerator, twisting the wheel until the car whirled and we faced back the way we had come. I clutched the handle mounted to the ceiling and planted both feet against the windshield. Graeson wrapped his arms around my waist, buried his face in my neck, and we both held on for dear life.

CHAPTER SIXTEEN

Hospitals were out of the question for the injured, so we returned to our hotel. The wolves trotted off as soon as the car doors opened. I trusted they knew their way back to the RV park. Abram could take it from there. Mom did recon, making sure the path was clear before Graeson hauled a blood-soaked Theo inside and up the elevators before returning to help me with the others. Isaac limped alongside me, but Graeson carried Aunt Dot since her eyes kept crossing.

Back in my room, I ran a bath for Isaac and let him relax while Mom and Graeson situated Theo on my bed. She put in a call to a local doctor, a dwarf, who made house calls. While we waited, we fished Isaac out and put him to bed in Theo's room wearing his brother's clothes. Aunt Dot we cleaned up, changed into a hotel-issued robe and tucked in beside Isaac. Graeson, being the thoughtful man he was, had ordered room service while we were elbows-deep in suds, but no one was in the mood to eat while Theo's fate remained uncertain.

I was visiting with Aunt Dot and Isaac when firm raps next door sent me jogging out of the room. "Dr. Wayne?" The stocky man whose head came up to my shoulder nodded, and I stuck out my arm. "I'm relieved you could come on such short notice."

"Short notice is my specialty." He grasped my hand, and clean, bright magic tickled my palm. Not a trace of darkness blighted him. He indicated the door behind me. "Is the patient in there?"

"No." I used my room card to grant us access. "My cousin is this way."

I led him to Theo's bedside then went to stand with Graeson. Mom kept her spot on the mattress with his hand on her lap, standing in for Aunt Dot even though Theo had been combative and snarky to her from the start.

A quick examination left the dwarf sporting a quizzical brow. "How did you say this happened?"

"We didn't," Graeson rumbled.

The doctor pinned on a frown and twisted to face us. "I have a reputation to maintain, and I won't be a party to anything unseemly."

"I'm an agent with the Earthen Conclave." I reached for my badge on instinct before remembering I no longer carried it. "I don't have ID on me right now." I mentally prepped a lie. "I'm working undercover on an ongoing case and can't afford to have any ties to my organization on my person. You can call Magistrate Vause, and she will vouch for me."

He panned his gaze toward Mom. "Is what she says true?"

"Yes." Mom offered him a watery laugh. "You don't see the resemblance?"

"Well, I'll be a toadstool's cushion." The dwarf studied me again, and his lips parted. "You're Camille." He shook his head as if to clear it. "I was too caught up in what happened to this young man to process it." He stood and approached me. "I've treated your sister off and on for several years. Your parents are good people." He brought me in for a hug I didn't expect, and I went stiff. Touch was a necessity I was growing used to among friends and with the pack, but stranger etiquette eluded me. I suppose he felt like he knew me after treating Lori for so long. "Thank you for your service," he added. "Your job can't be an easy one."

"It's no harder than yours." I offered him a polite smile, which he returned. "So what can you tell us about my cousin?"

"He's suffered five broken ribs, one of which punctured a lung, and there's damage to his spine. One of his shoulders was crushed, and that will be a long time mending."

I swallowed the sour taste in my throat. Theo had been at the cabin because of me. Sure he had wanted to help his mom and brother, but wasn't their involvement my fault too? How would I tell Aunt Dot...? What would I tell her?

"Sit down before you pass out." He shoved me into a chair and pushed my head between my legs. "I'm very good at what I do. Your cousin has been stabilized. The magic I've pushed into him has already begun mending the damage. He will survive. He will be in a great amount of pain, but he will live."

The room stopped whirling long enough for me to sit upright again. "Thank you." Magic zinged over my lips, sealing my vow. "My cousins are like brothers to me."

A pleased expression wreathed his face as my debt registered. "I understand there are more patients who need to be seen?"

"I'll walk you over." I guided him back to Theo's room. "This is Dot Cahill, my aunt, and Isaac Cahill, my cousin, Theo's brother."

I stood back and gave the doctor room to work. Now that Aunt Dot and Isaac were cleaned up and resting, I began searching them for signs of Charybdis's tampering. As relieved as I was to have my family back, mostly in one piece, I had to keep myself honest. They were ticking time bombs that could explode in our faces at the drop of a hat. We had no way of knowing what Charybdis had done to them, but I had no doubt he had infected them in case I managed to recover them.

This morning's rescue operation left only one victim in his grasp. Harlow. All this time, and I still hadn't managed to free her. That was about to change. By removing his leverage, I had wrecked his plans a second time. Ruining his circle and putting down his kelpie had painted a target on my back, and foiling his plans meant I might as well have neon tubing for veins. The bull's-eye between my shoulders was about to glow fluorescent.

"No permanent harm was done to them." The doctor's voice snapped me to attention. "They're both dehydrated, and they should stay in bed for the next few days. I recommend a diet of soup or broth, and plenty of fluids."

"Isaac?" Dell bulldozed into my thoughts.

"Your timing is impeccable." I had expected her to pounce me much sooner. Graeson might be to thank for her perceived restraint. *"The doctor is leaving now. He says Isaac is fine. He just needs time to regain his strength."*

"I could come by and—" She stopped herself. *"No. I can't. I have to tend the pack while Graeson is away."*

"Do you want me to pass on a message?" I could do that much.

"No." Zero hesitation. *"I— It's probably best if I wait until I can see him in person."*

So whatever she had to say, she didn't want me to overhear. I could respect that. *"Okay. I have to see the doctor out now. I'll check back in with you later."*

"Be careful out there, Cam. Take care of Cord too."

"Always," I promised.

The doctor skirted me, easing into the bathroom to wash his hands, and I joined him. One eyebrow rose, but he didn't startle. "Is there something else?"

"I need another moment of your time." Using the vaguest terms possible, I framed a scenario not too far off from the truth, giving him a rundown of our situation without expanding on the fine details. "The danger should pass in the next forty-eight hours." That was my most fervent wish. "Until then, Aunt Dot and Isaac are a danger to themselves and to others. Can you help me?"

"This is highly unorthodox." He rubbed a hand over his head. "I can bring them to my clinic and sedate them. As depleted as they are, it might be the best thing for them, but forty-eight hours is my limit." He pushed out a sigh. "I suppose I'll stay on-site. I can't risk contaminating my family or other patients."

"We're happy to compensate you for lost time." It might drain my savings, but keeping my family safe was the best use of those funds. "We have no reason to believe Theo has been contaminated, but I would rather you keep an eye on him as well. Graeson and I won't be around to monitor him, not if we want to end this."

"I assume your mother will return home?"

"I haven't asked her, but yes. That's what I expect she will want."

Negotiations over, we shook on the deal.

The doorknob dug into my hip as I kept him corralled. "There is one more thing you might do for me."

"Let's hear it." Acceptance smoothed his features. "I get the feeling you won't let me go until I agree."

The doctor wasn't wrong.

Graeson and I stood on the curb, watching the private ambulances pull away with Theo, Isaac and Aunt Dot tucked onto their stretchers. A sense of calm descended over me, and I exhaled a deep sigh of relief.

"Are you going home?" Graeson studied the red taillights. "Do you need a ride?"

"I am, and no." Mom angled herself toward us. "I have my truck. I can manage." She clasped her hands. "Cammie..."

"It's okay, Mom." I crossed over and gathered her in my arms. "I forgive you and Dad. I know you did what was best for me." How could I deny what I had experienced myself? "That's not to say I don't have some issues to work through, but I want us to have a relationship. Even if it's just letters or phone calls, I want that."

Tears wet my throat and soaked into the neck of my shirt as she sniffled. "I'd love that, honey. Your father would too." She drew back and wiped her cheeks. "We'll figure something out so you girls can visit too."

For the first time since learning my sister was alive, I had hope. The pack bond was strong, maybe enough to allow me to visit Lori a couple times a year. It wasn't much, but it was ten thousand times more than what we'd had only days ago.

"That would be great." I stood there, not sure what else to say. "Text me when you get home." She had my number now. "I want to make sure you got there safely."

Keys in hand, she crossed the lot and headed toward her truck. I shifted my weight from foot to foot, waiting on her to get in and crank the engine. We watched her pull out and head in a different direction than the one I had anticipated. Mom was smart, a survivor. Like me. I bet she was covering her tracks by taking a winding route home.

"Something tells me I won't much like the next phase of your plan." Graeson draped his arm across my shoulders. "Lay it on me."

A notification chime interrupted me. "That can't be Mom already." Unless she was reaching out for help. I whipped out my phone, and my shoulders sagged. Crisis averted. "It's Thierry."

His fingers toyed with my collarbone. "I thought you said she was out of the office."

"I guess this means she's back." I thumbed the icon and opened the message. "She wants to meet." I tilted my head back. "Here. Tonight."

He took the opportunity to caress the length of my throat. "All this over a prophecy?"

"Maybe she knows something we don't?" These days, the more I thought I knew, about anything, the more wrong I was. "We have a few hours until then." I scanned the empty street. "It's time to push."

"Are you sure about this?" He followed my line of sight to the gas station. "The clerk, if he's there, is a host."

In my mind, I was starting to classify hosts as people Charybdis popped in and out of while avatars were vehicles he drove for long periods of time. What qualified a victim for one role over another? I had no clue. I couldn't say he stuck to fae, because we were stronger or had magic, because Harlow had become his favorite new ride. Her humanity should have made her weak and unappealing to him, but of course where she was concerned, his fascination was only for me.

"I have to poke the hornet's nest. Otherwise we give Charybdis too much power. He took a loss today. We need to nudge him into a rash action while his temper is up."

We strolled down the street, Graeson's arm hooking me against him, until we passed the general store. An old wrought-iron bench crowded the curb, and he angled that way.

"Be careful." He pulled me in closer, kissed my temple with warm lips. "I told myself I wouldn't ask, but are you sure you don't want me to go in there with you?"

I shoved him down until he sat, and tapped his knee so he kept his seat. "He's more likely to put in an appearance if I'm alone."

He cuffed my wrist with his wide palm. "I'm going on the record to say I don't like this."

"Duly noted." I bent down and pressed my lips right over his scowl. "We have an advantage. We can't afford to lose it now."

Releasing my hand, he assumed a casual pose. "Ten minutes, and then I'm going to have an irresistible urge for chewing gum."

My shocked expression wasn't feigned. "That's five more than I expected."

"I'm trying," he grated. "For you."

Before I caved to the wish I could sit beside him, cuddle against his warmth and forget the rest of the world, I had work to do. With or without the badge, I had a killer in my sights, and I wasn't going to let him play games with my life or anyone else's.

A tendril of disappointment unfurled in me. I wanted the conclave to be more proactive than it was, to be better than it is, to not turn a blind eye when it suited them, but fae were fickle creatures. No wonder most Gemini avoided the law altogether.

I kept my stride casual as I pushed inside the store. A clerk greeted me, and my mood plummeted. This wasn't the right guy. The odds had been slim, but I had to try. If I had my badge, I could have flashed it and requested the schedule for the week. But I didn't, which meant the only guaranteed method of locating the guy was staking out the gas station.

Scowl deepening, I snagged a couple of jerkies and two bottles of water then paid and left.

"Does this mean it didn't go well?" Graeson kept his easy pose, waiting on me to join him. "What did you find out?"

"Nothing." I passed him a bottle of water and a jerky, and the latter tore a snort out of him. "The clerk wasn't there." I ripped open my package and took a big bite. "It was stupid to think he would be waiting for me."

"No, it's not." Graeson tugged a small plastic bottle out of his jeans pocket and handed it to me. "He's been one step ahead of us this entire time. You were right to think he would monitor this point of contact after he figured out we wrecked his cabin this morning."

"Do you always carry these on you?" The bottle of flavor enhancer was my favorite brand and my current favorite flavor. "I should shake you down sometime and see what else falls out of your pockets."

An amused bend shaped his lips. "It's my duty to see to my mate's needs."

A fission of warmth sizzled through me. "You're better at this mate gig than I am."

"You give me so much more than you realize." He tapped my flavor enhancer. "What you do for me can't be bottled, bought or sold."

"You've got a way with words, I'll give you that." I let him pull me against him. "You're very smooth."

"You sand my rough edges," he murmured against my hair. "Look at my wolf. He's ruined. Defanged."

"His fangs work just fine." I had the scars to prove it. Under my cheek, Graeson tensed until I patted his chest. "It's okay that your wolf is a bit of a caveman." Instead of clubbing me on the head and dragging me to his cave, he had been content to tear into my calf to stop me from running and then follow me home to my den. "We're friends now."

His grumbled response reminded me how gutted he had been to realize he was capable of hurting me. Graeson had been out of his mind with grief at the time, and his wolf had taken over their body, shifting him and taking control of their actions. What made sense to the wolf didn't please the man, but maybe the wolf was on to something. After all, I had fallen for his playfulness and fluffy belly that loved rubs before I realized that my heart already belonged to the bossy, grumpy, sometimes domineering man within him.

"How do you want to play this?" He let me doctor his drink and appeared pleasantly surprised with the end result. "If we're doing surveillance, shouldn't we move to a less-conspicuous spot?"

"Let him see us." I was bone-tired and heart sore, and the pack was splintered. They deserved a home, a place to put down new roots where they would be safe. "I want this finished."

So we sat there, holding on to one another, each of us lost in our thoughts. Besides the jerky, I hadn't eaten since breakfast, and all the shifting had depleted me. My eyelids grew heavier as the minutes ticked past, until I had to stand and stretch the kinks out of my back just to stay awake, though standing convinced me I might fall asleep on my feet.

A chime rang out, and I fumbled my phone in my haste to check the message. "Mom is home." That was one less worry. "The dryad touched base with them. She's participating in a grace ceremony, a vigil where they use the stones to put a dryad in an ailing tree to sleep. It will be three or four days before she can deliver the gems." I worried my bottom lip with my teeth, but Graeson kept his calm. "There goes that idea."

Contagious as a yawn, Graeson sat upright and stretched his upper body as if unable to resist after watching me. "How much longer until we meet Thierry?"

"We have about an hour." I plopped down beside him. "Do you think we spooked him?"

"You know him better than anyone." His lips pursed, a sour pucker at tasting that truth. "Do you think he'll run again?"

"No." I jiggled my knee, in desperate need of a restroom after downing my water an hour earlier. "We interrupted his timeline by killing the kelpie. My involvement might have made this personal, but I can't shake the feeling he's the one running out of time. He's not as careful, not as composed." The more I considered his actions, the more sense my theory made. "He's desperate to salvage this— whatever this is. I tie into his plans. He's made that much clear. Maybe I'm a nexus point since I was involved in the case?"

"Revenge is a simpler motive." His expression tightened. "He's put a lot of effort into hurting you."

Feeding off my pain and misery as he lashed out at my loved ones. "Do you believe in divination as prophesy?"

"The future is too malleable," he decided. "I don't believe anything is set in stone. But the Garzas are experts at choosing the most likely path and following it to a logical conclusion."

"Does that mean you think Faerie is about to throw open its doors and release the Wild Hunt?"

Expression thoughtful, he rolled his shoulder. "Stranger things have happened."

"You can say that again." I settled in against him to finish our shift. "I get the feeling stranger days are ahead."

How did you end a fae who could be anyone, anywhere and at any time? A possibility had occurred to me, a solution that required minimum sacrifice to protect all those I loved, and Graeson wasn't going to like it one bit. If he caught wind of my plan, he would lock me in the hotel until I was gray-haired and wheelchair-bound, and my family would help.

Forty-eight hours until the doctor released Aunt Dot, Isaac and Theo from his care. Forty-eight hours to bring down this monster once and for all. Breathing in Graeson's pine-and-musk scent, I curled tighter against him. Forty-eight hours to love him with all I had, in case my plan cost more than I could afford to pay.

CHAPTER SEVENTEEN

The gas station clerk was a no-show, and we ran out of time to wait him out. Thierry had sent another email, this one indicating she was minutes from town. With no choice but to resume our very public stakeout later, we returned to our hotel room and listened for a knock at the door.

A peculiar sense of anticipation swept over me when it came, and I rose to answer. Graeson crossed in front of me and took up position behind the door. I cut him a scowl for mistrusting her, but who was safe to trust these days?

I checked the peephole before Graeson could eyeball it, and saw the person I expected. Which, I allowed, didn't mean much when it came to Charybdis. Built lean with jet-black hair and piercing green eyes, Thierry didn't need more than her jeans and ratty T-shirt to be striking. Even through the distorted lens, the runes covering her left hand and arm stood out against her tanned skin.

"Hello?" she drawled, Texas thick in her voice.

One final check with Graeson, who nodded, and I opened the door. "Sorry about that. We're jumping at shadows lately."

"Understood." Her nostrils flared. "Graeson, so we meet again."

Scowl pinching his forehead, he circled behind me until he stood in front of her and dipped his chin. "Thierry."

"I'm going to invite myself in." She shuffled past us. "I'm being followed." She peered up at him. "Unless that's one of your people?"

"Our pack is all accounted for." He cocked his head. "Why do you ask?"

"The person tailing me is a warg." Thierry pulled out the task chair and sat. "Black fur if that helps with the ID."

Graeson and I exchanged a glance. I broke the standoff. "Aisha?"

"It's possible." He rubbed his jaw. "She does blame you for her expulsion from the pack."

"Of course she does." Me, and not Imogen, the female warg who had claimed her title, and her mate.

"I hate to bring bad news with me." Thierry crossed her legs. "I'm afraid that's not the worst of it."

"The prophecy means something to you?" I sank on the mattress and folded my legs under me.

"Let's make this private first." She took a charm from her pocket and crushed it. My ears popped as the spell sealed the room. "Decide amongst yourselves if Graeson is privy to this information. I will require an oath sealed in blood before we go further."

"I want in," he said before I could ask him.

"You okay with that?" she asked me. I nodded, and she pulled out a charm resembling a charred bird's nest and a slender dagger. She pricked her finger and fed it a drop of her blood, the wound sealing before our eyes. "Who wants to go next?"

I volunteered, leaving Graeson for last. My thumb was still bleeding when magic raced up my arms, stinging my throat and pricking my lips, binding us to shared secrets. The charm vanished in a puff of smoke, and Thierry dumped the ashes into the small trash can beneath the desk.

"Okay. Where were we?" She dusted her hands. "Oh yeah. The prophecy. It could mean a great many things to me, personally." She squinted up at me, lips pursed, debating. "You don't know who I am, do you?" She laughed. "God that sounds cocky, but you were alone with Mai, and she tends to be overprotective. I wasn't sure whose names she might have dropped to threaten you if you hurt me."

In my periphery, Graeson bristled. "She threatened you?"

"We worked it out," I soothed him. "It's fine." Focusing on Thierry, I got butterflies in my stomach, like I was at the top of one of those rickety National Fair coasters, high above a crowd with miles of track in front of me. "All I know about you is what I learned the first time we touched. You're a legacy, so one of your parents is Faerie-born." Her expectant look pushed me to continue. "You're a half-blood fae, a very powerful one."

Thierry sobered. "My father is Macsen Sullivan."

My gut rocketed into the soles of my feet, and that rollercoaster sensation blasted it right back up in my throat. *"You're the Black Dog's daughter?"*

"Yeah." She shrugged like it was no big deal to be the daughter of a legend. "I don't lead with that, you know? I don't like to name drop, and I like to keep my private life as private as possible."

"Who is the Black Dog?" Graeson expected me to answer, but I was too busy scraping my brains back in my head from where her announcement had blown the top off my skull. "Ellis?"

"Let me start at the beginning, okay?" Thierry started cracking her knuckles. "The story is easier to follow that way."

"All right." Graeson sat beside me and started rubbing my back.

"The purpose of the Wild Hunt for centuries was to ride through the mortal realm on All Hallows' Eve, collecting the wayward souls of fae who died on Earth. They returned them to Faerie, where they could sort of evaporate into the afterlife." She made a slashing gesture. "It's complicated. Anyway, the story goes that on one such hunt, the Huntsman and his pack of sleek, black hounds crossed a battlefield." Her voice fell into the cadence of someone used to telling the story. "Their hunger had been temporarily sated, but their noses led them to one last feast. Two souls, one Seelie and one Unseelie, stood with their hands clasped as though unaware the hunt was upon them."

"The Seelie are light and the Unseelie dark, right?" Graeson leaned forward, listening.

"Yes, well, sort of. Again, it's complicated. Nothing is black and white." She gusted out a breath. "Okay, so the pack leader ran ahead of the others. Confused when the spirits stood their ground, he approached them, sniffed them and allowed each to stroke his silky, midnight fur.

"The Seelie held the hound's gaze while the Unseelie spoke. 'Only in death have we known peace. If we had raised our voices instead of our swords, much of our grief might have been circumvented. Loyal beast, reaper, it is our final wish that Faerie never endure the misery of another Thousand Years War.'

"'Mark this day, Black Dog,' the Seelie intoned. 'Tonight you are the hunter, but one hundred years hence, you shall become the hunted. One prince from each of our houses will hunt you across Faerie wearing the skins of hounds, goaded by your own Huntsman while you wear the skin of a sidhe noble. Your blood will anoint the new ruler and usher in one hundred more years of prosperity for the fae.'

"Instead of consuming the spirits as the Huntsman had decreed, Black Dog bowed his head to their will. That simple act of defiance shattered the bonds between himself and the Huntsman, and Black Dog gained awareness. As a gift to aid him in the trials ahead, the Unseelie entered his left eye and the Seelie his right, so that Black Dog might always view both sides of any argument with impartiality.

"Black Dog also gained the form of a man so that he might stand toe-to-toe with kings. He named himself Macsen Sullivan and established the Faerie High Court, choosing one Seelie and one Unseelie consul to join him, and instituted the Right of the Hunt.

"Once a century, he was run to ground and torn to pieces. The blood of one man was spilled to determine a king. His sacrifice avoided the slaughter of thousands had the houses gone to war for the crown. For the seven days after he was laid to rest in Faerie's soil, the realm mourned him. Lore said those tears seeped into the ground and restored him, and he rose at midnight on the seventh day made whole again."

"Is any of that true?" Graeson wondered out loud.

A shudder rippled through Thierry. "Every word of it is true." She composed herself. "The Huntsman considers himself my grandfather. Not that I would mind a family reunion, but he shouldn't be able to cross the thresholds my father set." Her voice lowered. "I severed the tethers leading into Faerie myself. Only one remains, and it is hidden and guarded."

"You—?" I choked out.

"Yeah." She wiggled rune-marked hands at me. "Me."

Stunned as I was, my brain recovered faster this time. Pieces were clicking together all over the place.

"That's good news." Relief coasted through me. "I thought the divination meant the worlds would have to collide for the Wild Hunt to have access to this realm, but it could mean your grandfather came through the tether."

"The Wild Hunt free in the mortal world is not good news," she disagreed. "I'm not sure there's any merit to this divination, and I can't swear—if this does come to pass—that it won't be as you say. The Huntsman could use the tether. It's not outside the realm of possibility."

"If there is a functional tether, can you get word to Faerie? Find out what reason he might have for coming?" Another thought occurred to me. "What about your father? Can he help?"

"Dad is honeymooning with my mother in Summer." She grimaced.

So they hadn't been married when she was born? Or hadn't been together? She caught my expression and grimaced. I spared her an amused smile. "Let me guess, it's complicated?"

She huffed out a laugh. "Exactly that. There's no way to reach them. Not for ten more days when the glamour concealing their hideaway dissipates." She rubbed her forehead. "They wanted privacy to reconnect. They've been through so much."

"I get your interest based on your familial connection," Graeson started, "but Tennessee is a ways from Texas. Did you come in person to extract the oaths? Or did you have something else in mind?"

"I did need the oaths." She bobbed her head. "But if the Huntsman comes, I need to be here to greet him." Her lips flatlined. "Gramps hasn't been to this world in a long time, and his hounds will be ravenous. A little-known fact is parents who tell cautionary tales to naughty children about the hounds ripping souls from the living as easily as they capture the lost ones aren't wrong."

I blanched, but Graeson appeared torn on the edge of disbelief. This was not his culture, and Faerie was not his world. How strange it must be for him to accept our bizarre history as truth instead of fairy tale.

"You're here to stop him," Graeson said, rolling the implications around his mind.

"Not him so much as what else might follow him through," she demurred. "I'm more concerned about what the implications are that he was mentioned at all than he himself." She hesitated. "The rules change as rulers change in Faerie. No one has let the Huntsman off his leash in centuries, and the current king is..." She rolled a hand. "He's a decent-enough guy. Manipulative as hell, which he gets from his mother, but what fae aren't?"

I shrugged, not agreeing or disagreeing. Thierry was a protector of humans, most likely because one of her parents was one. Her stance on fae seemed...skewed...to me, but I would have to walk a mile in her shoes to understand her position, and I already had blisters on my heels. All that mattered to me was she was here, she was a powerful ally, and whatever was about to go down had a better chance of ending well with her on our side. "So you're saying you don't think he would let slip the hounds?"

"No." She shook her head. "Not without a direct order."

"How does this change our plan?" Graeson looked to me.

"It doesn't." I patted his thigh. "We still have to press Charybdis, and that means we have to find the clerk." I frowned, thinking it over. "He gave me permission to summon him when I 'made my peace.' I think that means he'll answer me if I can get near enough to one of his hosts."

"What does that mean?" Graeson snapped his head toward me. "Made your peace with what?"

"I could be wrong." I really, really didn't think I was. "I believe he wants me as his next avatar." Gold bathed Graeson's irises, and he snarled. "He wanted to punish me, and he failed. Harlow is all he's got left, and she's human. His kind of power will burn her out. She ought to have a higher resistance than most, given she's been exposed to magic all her life, but she won't last forever."

"You're not trading places with her." He made it an order, not a question.

"No, I'm not," I hedged. "But the only way for us to win this is if he thinks I am."

Thierry threw out a hand to forestall more growling. "No, listen. This could work." She stood and began pacing. "We isolate Charybdis while he's riding Harlow. Ask for a meet somewhere remote. You'll have the upper hand, and he'll know it. Harlow is his last bargaining chip. Offer to take her place, and before he makes the jump, we take her down."

I leapt to my feet. "We don't hurt her."

"I'll tranq her. From a safe distance." Thierry tapped her head. "I'm protected by layers of heavyweight spells these days, mostly to keep fae out of my noggin who might have heard about the tether and want its location. That ought to keep me safe from this guy too."

"Then why don't you—?" Graeson started.

"He doesn't want me." Thierry faced him. "I'd do this in a heartbeat if I could, because I'm confident I can walk out the other side. My mate is too, or I wouldn't be here. I'd be tied to a chair in the basement of a building half a world away. But I can't provide the incentive. He wants Cam. That's what we have to give him."

"I don't like this, Ellis." All the jumping and pacing must have irritated Graeson's wolf, because he rose too. "I know you have to do this." He clenched his fists. "Your sense of honor won't allow anything less."

"We've tried to catch him for months, and so many lives have been lost in the process." I didn't mention Marie, but he flinched the same as if I had. "I have one shot to end this now before anyone else is put at risk. He's fixated on me." I kissed him tenderly. "Let it end with me."

Let the ghosts of all those murdered by his hands be laid to rest. I owed them that peace for my role in their deaths.

He circled my wrists, his grip iron. "You are not *ending*."

"Poor choice of words," I allowed. "That's not what I meant." Mostly.

"This can work." Thierry sounded certain. "I've had the same training as Cam. I can handle a gun. They're just not my favorite thing."

"What about the tranqs?" Butler was tiny, and I doubted she could root out the supplies she needed locally.

"I'll put in a call." She pulled out her cell. "I can have the gun and ammo here by morning."

A tiny pang of longing zipped through my chest. Once upon a time, I'd had all the conclave's resources at the tips of my fingers, and it had been a beautiful thing.

"You do that." I was glad one of us could. "Graeson and I will resume surveillance of the gas station."

"After you eat." His tone brooked no argument. "You have to refuel or you won't have the energy to shift when you need to."

"He makes a good point." A haunted expression ribboned across Thierry's features. "We should both top off before the ball gets rolling."

I eased closer to her. "Would you like to join us?"

"No." Her voice went gritty. "I should feed alone."

Chills swept down my arms. Feed? I didn't want to know. "If you change your mind, let me know."

"You kids go have fun." A faint smile lifted her lips. "I have a date with Shaw." She waggled her phone. "Whatever passes for Chinese around here and Skype."

I smiled back, hoping he could shake her grim mood. "Where are you staying?"

"Here. I figured it would be easiest." She glanced around the room. "I'm one floor up, room two twelve."

"We'll leave you to it then." Graeson held the door for us, pulling it closed behind him and testing it as if not quite convinced he ought to trust Thierry. Or maybe his mistrust had morphed into something else seeing as how she supported my Cam-as-bait plan. "Good night," he told her, almost managing not to snap. "We'll plan on meeting across the street at six in the morning."

"So early?" Thierry groaned. "Okay. Fine. Yeah. Six works."

We left her to make her calls and went in search of dinner and the patience to wait out Charybdis.

Full of burgers and fries, we resumed our position on the bench in front of the general store. Night had fallen, and a cool breeze whisked away the day's heat. Light poured through the grimy windows of the gas station, casting slanted rectangles onto the pavement. One of the bulbs had blown over the pumps, but the other valiantly held back the night for wayward drivers in need of fuel.

"There is another option that might net us quicker results," Graeson rumbled from beside me.

"You mean Bianca?" I sipped at my drink and rechecked my gut. "I can't do that to her. I can't invite Charybdis back into her body, not after what he did—what he made her do—last time."

Tension eased from his shoulders, a sure indication he was relieved I had chosen to spare her more pain.

"By now he must know Aunt Dot and Isaac are gone." Any hope of getting the drop on him had vanished.

"It might work in our favor." Graeson crossed his ankle over his knee. "We need him desperate. We need him to make a mistake. We need him to underestimate us."

Watching his plans unravel a second time might be all it took. "I agree."

Shift change came and went, the teen clerk replaced by an older man with a ring full of keys hanging from his belt that screamed supervisor. I'd had enough. I stood and twisted out the kinks. "I say we head back to our room and crash while we can."

"We do have eight hours before shift changes again." A smile tipped his lips. "I don't know about sleep, but I'm definitely ready for bed."

Flush riding my cheeks, I took his hand and led him back to the hotel.

The night passed too quickly.

CHAPTER EIGHTEEN

Morning arrived between one blink of my eyes and the next. Confident we had the shift changes down at the gas station, Graeson and I headed out to breakfast. Cheeks flushed and eyes shining, Thierry joined us only ten minutes after six. Feeding, whatever it entailed, agreed with her even if she didn't agree with it.

"You guys are morning people." She plunked down on the bench seat across from us. "Ugh." She gestured to the waitress and indicated she wanted coffee. Lots and lots of it. "Tell me something good."

"I wish we could." I toyed with the paper banding my utensils. "We bombed last night."

"Shift change is in forty-five minutes," Graeson reminded me.

"How about you?" I asked Thierry. "Tell me your night went better than ours."

"I suppose it did." A somber thread wove through her voice, and she flexed her rune-marked fingers. "I do have some good news." She reached in a pocket and flashed three green postal receipts stamped with a wizard's hat. "Pointed Hat Deliveries made a pit stop last night around midnight. We're set on that end."

"Pointed Hat?" Graeson asked, puzzling over the slips of paper. "As in a witch delivery service?"

"Ha." She slapped a hand over her mouth. "Um, no. The conclave's pockets are deep, but they're not that deep. Pointed Hat is operated by a gremlin couple. Harris is an avid Harry Potter fan. The patch on his shirt says *Harris Potter*."

"Order up," a cheery voice intruded.

"We haven't ordered..." I glanced up and sweat popped down my spine, "...yet."

Under the table, I rested my hand on Graeson's thigh, cursing myself a thousand times for not taking the aisle seat. Across from us, Thierry's runes glittered emerald green.

"I saw you last night," the waitress continued, all smiles. "You were waiting for the boy, but I'm afraid he's no longer with us." She plunked down one of the plates on her tray, black eyes gleaming. "He had a heart condition. Who knew?"

"Why didn't you approach us?" I inched closer to Graeson, until our thighs were plastered together.

"Approach a conclave agent and her warg lover in the middle of the night?" She clicked her tongue. "Come now, I do have some sense of self-preservation." She kept unloading her tray. "I thought meeting this morning, as you've done the past two mornings, would make the most sense." She surveyed the area, ignoring an elderly man attempting to flag her down for a coffee refill. "Witnesses abound."

Hmm. This was new. If she cared about witnesses, that meant she was vulnerable, didn't it? Too bad there were no obvious means of capitalizing on her weakness. "What do you want?"

"You're the one who came looking for me." Her speech pattern was much more human and natural. A show for the customers? A result of spending enough time in this world to adapt to its people? Or had Charybdis been making a point by speaking to me formally before? "What is it, Camille Ellis, that *you* want?"

"I want you to release Harlow Bevans." And die a horrible, fiery death for what he had done to those girls, to Bianca and Jensen, the gas station clerk, all his victims.

"Releasing her will cost me an avatar." The waitress pulled straws from her pockets and tossed them at us, clearly relishing the role. "Are you offering a substitute?" Her gaze lit on Thierry. "Not that one. No." She retreated a half step. "Your lineage is as clear as the runes branded on your skin." She whipped her head toward Graeson. "That one, though. He's strong. He would last. For a while." She snaked her hand over the table toward Graeson, chest heaving at the shock of terror radiating from me. "Yes. This one will do—"

"No." I stabbed a fork through the back of her hand. "He won't."

The waitress's expression didn't change as she ripped out the fork and tucked her hand in her pocket before we created a scene. More of a scene. "There is something to be said for mated wargs," she mused, voice losing its modern edge. "Once I claim you, his mind will shatter." She grinned at him. "She has no idea how close you are to the edge. How losing her would shove you over it."

A cold ache took root in my belly. Graeson was healing. He was moving on from his sister's death. He loved me. Losing me to the same killer, especially if my physical body were still viable, might force him back several dangerous steps in his recovery.

Unless I told him the truth, that Charybdis had been hunting me all along. That Marie was a casualty of his greed, that her blood was on my hands. Once I told him that, he might not care what the murderous fae had in store for me.

Coward that I was, I caged that admission behind my teeth. I wanted to enjoy Graeson for as long as I had him. It was selfish and wrong of me, but there it was. There would be time enough for him to hate me later, once this was done.

His warm hand covered mine where my nails dug into his thigh. *"She's trying to get under your skin. Don't let her."*

"So we have a deal?" I forced her attention back on me.

"I would shake hands—" her grin flashed dimples, "—but I might get too eager." Fetching her order pad out of her front pocket, she flipped to a clean page and brought out her bloody hand with a pencil gripped between those fingers. "Meet me here, at midnight." She scribbled. "You have the rest of the day to say your goodbyes." She tore off the top sheaf and slapped it on the table. "Come alone, or the changeling will be a gibbering fool by the time you wrest her from me."

"Understood." I tucked the paper with precise coordinates into my pocket.

Spinning on her heel, the waitress crossed the room and entered the kitchen. I tossed a handful of bills on the table to cover the food we hadn't ordered, and we exited the building before the police got called. Assaulting an innocent woman in a restaurant was not my brightest move ever, but my she-wolf had been a whisper away from bursting from my skin since Charybdis revealed himself.

The three of us hotfooted it back to the hotel. Thierry had work to do, so she left us to spend the final hours together while she figured out logistics of the area the coordinates indicated.

With more than twelve hours to go until midnight, I made phone calls to Mom and Dad and then to Dr. Wayne to check on Aunt Dot, Isaac and Theo. Too antsy to stay cooped up in our rooms a minute longer, Graeson and I went for a drive to visit the pack. He needed to see his people, and I did too. Dell had been blowing up my mind wanting details on Isaac, and I hoped reporting in person might help the details stick. She had managed to slip in jabs of concern for me too, but when I was in her head, the walls were painted the clear blue of his eyes.

Stone's Throw RV Park was cramped and lacked the polish of the site the pack had abandoned in Chattanooga. But it was quiet, and the view was spectacular if mountains and forest were your thing. Needless to say, for a warg pack it was exactly their thing.

The pack, minus Bianca and Zed, who was pulling guard duty, met us in the parking lot. Graeson took my hand and led me forward when my knees threatened to lock with uncertainty. A transient childhood meant I feared absence hadn't made their hearts fonder but forgetful. He guided me through the gauntlet of hugs, and I ignored when the guys sniffed my hair or exhaled their relief against my skin that I was home.

Home.

Muscles relaxing, heart lightening, I breathed out my own blissful sigh. This place did feel like home. The familiar trailers had nothing to do with it. These people made it—made me—feel that way.

"Cam." Dell smashed into me, squeezing me until my eyes bulged. "I'm so glad you came." She pushed me back to better read my expression. "You are staying, right?"

"I can't." Tension met my announcement, crackling in the air. "I have a meeting tonight. After that, if all goes well, we can put this behind us."

Several faces turned toward the trailer where Bianca rested. Point taken. We would never move past Jensen's absence, never look at Bianca without remembering it all over again. We would have to address her care and the baby's when this was finished, when she was truly safe and could begin healing.

"This meeting sounds serious." Dell studied me. "Do you need extra eyes or ears or..." she peeled back her upper lip, "...teeth?"

"I can't risk you." I glanced around the tightly packed gathering. "Any of you."

"You're alpha," Abram rumbled. "We can't risk you, either."

Graeson slung his arm around my waist and anchored us together at the hips. "We've brought in outside help that's not susceptible to the tricks this fae employs." He kissed my temple. "Ellis won't be alone."

I heard a deeper meaning in his voice and pondered it, deciding I would have to extract a promise that, no matter how sure he was that his idea was better than mine, that he was in the right to protect me, he had to trust me to handle business this time.

Behind us a horn honked. We turned as one to greet a pickup with a lit sign decorated with a pizza slice on top.

"Come to momma." Dell rubbed her hands together. "We decided to have a welcome-home feast in your honor."

"That was generous of you." I aimed the remark at Graeson, who appeared as innocent as a lamb among wolves. I got the feeling he was so intent on stuffing me that I would have to waddle out to meet Charybdis.

The guys rushed the delivery driver, who did a double take at being crowded by such large men with a singular interest. He shoved the boxes into their hands and retreated a few steps, until his back pressed against the side of his car. Cash was shoved into his trembling palms, and the guy hopped in his ride and left without a backward glance.

Graeson and I passed several hours in the company of friends, eating and joking and eating some more. We ran together to burn off the jitters making us all antsy. By the time we finished, the tightness in my shoulders had lessened. I was leaning against Graeson's side, hand resting over his steady heart, when my phone pinged.

"I don't want to get that," I confided in him.

"We can't afford not to." He tipped my head back with his finger under my chin and kissed me. "Thierry might need us."

Knowing he was right, I checked my messages. "She's got the location mapped." I swiped my thumb over the attached graphic. "She wants to meet and discuss strategy."

"Then we should go." He stood and pulled me up with him. "I want tonight to go off without a hitch."

"Me too."

I wanted tonight to be the end of Charybdis's reign and the start of our new beginning.

Thierry met us at the door of her hotel room with her hair in a bun, a pencil clamped between her teeth and a gas station map folded in her hand. *Vindication.* I wished Theo was here to see her going paper versus digital. It sprung to mind that perhaps since we'd had the same training we gravitated toward using the same means of deductive reasoning, but I took victories where I could find them.

"We have about two hours until go time." She tucked the pencil behind her ear. "It takes about thirty minutes to reach our destination, so that cuts us down to an hour and a half." She ushered us inside and gestured toward her bed, which was covered in electronics and scribbled-on paper maps. "He wants to meet in this area, on Watauga Lake. I mean literally on the lake." She indicated the map at the foot of the mattress. "The coordinates are for a section of pier at the marina."

Graeson tapped a few buttons on the laptop and switched from the road map to earth view. "This limits Thierry's line of sight." Sailboats and pontoon boats crowded the dock, making it difficult to isolate the exact spot Charybdis had specified. "This tells me he's been out there before and knows the lay of the land." He straightened with a scowl. "He could hide a dozen hosts in those boats, and we would never know." He shook his head. "This is too dangerous. There are too many unknowns."

"I know you wanted to end this tonight," Thierry chimed in, "but he's got a point."

"This is why he agreed so easily." The first phase of my plan had backfired. Instead of making him sweat, I had tipped our hand. "He used that extra time while we were staking out the gas station last night to set this up."

"We'll have other opportunities." Graeson reached for me.

"At what cost?" I skirted his grasp. "Who will be next?"

The flattening of his lips before he glanced aside confirmed he suspected it would be him. Me? I knew it would be. He was the most precious thing I had left.

"Please," I begged him. "We can do this. We can still turn this in our favor."

"Thierry?" That he looked to her for advice cut me.

"We have an hour." She cleared off room for us to sit. "No promises, but let's put our heads together, and see what we come up with."

"I debated giving this to you." He removed a crumpled foil ball from the back pocket of his jeans. The imprint on the material told me it was a used gum wrapper. "I'm not sure why you asked your parents for some of these, but maybe one is enough?"

The thin metal crinkled as I folded back the edges, revealing a gem the size of my thumb. "I thought this was lost." It was the stone I had found in Aunt Dot's pocket. "You're sneaky." No wonder he hadn't reacted to the dryad's news. "Very sneaky." The metal dampened its magic to a bearable level, unlike the porous fabric I'd used. "You told me to leave this."

"I didn't want you to get hurt." He covered the gem again before I got a good look at it. "An opportunity presented itself, and I took it." He crimped the foil shut. "Keep it wrapped up tight, or the magic leaks."

A single gem wasn't what I'd had in mind when I asked my parents to procure them for me. Actually I'd had no specific application in mind. Maybe that's why the deal had fallen through. Karmic retribution. I had gotten greedy. I was grasping, adding weapons to my arsenal while the thought continued to tickle the back of my mind that all this preparation might not be enough.

"I appreciate this." I kissed his cheek.

"Sorry to break up the moment, but time is ticking." Thierry checked her phone. "If we're not solid and all in agreement by eleven fifteen, then we abort the mission. Deal?"

"Deal." Graeson almost spoke over her in his haste to lock down his vote.

Trapped between a warg and a hard place, I clutched the gem as an idea formed. "Deal."

CHAPTER NINETEEN

I wore my jogging clothes and tennis shoes to the meeting. The tag in my shorts had never itched me before, but it urged me to scratch my lower back now. Psychosomatic irritation was my self-diagnosis. Thierry had crafted a hodgepodge privacy spell designed to keep the wargs out of my head, and clear of Charybdis's influence, then cast it in a place no one would think to search.

I arrived ten minutes early and scouted the area in person. The marina was well lit, but shadows prowled the corners of my vision. Reflections off the water. Probably. The pier was long, portions of it covered by tin roofs. Dozens of boats were moored in their slips. Their bright colors glinted, cheering me up despite myself. Even the punny names earned a huff of amusement from me despite the circumstances. Or maybe because of them.

"Camille Ellis, you're early." The cultured tone came from Harlow's throat, her natural voice a faint memory at this point. "I hope that is a sign of your willingness to submit and not one of rebellion."

Even with her blacked-out eyes and stiff posture, Harlow's presence lifted my mood. Her cotton-candy-pink hair had grown out so the roots showed blonde. Charybdis had dressed and styled her like a doll, in the image of the woman who was now a pale echo of her former self.

"Did you show the same faith?" I kept several planks between us. "Did you come alone?"

A smile played on her lips. "Those were not the terms we negotiated."

I rolled my shoulder like I had expected as much, and I had. The double standard didn't surprise me. This location was all about secreting away hosts or whatever other supplies he required.

"What proof do I have that you'll release Harlow once I submit?"

"Her body is failing," she admitted. "Soon I would have no use for her, so why not sacrifice her for you?" Her expression turned wistful. "Your form pleases me greatly. I look forward to wearing your skin." That wasn't creepy at all. "Pity it won't survive the night." She laughed. "That is the marvelous thing about Geminis, is it not? There is always a spare."

"What does my sister have to do with this?" I took a careful step back. "I want your word you won't harm her or my family. That includes the pack."

"That I cannot do." She cocked her head at me. "The magistrate's warrior visited you. I thought...but she didn't tell you, did she?"

Aware I was taking the bait, I couldn't help biting. "Tell me what?"

"All of this was for you." She twirled a strand of hair around her finger. "The drownings. The sex of the victims. The loving families. I selected them based on Lori's profile. On *your* profile. I used twofold magic to protect my investment. I anchored the circle using their pain, their misery, their anguish, but I made certain Ayer put a bug in Magistrate Vause's ear. I made sure you were positioned to lead the investigation so that every echo of your grief, remorse, pity wove its own filament in the spell. So that even if one layer was broken, the other would survive."

Acid stung the back of my throat, and a familiar wave of self-loathing crested in me. Hearing Vause pontificate was nothing compared to Charybdis confirming that I was the cause of so much death. So many lives lost, and for what?

"Your Marshal Ayer was the first contact I had in this world. I had to cross the portal in my natural state, incorporeally, a gamble that might have cost me my life had not she appeared." Her gaze went glassy as she absorbed the grief spinning off me. "She held so much private knowledge about the inner workings of this world, but the item in the forefront of her mind was a girl, Lori Grace Ellis. She was fresh from visiting your sister, on her way to speak with Magistrate Vause, and her memories astounded me. Gemini are legend in Faerie. They no longer exist. I had not dared hope I would find such a match in this realm, but she offered up not one but *two* such morsels with the promise of more."

"Why fixate on her—on us?" Revenge aside, it made no sense. "We aren't the strongest or the most powerful fae."

"No, but you have other redeeming qualities." She took one calculated step nearer. "Do you know the reason why my kind exhaust our hosts in Faerie? They lack emotion. We're forced to feed on their magic instead. Most have a finite supply and no means of tapping into power outside their own. We devour that spark, and they die. We keep several hosts tapped for such occasions so that we might minimize the amount of time we are exposed as we claim a new primary, a true avatar."

"You want a Gemini host so that when the magic runs dry, we can tap into someone else's." I inched back a foot. "You realize that fix is temporary, right?"

The fact was, I had traded on this very bit of Gemini biology not a week ago. My ability to filter magic from others and claim aspects of their power as my own had led Miguel Garza to theorize my blood was a universal donor. Charybdis was hinting that same ability would enable him to sustain himself off the magic of others while my body acted as a filtration system.

"Perhaps the issue is not you, but the weak stock available to you." Her eyes gleamed with malice. "I would drink rivers of fae blood to quench my thirst, but earthborn are watered down, near flavorless. Their excess of emotion is their only saving grace." She wet her lips. "What this world needs is an infusion. Fresh blood."

The prophecy tickled the back of my mind. What was his endgame? "Why burn me up in one night if I'm that valuable?"

"I have no choice." She frowned, seeming unhappy at the prospect. "All that remains of your sister is a shell, which suits my purpose, as sharing one body with two minds gets rather tiresome. My hungers are aroused by an active mind, by emotion, the darker the better, and she possesses neither."

"Leave her out of this." Hearing him dismiss my sister raised my hackles.

"That is an impossibility, I'm afraid." She studied the star-studded sky. "Your pain, your anger—your self-loathing—will enable me to salvage what you cost me when you ended the kelpie too soon. I would have taken you once completing the circle, but perhaps this was all for the best." She gave a decisive nod. "The sterility of Lori's shell will make claiming her much simpler than my possession of you." She pressed me back another step. "You'll fight me. I can read it in the set of your shoulders and that smoldering fury in your gaze. Eating you from the inside out would sate me for some time."

"It would?" Nothing she said made sense. "Why not *it will?*"

Harlow advanced another step on me, and I eased back only to realize I had run out of pier. The only escape now, if I took it, was the water.

"I might have been hasty allowing you the full credit for my actions." She traced a finger down my forearm. "I came to this world with a goal. Marshal Ayer granted me a gift beyond compare, the knowledge of your species, and evidence the gods were rewarding my efforts by granting me that which none of my kind have ever possessed."

"A body," I surmised. One capable of sustaining one of Faerie's many bizarre creations.

"Yes," she hissed, fingers circling my wrist. "I will become singular among my kind—an Iezu made flesh. All will fall on their knees and worship me."

Iezu? Is that what Charybdis was? From what I recalled during my training, those were a rare subclass of fae skilled in illusion. What Charybdis did was no mirage. Perhaps the truth of them had been as lost to us as the existence of Gemini had been to them.

I eased my hand into my pocket, talking over the crinkling of foil. "I want to say goodbye to Harlow."

"Speak, and I will allow her to hear." Her grip tightened. "I will not leave this form yet. I need my strength for what is to come."

"Cam?" Comprehension widened her gaze. "You can't be here. Don't do this. Get out while you can." Harlow cried out, releasing me to clutch her head. "Kill me. Kill *him*. You can't let him complete the ritual."

I gripped her shoulders. "What ritual?"

"He's coming back. He's coming..." She doubled over. "Run. Please. *Run.*"

Ignoring her struggle, I brought her in for a hug. "You're going to be free, Harlow. Everything will be fine."

The fight drained out of her, and I knew before I withdrew that Harlow was gone. I peered down at the fragile teen, and malice slammed into me as solidly as a fist. She raked her nails down my arms. Her fingers snagged the pearl bracelet, and the string broke. Beads rolled across the dock, dozens of tiny *plip-plops* sounding as they hit in the water.

"No," she slurred. "What...have you...done?"

"I just returned what you stole from my parents." The gem rested precariously in the tiny pocket of her barely there jean shorts. It was a hip wiggle away from falling out and thunking into the water too.

As much as I hated to lose the bracelet, I hoped after tonight I would no longer require the talisman.

Dark eyes blazing hatred, Harlow bared her teeth. Her lips slid together as her lids began fluttering. The last I saw of Charybdis was the seething vengeance in Harlow's eyes before the charm snared her an instant later. Grunting under her sudden weight, I held her until she slumped against my chest.

Booted footsteps pounded on planks, growing louder. Thierry rounded the corner, runes casting soft peridot shadows, with the tranq gun primed, ready and aimed at Harlow.

"I wish I had thought to ask for life vests while I was at it," I admitted. Thierry had called in a favor and gotten a johnboat delivered. I didn't know much about watercraft, but Graeson had talked me through operating this lightweight aluminum one. Its neighbors dwarfed it, but I wasn't comfortable handling one of the larger vessels. "This is going to be one of the less-fun things I've ever done."

Driving a boat. On open water. Sure it was a lake, but its mean depth was fifty-two feet. Near the dam that plummeted to two hundred and sixty-five feet. Considering the Tennessee River was a bare twelve feet deep, I got hives thinking about navigating the Watauga.

"Are you sure you want to do this? We've got your friend sedated. There's a decent chance Charybdis didn't have time to jump." She held the gun steady. "We could walk away."

"I can't back down now." We might never get this far again. "I won't know if he's in there until I remove the gem, and I need to be dead center when that happens." I settled Harlow in the boat as best I could, and joined her before flipping on the spotlight mounted to the front of the boat. I fumbled with the trolling motor until it caught, futzing with the controls until I felt confident. "We couldn't have made it this far without your help."

"Don't make it sound like goodbye, Cam." Thierry's aim never wavered as she shouted over the noise. "We've got your back. You're coming out the other side of this. That mate of yours won't have it any other way."

I raised a hand in farewell, the engine's roar too loud to fight, then gripped the edge of the boat until the metal bit into my hand. Mindful of Graeson's instructions, I maneuvered us toward the center of the lake. Fifteen minutes later, a quick check of my phone's GPS told me we had reached our destination. I flipped on the spotlight mounted to the rear of the boat and dialed Thierry. "Have you cleared the marina?"

"We found three fae and two humans, all unconscious. The pack volunteers are here, and they're moving the bodies out of range. I'm going to run the heartbeat spell one more time to make sure there aren't any more hosts tucked away, but I think we got this. He cast an erasure spell, but that can't hide an active pulse. The area should be clear in about ten minutes."

"I'll give you twenty." I hung up the phone and set a timer, gut churning at her mention of pack volunteers. I hated to think of the wargs so close to Charybdis, but we needed the manpower to make sure the sweep was successful. Illuminated by the spotlight, Harlow's pale skin drew my eye. "This is not how I pictured our friendship going, Flipper."

I patted under the bench seat she occupied and located a built-in drawer that pulled open to reveal a tray of tools. I selected the ones I needed, then set to work removing the motor from its mount. Thank the gods breaking equipment was always easier than assembling it. Once I had the unit clear of the boat, I dumped it backward into the water and sat down to rest and give it time to hit bottom.

The temptation to reach out to Graeson buzzed in my head. Good thing the tag was running interference. I was too weak to resist temptation. Knowing the pack was close, being certain that meant he was too, had me itching to touch minds with him one last time before—

The timer clanged.

Unable to find my voice for a second call, I shot Thierry a text. She replied seconds later. *All clear.*

Leaning over Harlow, I shifted her weight enough to remove the stone from her back pocket. It too hit the water with a *plop*. As much as I wanted the insurance, I couldn't afford to risk Charybdis using it against me.

Several minutes passed before Harlow's eyes sprang open. She woke slower than Aunt Dot had after being exposed to the gem for days, meaning Harlow was far weaker than she appeared. The shine from the spotlight forced her to squint, but there was no hiding the feral presence moving behind her eyes.

Harlow lunged, hands circling my throat with inhuman strength, and flung me onto my back. Crawling up my legs, she settled her hips over my waist and pinned me. Torn between clutching the edges of the boat to stabilize it or prying her fingers off me, I lay there while her chest heaved and obscenities poured over her lips. My fingers found the tray beneath the bench I had been sitting on, and I tugged it out, fingers tickling over Dr. Wayne's contribution to our operation. One with less-permanent results than the gem.

"Take me back." Her nails pierced my skin. "Return me to the shore."

"Can't," I wheezed. "No...motor."

Stars danced at the corners of my eyes, and I struggled to stay conscious.

Relaxing her fingers, she leaned back and oriented herself to our surroundings. "You will not cost me that which is owed to me."

"Yes." High on the rush of oxygen, I grasped one tube from the tray and fisted it. "I will."

With my thumb and finger, I shoved the plastic cap off the needle tipping the syringe full of Propofol. I slammed it into her exposed thigh, readjusted my grip and depressed the plunger.

"Jump into me," I ordered in my best co-alpha voice. "Or this is goodbye."

Harlow began relaxing muscle by muscle, her chin dropping to her chest. Only Charybdis's will kept her upright. For a span of several heartbeats, I thought he would stick it out, cling to her until I had no choice but to deliver Harlow to the conclave and let them figure out how to extract the crazed fae living inside her.

Unseen force punched me in the chest, and I gasped, all the air I had sucked in expelled on a scream of shock. I bolted upright, arms flailing, and Harlow crumpled in a tangle of limbs.

"Let me in," an alien voice hissed on the periphery of my thoughts. *"You invited me. I am here."*

"No." His was not the warm caress of the pack bond. His invasion turned my veins to ice, glazing my brain in hoarfrost until he gained a toehold in my shivering psyche. Was this what he had done to the others? This frigid paralysis? How cruel that the only treatment up to this point had been further sedation. What a special hell that must be for his surviving victims. *"You don't get me too."*

Needles of ice skewered my mind, ripping it to shreds. Tattered remnants of my careful plan fluttered out the window of my thoughts into an arctic storm I had no hope of surviving. *It hurts,* became my mantra. *Make it stop,* my prayer.

I was forgetting something. The plan. *Remember the plan.* There was something...

"Surrender to me," he screamed, crystal fissures crackling, exposing the raw core of my tender mind.

Fear of the water abandoned me on that first brutal assault. Now the gently lapping waves offered me comfort. All I had to do was reach their embrace before he took full control of me and swam for the shore to escape capture yet again.

I couldn't let that happen. Not after what he had confided. All those deaths, those ghosts, howled for justice, and once upon a time I had worn a badge, hadn't I?

Gripping the boat's edge, I hauled myself to my feet.

"No." His horrified screech raked nails down the blackboard of my mind. *"Stop this. I command you."*

Already his strength suffused my fingers, making them harder to pry up one by one until I stood tall in the boat. The urge to wave farewell to those watching from the safety of the shoreline was strong, but I wasn't about to blast up a signal flare now.

Head pounding, I jumped.

"No." Charybdis flung himself against my skull, but the bars of his cage held strong. *"Stop."*

Water shot up my nose. I didn't fight it, I embraced it. I couldn't rescue myself without saving Charybdis too, and I had come too far for that. The fizzle of bubbles rushed from my lungs to tickle my cheeks. Pressure filled my ears with the sound of my frantic heartbeat, muting the vitriol my parasite spewed.

"Cam?"

A shocked laugh teased my eyes open onto darkness. Moonlit waters folded over my head while grim depths swirled around my toes. Caught somewhere in the middle drifted a familiar ghost.

Blonde hair floated around her head as she cocked it at me. "What are you doing down here?"

Gone was the sallow child of my nightmares. This Lori appeared healthy, a glowing reflection of her adult self. The nightgown that had haunted me for so long had been replaced by a shorts and camisole set in baby pink, an outfit I must remember from her closet.

Serenity ebbed from her, encapsulating me, my own struggles forgotten. Charybdis scurried to the far reaches of my consciousness, a cockroach exposed to light. Lori drifted forward, following the same ebb and flow as me, embracing me in arms that were both solid and warm.

"You have to take better care of yourself."

I held on tight, squeezing until she chuckled, so damn glad not to be alone.

"You did it." Her form splintered, shattering into a million fragments. "We're free."

The vise clamping my brain eased enough she might have been right.

"I love you." Her fractured voice faded.

I love you too, I thought, before the tension in my body burst like a bubble.

No, that's not right. Magic exploded from me, an atom bomb detonating, leaving me in the eye of a great and terrible storm.

CHAPTER TWENTY

I jackknifed in bed, bolting upright on a gasp that sucked antiseptic air into my lungs. Lakes were many things, but chemically sanitized they were not. Or, you know, oxygen-producing. Afraid of what I might find on the other side, I opened my eyelids...onto a hospital room.

"She's awake," Graeson whispered at my elbow. I hadn't even seen him there. He shot to his feet and leaned over the bed. "Sweetheart?"

I smiled at him. I'm pretty sure I did. I couldn't feel my face.

Turning his head, he bellowed louder, "She's awake."

Two nurses decked out in vibrant yellow scrubs with black seams running down the sides burst into the room and began checking my vitals. Dr. Wayne strolled in on their heels, hands shoved into his pockets. Exhaustion cast dark shadows under his bloodshot eyes, and his bedside manner left me wishing my vocal cords were online.

"You can turn down the drip," he instructed Banana One. To Banana Two, he said, "Get her a cup of ice chips and a pitcher of water. She'll need it if she wants to talk."

The good doctor pulled out a pen. "Camille..."

"No." Graeson stepped between us. "She doesn't need to hear this now."

"Believe me when I say the last thing I want to drop in the lap of a trauma patient is more trauma," he argued, "but not telling her doesn't make the threat any less real."

The growl leaving my mate's throat lacked heat, meaning he agreed on some level. He just didn't want to admit it, even to himself.

Doing my best with the saliva I had, I forced out, "Charybdis?"

"Shh." Graeson covered my hand with his. "The nurses will be back in a minute."

On cue, Banana Two arrived with the promised drink. She stuck a bendy straw in a small Styrofoam cup and poured water to the top line before passing it to Graeson. I'd meant to reach for it, but my hands weren't working all that well. Had I been sedated too? Just in case?

Graeson removed a plastic bottle from his pocket and squirted a few drops of berry flavor enhancer into the cup, stirred and then held it, positioning the straw at my lips while I drank.

"I have distressing news to share," Dr. Wayne resumed in a calm voice.

I hit the bottom and indicated I wanted more, which Graeson was happy to provide.

"We'll talk to her." New voices entered the fray. Mom spoke again. "It's our place."

Finding strength to twitch my fingers, I got the message across to Graeson, and he set the cup aside and hauled me into his lap, tubes and all.

Dad lumbered in behind her, and they stood on the side of the bed opposite Graeson.

I did my best to curl tighter against his side. "What's...wrong?"

"What you did was a very brave thing," Dad soothed. "Your mother and I are so proud of you, and we're so grateful the gods returned you to us."

When he stalled out, Mom took over for him. "You died, honey. You drowned." She ducked her head. "It wasn't for long." Pride filled her gaze when she looked to Graeson. "Your mate had the forethought to bring a doctor with their team, just in case." She must have meant Abram. "He was able to revive you within minutes."

Minutes.

I had been dead for...whole minutes.

"Charybdis is gone" was my first coherent thought after that. Why that merited an intervention, I had no idea.

"Yes," Graeson rumbled, forcing another cup of flavored water into my hand. "He is."

"The plan worked?" I sipped and sipped until my straw made sucking noises.

"*A* plan worked," he confirmed. "Not *the* plan, the one I approved before letting you out of my sight."

"Cord," my father warned. "Now is not the time."

"You're right." He reined in his wolf before his eyes did more than flicker with a promise of gold. "I apologize."

"I don't understand." The drugs keeping my brain hazy refused to connect the dots for me. "What happened?"

"The plan," he grumbled just shy of a growl, "was to get Harlow isolated in the boat on the lake, wake her up and then force Charybdis to take you as his avatar." Metal groaned where his fingers left indentions in the bed's chrome railing. "You theorized that you could metabolize him, the same way your body responds to all foreign magic, and we decided it was worth a shot if the right conditions could be met. Thierry was instructed to tranquilize you after one hour unless you showed signs of distress, so we could reclaim you and evaluate your success."

Bits of what he said sank in and tickled distant memories. Whoever had dreamed up that plan, it was a good one from where I was sitting—laying.

"Except you showed signs of distress," he continued, "and before Thierry could take a shot, you hit the water."

That must be the drowning part. Still, I had survived. I was here, sitting and talking to them. By some miracle, I had full use of my faculties. Maybe. It was hard to tell with the drugs pumping feel-good vibes into me.

"What am I missing?" I looked to Graeson for answers, but his solemn gaze rested on my parents.

"Lori passed yesterday," Mom said quietly.

Adrenaline dumped in my veins, and the comforting shroud of medicine evaporated. I pushed away from Graeson and sat upright in bed, gaze darting from face to face. "No." I jabbed a finger at the IV pole. "That is messing with my head. You're not here. You're not real. None of this is real. I died. I'm dead. This is—I don't know what this is, but Lori is alive. I saw her." A sob burst from me. "She's *alive.*"

Graeson attempted to wrap his arms around me, but I shoved him away. I didn't want comfort. I didn't deserve comfort. Not from him, not from my parents, not from anyone. Hadn't my specialness in life been derived from being the Gemini who survived as an individual? Hadn't I been treated as different because of my perceived immunity to the curse of our species? Except I hadn't ever been special or different. Lori had been there, anchoring me the whole time.

Never once during our meetings had I considered the ramifications of what might happen to her if I failed or what the cost of my success might be. I hadn't planned to go out in that boat on a suicide run, but I had been so caught up in the notion of vengeance that I left my sister unprotected.

Lori was dead.

It was my fault.

All this time I'd spent hunting monsters, never understanding I was one.

"Get out," I whispered, curling into myself. *"Get. Out."*

I counted the drips in the IV line until Banana One took pity on me and returned me to oblivion.

CHAPTER TWENTY-ONE

The irony was not lost on me that the next time I woke was to a private suite at Edelweiss. Days slipped past in a drugged haze that took the edge off, so I didn't mind much. I spent hours in therapy each afternoon, dealing with my grief and my guilt, and I didn't mind that either. I was kept high in the beginning to lessen the mind-searing agony of my brain forging fresh neural pathways to erase the overrides Charybdis bored into my gray matter. Life became eat, get shrunk, get medicated, wander around in a daze, sleep and repeat.

The monotony didn't bother me. Until the day it did.

A month into my stay I experienced an epiphany brought on by a single question at group.

Would you be this hard on Harlow if she had done what you did to save her?

Harlow occupied a room down the hall from me. She hadn't spoken since she was retrieved from the boat, even though I sat with her every weekend in the visitation lounge. But she was alive, and once or twice a week she slept through the night without waking the entire ward with her screams.

The answer, after much deliberation, was no. Harlow's suffering made it easy to forgive hypothetical her.

The crack in my reasoning spread wider when the shrink followed up with a question equally profound.

Is your suffering any less that you can forgive her and not yourself?

I had endured what few, if any, Gemini survived, and fate had repaid me by twisting my life around until I was truly what I had believed myself to be since that night on the beach.

Alone.

The pack bond had saved my life, the psychic feedback of all those minds nourished my soul. Even after what I had cost him, Graeson paid me visits on Sundays and played donor. When his attempts at conversation met with silence, he accepted I wasn't ready to talk and started spending his hour reading *Bunnicula* to me. I almost cracked a smile once or twice, but my lips had weighed too much to haul up the edges at the time.

At night I reflected on what I could l remember of that last fleeting glimpse I'd caught of Lori. Her next-to-last words replayed in a loop in my head. *We're free*, she'd said. Hanging on to life by my fingernails, I'd thought she meant free from Charybdis. Figment of my imagination or not, now I wasn't sure that's what she meant.

Why would I picture her in those clothes? Pick those words as her last? Unless I hadn't. Was it crazy to believe it might have been real? Looking around, this was the place to be if I had lost my marbles. *Unless I hadn't.* Had some tendril of the bond Lori and I shared stretched out to find me one last time before it snapped for good? What if her words—*we're free*—meant she was too?

I am alive.

I kept circling back to what a miracle that was in so many ways. I made a choice. I decided it wasn't enough to live, I wanted to be *alive*. Ghosts might haunt me the rest of my days, but I would lay each one to rest as best I could by continuing the work I had begun with the conclave, and by greeting each day with a blessing that I was here to witness it. I might not deserve a second chance—or was this my third?—but I wanted one.

Recovery went quicker after that. Three weeks after my epiphany, I cleared the psych eval necessary for release.

Something told me they had been waiting on me to make up my mind all along.

Funny how the simple, defiant act of deciding to live manifests the will to survive.

Today was my final day at Edelweiss. Blue sky stretched for miles on the other side of my window, an omen if I ever saw one. I had no idea who to expect downstairs, no clue who would take me home or where that home might be. I hadn't worked up the nerve to speak to anyone from the outside since I was admitted, leaving the choice of escort up to my doctors. That had been a mistake, granting a window of opportunity for paranoia and those old feelings of unworthiness to creep in. Graeson hadn't visited this week. He hadn't read to me. Had he finally given up? Right here at the end? Was fate that cruel? Yes. Yes, she was. What awaited me downstairs might be a shuttle bus to the nearest town and an empty hotel room reserved in my name for all I knew.

"Are you ready, Ms. Ellis?" a curvy nurse with a pin-tight bun greeted me.

As I ever will be. "Yes."

She held open the door, and I crossed the room to her, hesitating inside what had become my sanctuary. Crossing the threshold meant re-entering real life. As certain as I was that was what I wanted, I still paused before my foot hit the tile in the hall.

"You're doing fine," she assured me. "Everything has been handled. All that's left is for you to sign out at the desk."

A few cautious steps later, I bumped into a man I hadn't noticed, who appeared to have been caught peeping into the slender rectangle of glass that allowed nurses to observe patients at a glance. He was a stranger, but the room number was familiar. It was Harlow's.

Pinpricks of discomfort radiated up the base of my neck as I saw myself reflected in his aviator shades. "Do I know you?"

"I don't know." He slid the frames on top of his head and peered at me with mercurial eyes reminiscent of a quicksilver whirlpool. "Do you?"

"No," I decided, not sure I was telling myself the truth. "What are you doing outside Harlow's room?"

"Harlow," he echoed then flipped down his shades. "I'm one of the guards here at Edelweiss, ma'am. I'm just making my rounds is all."

He set off whistling a tune, and I approached the window to check on her myself.

"You're still welcome to visit her on the weekends," the nurse informed me.

"Can I...?" I pressed my palm to the cool glass. "I don't want Harlow to think I'm abandoning her."

"I'll break the rules this once, because you're the only visitor that poor girl gets." She jingled the keys at her hip as she searched out a particular one. "Make it quick, or we'll both get in trouble."

The nurse opened the door, and I eased inside the room identical to mine. A fragile young woman curled on her bed, facing the large window overlooking the largest fountain out front. Blonde hair so pale it was almost transparent fanned her pillow. The tail of her scrublike top had rucked up, exposing her bony spine.

"I'm leaving today." I didn't expect an answer. Harlow wasn't ready to talk just yet, and I respected that. "Non-family visitation is on the weekends, so I'll see you on Sunday."

She didn't move or speak to acknowledge me. She gazed forward, seeing but not seeing.

"If you need anything, you know how to find me." I went to my knees beside her bed and rubbed soothing circles on her upper back. "When you're ready to leave this place, you can come home with me. Or I can help you get back to your parents. Whatever you want." I leaned over and kissed her cheek. "Just get better, okay?"

The glitter of moisture gathering at the corners of her eyes was more response than I had expected.

"Ms. Ellis," the nurse said, poking her head in the door, "we really have to get going."

"Bye for now, Harlow."

The nurse hustled me into the hall and secured the door behind us. Harlow missed my goodbye wave.

Labyrinthine twists meant to confuse patients worked well enough on me, even clearheaded, that I drew up with surprise when the nurse shoved through a set of swinging doors that fed into the lobby. I forced my head up and gaze out toward the open space lined with chairs for visiting family members.

It sat empty.

Heart stuck in my throat, I signed out with a brittle smile and turned to the nurse.

"You get to go home now." She patted my cheek. "Be well, Camille. You deserve happiness."

I murmured nonsensical syllables and made my way to the parking lot, expecting the shuttle bus to be waiting. I mentally prepared a pep talk to get me on the public transpo without sprouting leaks that might force the driver to question my readiness to rejoin society.

I hit the pavement as a deafening cheer rose across the lawn.

Struggling to comprehend the streamers hung from topiaries and the catering tables laden with food, I drifted under the portico in a daze. Dozens of smiling faces milled on the grass, Mom and Dad among them. Aunt Dot stood next to Theo, who sat in a wheelchair, Isaac gripping the handles. Dell waited behind them, eyes puffy, but her smile for me was ten miles wide. The rest of the pack flanked her, creating a wall of bodies. But the face I longed to see most was the one absent, and I couldn't stop the rogue tear from wetting my cheek.

"One day you're going to believe me when I say I love you." Strong arms encircled me from behind. "That I will always love you." Warm lips brushed my ear. "That not even death will keep you from me."

More tears leaking down my face, I turned in Graeson's arms. "How can you ever forgive me?"

Between therapy sessions, I had given interviews and called in yet another favor to make sure the transcripts reached my parents and Graeson. I wanted the truth out there, so that if I never had the courage to speak it again, they knew every last detail.

"For avenging my sister? For saving me from myself?" He cupped my face. "What is there to forgive?"

Throat gone tight, I buried my face against his chest and let him hold me until I almost believed I might not shatter after all.

More hands touched my shoulders, and I turned my head without lifting to see my parents.

"Hey, baby girl." Mom smoothed my hair from my face. "I'm so glad to see you."

I was a long way from healed, but I would get there. I couldn't look into their faces and believe otherwise.

"Are we getting hugs or what?" Dad restrained himself, mostly, and half-pried me away from Graeson so he could wrap me in a bear hug that popped my spine. "That's better." He kissed the top of my head. "One day, when you're ready, we'll all sit down together and let you say anything you want."

"Listen to your dad, pumpkin." Aunt Dot swatted my butt. "We're all here for you, for whatever you need." She stole me from Dad with a hard yank. "I'll warn you now that if I hear you try and claim one ounce of blame, I will break off a switch and tap your calf every time you try." Moisture pooled in her eyes. "You saved me. You saved my boys." She let her tears fall against my cheek where they mingled with mine. "Your sister would be so proud of you."

Once upon a time, I would have held on to my anger and railed against the knowledge Aunt Dot had kept Lori from me, but I understood now, and I was too grateful to be able to breathe in her rosewater scent to hold on to grudges.

"Save some for me." Isaac caught me next, squeezing me tight, his burnt-metal scent as welcome as Aunt Dot's had been. "You saved my bacon, coz." He stared down into my face. "What Mom said about the switch? Just remember that when her arm gets tired, I'll take over for her. Got it?"

I bobbed my head and spotted Theo over his shoulder. My least-favorite cousin made a *come here* gesture, and I went to stand beside him. He offered his hand as though he meant to shake mine, but I bent down and wrapped my arms around his neck.

"I love you, Cammie." He brought his arms up to hold me. "I'm shit at showing it, but I do."

"I love you too." I grunted when slender arms caught me around the middle and hauled me backward.

"You love me too, right?" Dell rested her chin on my shoulder. "I'm nicer than Theo, and I smell better too."

"I love you too, Dell." I patted her flushed cheek, and my palm came away damp. "Are you all right?"

"Good as gold," she assured me.

"Aunt Dot invited your parents to travel with her for a while." Graeson's voice came to me as though from a great distance. *"Theo is returning to Orlando, but Isaac is going with them."*

Suddenly Dell's tears made a lot more sense.

Nodding at Graeson, I let him know I had heard him. Between the lingering meds and an excess of emotion, I was too overwhelmed to zap him a mental response.

Beyond the tightknit group of my blood relatives, my chosen family dawdled in the grass.

"Well?" I flung my arms open wide. "What are you waiting for?"

They didn't need a second invitation. My pack mates embraced me, and the nearness of their wolves drew my own aspect closer to the surface of my skin. I relished her presence. I had missed her. She radiated happiness, gleeful to be among kin. Moore and Zed and Job sniffed my hair. Abram attempted to examine me, but Nathalie swatted his shoulder.

"Hey, wait a minute." I counted heads. "You're all here except..." Bianca.

Graeson's voice came from over my shoulder. "Bianca committed herself the day after you arrived." His warmth beat at my back, and I leaned against him. "She doesn't trust herself or her wolf. She doesn't want the baby harmed, so she's staying at Edelweiss in isolation until after she delivers."

"I wanted a better ending for her," I murmured.

"She had one," Nathalie chimed in, sticking her fingers in her mouth and blasting out a shrill whistle. "Remember when I said I didn't think Bianca had attacked Jensen?"

Wishful thinking, but I nodded.

"Well, it turns out she didn't." She jerked her hand toward someone out of my line of sight. "Oh come on," she yelled. "There's food waiting."

From around the corner strolled the last person I expected to see today. Or ever again. "Aisha?"

Head down and eyes darting, she approached me. "Alpha."

"I thought the drugs wore off," I muttered more to myself than the others. "What are you doing here?"

"Apologizing if she doesn't want to get kicked to the curb," Nathalie said.

"I followed you from Villanow," she grumbled. "I was pissed about Bessemer, and I wanted to take a chunk out of your hide." Her chin lifted in defiance but began wilting immediately. "I watched you jog the night of the ceremony, but Cord never let you out of his sight."

"I thought it was paranoia." I cut a glance at Graeson. "I figured he had posted babysitters to watch me."

He was all innocence when he said, "And let someone else enjoy that view for ten miles?"

Wrinkling her nose at him, Aisha continued, "I was hiding when you left with the others, waiting for you to come back, but then…" She studied her feet. "Bianca and Jensen were fine, all lovey-dovey and dopey-eyed for each other one minute. The next she started talking funny, real formal, and panting like she wanted to shift but couldn't." She shuddered. "Jensen was rubbing her back, and he just…snapped. He shifted and went straight for her jugular. She couldn't defend herself, so I shifted, and we fought." She cupped her elbows. "I killed him. She was in shock, I guess, and crawled to him. She was screaming at me and covered in blood." She rocked back on her heels. "I ran, and I didn't look back."

"Aisha came back to check on Bianca from a distance, I caught her, and she copped to the whole thing." Nathalie wrapped up the whole sordid tale. "Bessemer kicked her to the curb without a penny to her name, just the clothes on her back. I'm not saying stalking you with intent to kill was the best idea ever, but she did save Bianca's life."

Graeson's voice vibrated against my back. "Which is the only reason I didn't kill her to save us the headache of deciding what becomes of her now."

"What do you think?" I tilted back my head. "She's been living with the pack, I assume, for several weeks."

He returned my stare. "She's been the perfect guest."

"That makes you suspicious." It made me twitchy too. Or maybe that was Nathalie's expectation that I would know what to do about Aisha. "Honestly I'm too overwhelmed to make a decision of this magnitude right now."

"I understand." Aisha's face fell. "I'll figure something out."

"Nathalie, are you willing to take responsibility for her?" Sympathetic I might be, but stupid… Well, I hoped I wasn't that. Nathalie rubbed a finger over her lips for an eternity before nodding. "In that case, we'll take this one day at a time, unless you attempt to harm me or mine. Then we'll ship you back to Bessemer in a silver cage and let him decide what happens to you."

"That's...fair." Her brown skin paled many shades. "But there's more."

Nathalie did a double take. "What?"

Chin up, Aisha set her shoulders back. "I blew up your aunt's truck."

"It wasn't blown up." That might have left it salvageable. "It was spelled into an inferno."

"The Garzas owed me a favor, and I cashed it in before I left." Heat flushed her cheeks. "I'm sorry."

"Take it up with my aunt." I waved her in Aunt Dot's general direction. "She's the one you owe an apology to. Not to mention a new truck."

After raising three kids, Aunt Dot had elevated punishment to an art form. Insurance ought to cover replacing the vehicle, but Aisha didn't have to know that. I had no doubt Aunt Dot would find other ways for the former alpha to make amends.

"Enough pack business for one day," Graeson proclaimed as he threaded my arm through his, hauling me away from Aisha. "I would have let this wait until tomorrow, but Nathalie won't let Aisha out of her sight, and we had to explain her presence."

"I can't say I blame Nathalie." Aisha had a history of trying to kill me. As alpha, my pack was bound to take issue with her murderous inclinations. Yet she had saved one of us. "Maybe a new pack, a new environment, will set her straight."

"Maybe," he allowed, steering me toward the buffet line. He pushed a plate into my hands, giving me the chance to load up with favorites before the wargs decimated the food. "Either way, it's not a problem for today."

"What are our problems?" I mounded a generous portion of home-style potatoes beside a scoop of pulled pork. Clearly this was a Cam-themed meal. "Where do we go from here? Back to the RV park? Where do we call home?"

"Well, about that." For an alpha warg, he sure had trouble meeting my gaze. "I might have made an executive decision in your absence." He heaped more potatoes onto my plate as if that might fix the problem. "I would have asked you, if that had been an option. The arrangements I've made aren't permanent. We can leave if you want, if that's what your job requires, or if you want to put that place behind us."

"It sounds like you made the call to stay in Butler." I shook my head to clear it. "I didn't see that coming."

"That's where we're needed," he said cryptically.

"Okay, then Butler it is." I placed my hand over his before he dumped another mound of potatoes on my plate. "I trust you."

"Look how far we've come," he teased. "Not too long ago, I would have had to bribe you with homemade brownies to earn that endorsement."

"You can pay me a retroactive bribe once we get home." I leaned over and kissed him softly on the lips.

"Home sounds good." He hooked his arms around me. "We could slip away while the others are busy eating—"

"—my potatoes." I cradled the plate to my chest, laughing as he playfully growled in my ear. "I missed this." I rubbed my cheek against his. "I missed you."

"Wherever you go, I go." His breath blew warm across my throat. "I was never far. You realize that, right? I only gave you the illusion of privacy because it's what you needed."

I laughed at his earnest expression. "I'm almost afraid to ask."

"I rented a room."

Edelweiss's shadow peered over our shoulder, a party to the conversation. "This isn't exactly a hotel."

"Mai found me sleeping in my truck one night and introduced herself. The name rang a bell, and once we discovered we had Thierry and you in common, she hauled me inside and gave me the grand tour. There are four guest suites in the basement outfitted for supernatural out-of-towners unable to blend into human society who come to visit with their loved ones."

"You were here the whole time?" Two floors away from me, and I never knew. No one had told me.

No wonder he had decided to throw my party on the lawn. This place had been his home for months.

"Did you honestly think I would leave you when you needed me the most?" His fingers dug into my hips. "You're mine, Ellis, from the top of your blonde head to the tips of your pink toes. If you wanted out, you should have run a long time ago. Now you're stuck with me. You and me are forever."

"Forever." I breathed in his deep-woods scent, the smell of my true home, and exhaled with happiness too large to be contained. "I like the sound of that."

Allowing my lids to fall shut, I focused on the security of Graeson's arms as he stole kisses between bites of food snatched from my plate. Aunt Dot's animated voice carried as she swapped anecdotes with Mom and Dad about our childhood, earning groans and pleas for mercy from Isaac and Theo. Shouts and good-natured ribbing ensued among the pack as they scuffled for prime spots in the buffet line.

"Open up." Graeson pressed a crisp morsel to my lips. "You don't want to miss this."

Blinking the world back into focus, I bit down on the pad of his thumb, relishing his possessive growl, and had to agree. "I wouldn't miss this for the world."

EPILOGUE

THIERRY

Eight weeks earlier.

I planted my hands on my hips and squinted up at a burnt-orange sky that was a heck of a lot closer than it ought to be. Parts of the ceiling of this world dipped so low I imagined rising up on my toes to brush my fingers along its voluminous underbelly.

"Freaking monkeys," I muttered. "This is not great."

The churning vortex fraught with otherworldly winds whipped my long black hair into my eyes until I caved to annoyance and yanked it back in a quick and dirty bun.

"I don't have time for this." Cord Graeson stood at my elbow, glaring at the sky as if his pissedoffedness might sear the void closed. "Ellis needs me."

His mate, a Gemini woman by the name of Camille Ellis, had drowned herself in a bid to take a body-hopping serial killer with her.

All things considered, I got that he wanted to wash his hands of this place and bolt.

Too bad we didn't always get what we wanted.

"Make time, wolfman." I angled my head to better take in his disheveled appearance. "This was the endgame, and we all got played."

The words registered, and a growl pumped through his chest. "The circle."

"On a much, much smaller scale, yes." The same fruitcake fae Cam had died taking down had been wilier than any of us dreamed. "Charybdis used his sacrificial killings to create the circle around the entire state. When that fell through, he moved to plan B." The part of his plan I hadn't guessed at until my hiding place allowed me to overhear his villain monologue seconds before Cam knocked him unconscious with an enchanted gem. "Cam was his target all along. He tailored his victims and their deaths to echo her sister's drowning." Even though, much to her surprise, her sister had been alive. That part wasn't Charybdis's fault, though. He just wielded the knowledge over her like the sword of Damocles. "Thanks to his mind-bending tricks, he finagled Cam into position as primary on the kelpie case, which wasn't hard considering it was designed to appeal to her on a personal and professional level."

"Okay," he grunted. "I follow."

"What we didn't pick up on fast enough was he had a secondary reason for targeting Cam. It wasn't just that he believed she was capable of sustaining him indefinitely, because any Gemini could have, in theory, worked in a pinch." Fate, convenience or plain old bad luck led him to fixate on her. "The original spell, the circle, was woven with a secondary layer that fed entirely off Cam's emotional distress. He was priming her for this all along."

"The others..." his throat worked, "...they were sacrificed. Does that mean Ellis's death was the trigger for the spell?"

"You catch on quick." I pursed my lips and debated how to go about explaining this next bit. "He told Cam he chose her because the first contact he had on this world, Marshal Ayer, had knowledge of her that he exploited. From what I overheard, it sounds like his plan was always to use Cam as fuel for his spells and her sister as his permanent residence."

"He sent Ayer to attack the Ellis's home," the warg reflected. "He was attempting to lock down his preferred vessel before Cam caught wind of her sister's existence."

"That's how it looks to me too, in hindsight." Which always sparkled with twenty-twenty clarity. "The problem is, he feeds on emotion, and Lori didn't emote." I jerked a thumb toward the sky. "The only way he could hotwire his ride was by plying it with enough magic to kick-start its engine."

"You're telling me he ripped a hole in the fabric between worlds all for Lori?" Doubt sat heavy in his voice.

"Nah." Last night Charybdis, whoever he really was, had been eager to chatter once he got Cam alone and at his mercy. "He did it for himself. He might have figured out how to wear a Gemini suit long term, but fae here don't have the juice they do in Faerie. He was hedging his bets."

A black dot, a teeny-tiny speck, materialized in the center of the churning skies, and I got the feeling first contact was about to happen. Oh boy.

"I guarantee you Charybdis came here thinking Earth was a paradise of untapped resources." Read: Humans for snacking. "But once he got here and realized he was stuck because the tethers were severed, he went from skipping through daisies to wading through a briar patch. I'm betting he hatched this scheme to tap into Faerie's magic. He wanted that energy to leak into this world so that he could have his cake and eat it too."

"Freedom from Faerie's rule but access to her power," Graeson agreed with a nod. "Makes sense."

"Faerie has had her belly sliced open, and until we figure out how to close a gash this size, which will require my dad's intervention, she's going to bleed into this world."

The coolheaded warg snapped to attention as the reason I'd invited him out here despite his mate's declining health sank into his wolf skull. "Humans are going to learn about the fae."

His tone said he didn't give a damn about those consequences. His alpha brain was churning what-if scenarios that included wargs and vamps and all manner of native supernaturals having their cover blown too.

Earth was a sinking ship. Much like the dumbass who hadn't outfitted the Titanic with enough life rafts, I could tell him right now there wasn't enough glamour, illusion, deceit or sleight of hand to save us all. I had a fae working right now to slather glamour over the sky to block out the surreal anomaly until we figured out what the heck to do about this.

"I can't see any alternative." I leaned against a tree, wishing Shaw was here to bounce ideas with me. "I don't see the conclave sewing this rift shut fast enough to stop what's coming."

"Your father could stop this?" He examined my runes as he spoke.

"The current threshold to Faerie is his handiwork," was the best answer I had for him.

"Why did you want me to see this?" He angled so he faced me. "What is it you're asking without asking?"

Winding up my sales pitch, I let it fly. "Wargs are tough, smart and have the home field advantage." Lucky me, there happened to be an entire pack right here, right now. "Until the conclave locks down the area, we need sharp eyes—and teeth—on patrol. We need a buffer between what comes out of that hole in the sky and the people here on the ground."

The firm set of his jaw confirmed his decision. "We can help."

"Great." I did a mental fist pump. "What I need you to do is—"

"What you need to do is speak with my beta, Adele Preston." He spared the Vortex of Doom one last flicker of attention. "I'm going to Kermit, Texas to be with Ellis." His voice went deep, gold flecks in his eyes warning me the wolf was near the surface. "Where she goes, I go."

"I respect the sentiment." The loss of the alpha burst my bubble, though his defection wasn't totally unexpected. "Are you sure it's wise to leave your second-in-command?"

Diplomacy wasn't my strong suit, but I didn't mention he was a young alpha with a pack cobbled together out of troublemakers. As straight of an arrow as Cam was, Cord must have sweet-talked her to get them into her good graces. That or she hadn't seen the files the conclave kept on them.

"Part of the reason we left our old home is because the old ways weren't working for us." He gave his answer consideration. "This pack will be different. We're melding the strict control required to make our wolves happy with the flexibility to please my fae mate. We'll either succeed, or we'll fail, but I'm alpha. I didn't sign on to wipe their asses, and I'm no babysitter. They will honor the vows they made, or they will defect." A feral grin amped up with possessiveness split his lips. "I have Ellis. That's all the pack I need."

"All right." I respected a man dedicated to his mate. "I'll parse details with Dell."

He backed three steps closer to the road before speaking. "If that's all...?"

"Go on." I flicked my wrist. "I'll handle things here." Getting into a dominance fight with a beta held no appeal. "Just make sure Dell knows that's what I'm doing, okay?"

Not slowing to answer, he lifted his hand in what I took as a *sure thing* gesture.

Figuring I had a few minutes until impact, I pulled out my phone to call Shaw and startled when it rang with an unlisted number in my hand. "Marco's Pizza."

An elegant sigh worked as well as any greeting.

Biting my lip to keep from snorting at her haughty disdain, I tried again. "Hello, Magistrate Vause."

"Thierry," came her long-suffering acknowledgment. "I understand Camille Ellis suffered a rather unfortunate incident."

While I filled her in on Cam, and she updated me about how she had resumed her duties now that Charybdis was no longer a threat, I kept an eye on the dot in the sky. When its shape turned more birdlike than bloblike, I cut her loose with a promise to keep her informed that I mostly intended to keep.

Minutes later, a black bird the size of a Chihuahua swooped over my head. The bastard buzzed me, and I had to drop to avoid getting creamed. Still his talons raked through my hair, yanking down my bun, before he lit on the ground with a few hops and morphed into a striking fae man.

"Wife," he greeted me with a courtly bow.

The King of Faerie was almost as pretty as he was arrogant. Almost.

"Ex," I corrected him, middle finger extended.

Chuckling like I was the wittiest girl in Witville, he sauntered over to me and beheld the seam between worlds that appeared to unzip more the longer we watched. "What do you propose we do about this?"

Cute how he managed to make it sound as though we shared a side when, for as long as I had known him, the only cause Rook championed was himself. I played along, our union being amicably annulled and all. "We try and minimize the casualties."

His regal nod almost read as sincere. "Faerie, and her king, are at your disposal." A thin smile bent his perfect lips. "How may I be of assistance?"

The urge to roll my eyes left me staring at the patch of sky directly over my head.

The prophecy Cam emailed me had been a thorn under my skin for days. I had tap-danced around the truth with my new friends, but I was a beast apart from them. The thirst for judgment parched my throat, and the battle to hold Earth hadn't yet begun. This lake might soon run with blood, and if it did, I had made the decision it would be spilled on my orders.

Cam was hardcore, and the Lorimar pack was badass. Their involvement might persuade more native supernaturals and their human allies that earthborn fae could be trusted when the alternative was former apex predators getting bent over a barrel sans lube by first-wave Faerie mercenaries. So, yeah, the wargs made an excellent addition to Team Save Earth. But at the end of the day, I was half human *and* half fae, and I was an equal opportunity recruiter.

"Send me the Huntsman." Hunger coiled in my gut, my runes sparking to life as magic caressed my skin. I met Rook's intrigued gaze and held it. "Unleash the Wild Hunt."

And may God have mercy on our souls.

HAILEY'S BACKLIST

Araneae Nation

A Heart of Ice #.5
A Hint of Frost #1
A Feast of Souls #2
A Cast of Shadows #2.5
A Time of Dying #3
A Kiss of Venom #3.5
A Breath of Winter #4
A Veil of Secrets #5

Daughters of Askara

Everlong #1
Evermine #2
Eversworn #3

Black Dog

Dog with a Bone #1
Heir of the Dog #2
Lie Down with Dogs #3
Old Dog, New Tricks #4

Gemini

Dead in the Water #1
Head Above Water #2
Hell or High Water #3

Wicked Kin

Soul Weaver #1

ABOUT THE AUTHOR

A cupcake enthusiast and funky sock lover possessed of an overactive imagination, Hailey lives in Alabama with her handcuff-carrying hubby, her fluty-tooting daughter and their herd of dachshunds.

Chat with Hailey on Facebook or Twitter, or swing by her website.
www.facebook.com/authorhaileyedwards
@Hailey Edwards
www.HaileyEdwards.net

Sign up for her newsletter to receive updates on new releases, contests and other nifty happenings.